SHOEMAKER
Shoemaker, Sarah,
Children of the catastrophe :a novel /

CHILDREN
OF THE
CATASTROPHE

CHILDREN
OF THE
CATASTROPHE

A Novel

SARAH SHOEMAKER

HARPER

An Imprint of HarperCollins*Publishers*

HarperCollins books may be purchased for educational, business, or sales promotional use. For information please email the Special Markets Department at SPsales@harpercollins.com.

P.S.™ is a registered trademark of HarperCollins Publishers.

FIRST EDITION

Library of Congress Cataloging-in-Publication Data has been applied for.

ISBN 978-0-06-325427-5 (pbk.)
ISBN 978-0-06-327232-3 (library edition)

22 23 24 25 26 LSC 10 9 8 7 6 5 4 3 2 1

For families of all sorts,
and for my family in particular

CHILDREN
OF THE
CATASTROPHE

Starting a family is a venture into the unknown.

—ANONYMOUS

CHAPTER I

Smyrna, Ottoman Empire, 1908

THEY SAT LIKE FAT PASHAS, EACH WITH HER OWN RETINUE OF friends and hangers-on, each court ignoring the others, as if theirs were the only one that counted. Their pendulous breasts hung like overripe fruit, their stomachs dropped in folds on their laps or lay heavily between wide-spread, beefy thighs. They were past caring about their own appearances, and all the honey-soaked cakes and *baklavas* of their years of afternoon teas had exacted a toll. It would not have mattered anyway; a fat wife was the truest sign of a prosperous husband.

In the close, steamy atmosphere of the baths, the effect they made was as calculated as any other part of the delicate and all-important ritual in which they were involved. They were the watchers, not the watched; the judges, not the judged. Now, on this Saturday afternoon at the baths, each was at the height of her career, one that had begun years before on sweat-stained sheets, when the agony had ended and the midwife had triumphantly lifted the baby by its heels so that the new mother could see its sex and relax at last in the knowledge that she had done her duty to her husband.

In a small, private room—one of a warren of such rooms—
Theodora Demirgis briskly brushed her daughter's hair,
gleaming richly with a henna rinse. "Remember, Liana," she
said for the third or fourth time, "remember everything we've
told you and it will be just fine." She kept one eye on the hair
as it fell in soft waves down the length of her daughter's back,
and another on Liana's skin, turning to a rosy glow from the
fierce loofah scrubbing she had just given it. Theodora calculated how much longer until everything would be just right.
A few steps down the corridor, a moment or two, perhaps,
before the women noticed Liana, and then . . . "Liana," she
cautioned, "your eyes and your hair, remember that: your eyes
and your hair." But as she said those words, she stole a glance
at Liana's small buttocks, high and rounded like a child's, and
she said a quick prayer: *Dear God, don't let them notice her hips.
Let them notice her hair and not the rest.* But even as she prayed,
she knew that when one began by admiring the way Liana's
hair hung in gentle waves down her back, one's eyes always
strayed to her narrow hips. *Not good hips for birthing,* the others
would think.

Now Theodora stepped around in front of her daughter
and tilted Liana's chin up just a little. "Like this," she cautioned, "like you are a princess. Like they would be lucky to
have you." Then, quickly, she turned, crossed herself three
times, and tied up the bath utensils in a scarf of turquoise silk.

Liana watched her mother gather her things and step out of
the private room without even looking back. Proud Theodora,
who had wanted desperately to have a son and who had borne
only daughters; broad-backed, wide-hipped Theodora acted as
if this, her last daughter, were every bit as desirable as her first
had been. *I know what they'll think,* Liana told herself, *and I
don't care.*

In front of her, Theodora paused for the briefest of moments. Liana could see her mother's shoulders rise as she took in a deep breath, and despite herself Liana felt the blood pounding in her temples. *I don't care, I don't care*, she told herself over and over, but she knew she did care, and no amount of pretending would make it otherwise.

When Theodora walked across the threshold of the cooling room all eyes turned toward her, and she allowed herself the smallest of smiles. After three daughters, at least she knew how to make an entrance into the baths. They would be staring now, curious to see this last of the Demirgis daughters.

Liana waited a moment too long before following her mother. *Never mind*, she thought, *better too slow than too fast. I don't care anyway. It doesn't matter.* The women lounged the way her mother had described, on long white marble benches rising three or four tiers against the high marbled walls of the enormous room. Overhead, the ceiling formed a large vaulted dome of multicolored marble, flanked by two smaller, plainer domes. Painted angels graced the arches between the domes. The room glowed with muted colors as shafts of light shone through small, high windows of colored glass. Though this was Liana's first time at the baths, the place seemed oddly familiar: It was all exactly the way her mother and sisters had described it.

She saw someone she knew and smiled and nodded, and another familiar face—perhaps this would not be so unbearable after all. But there were still so many she didn't know. She saw hands held up to hide murmured confidences, heads inclined toward one another as comments passed back and forth, and she could only imagine the whispered words: *So that's Dora's youngest. Thin, isn't she? . . . Indeed, and you can't have healthy babies with such hips . . . No wonder they've been delaying with her . . . Not like her sisters, is she? . . . Dora? I don't know the family . . . Yes, you do. It's Emmanuel Demirgis's wife and daughter. Emmanuel Demirgis, the silversmith . . . Tall, don't you think? . . . Her father's tall, what do you expect? . . . Pity she doesn't take after her mother . . .* The marble floors and walls seemed to echo with whispered comments made behind cupped hands, with sudden muffled titters.

Perversely, Liana wondered what they would do if she laughed out loud. Or made an ugly face. But she knew her mother would be horrified—and humiliated—and she walked on demurely, enduring their staring eyes and murmuring mouths, following her mother, thinking *I don't care. I really don't care; it doesn't really matter.* Yet knowing still that it did.

Theodora turned slowly to face her daughter, watching now Liana's progress across the massive room. *She is sweet and obedient,* she would have liked to say to all those who stared so critically, *and she is earnest and loving. Her handwork, while not the best of all my daughters, is still quite fine, and she learns quickly.* If there had been an opportunity, she would have said those things aloud, but of course there was none.

Reaching her mother, Liana bent to adjust the strap of a wooden patten. As she rose, she used both hands to lift and rearrange her hair, letting it fall again in waves down her back, doing it just as she had been taught, and an appreciative murmur scurried around the cooling room. Theodora smiled again in satisfaction that the elegantly provocative movement had been noticed.

"You did beautifully," Theodora whispered, hoping no one else would hear.

Beauty is a state of mind, Liana repeated to herself. How often had her mother told her that? As if it did any good. As if any of these women were thinking that. She wondered how many visitors would come in the next weeks, and a sudden thought occurred to her: *What if no one came?* "There are worse things than being an old maid," she had said defiantly to Eleni just yesterday, but Eleni had stared at her in shock.

Well, then, suppose there wasn't anything worse. You could still live through it. Couldn't you?

CHAPTER 2

Theodora Demirgis was home to callers on Tuesdays. Liana usually loved those gatherings—her sisters almost always came, bringing their little ones, with whom Liana enjoyed cuddling and playing. Old friends and neighbors might come as well, and the women would eat sweets and gossip: the local news of who was engaged to whom, the new styles from France and the new dress fabrics at their favorite stores on the Corniche. Or who was building a house in the country, or whose children were ill behaved, or the new and very young assistant priest at Aghios Giorgios.

But not this day. On this first Tuesday after Liana's introduction at the baths, there was more to concern herself with. She knew there should have been a flurry of interest and an increased number of callers this week: mothers who were looking for a girl worthy of their precious sons. And, indeed, several women had spoken with Theodora at the baths, and two additional ones at Aghios Giorgios on Sunday, but Theodora had neglected to tell Liana how many had gone so far as to ask on which day Theodora received callers. Still, on Monday a message had come from a woman named Vaia Melopoulos that she would be paying a visit as well. Even Theodora had barely known who this Vaia Melopoulos was, though she thought the family was in tobacco. Liana tried not to worry whether any such mother would actually appear, and she forced herself not to daydream about a possible young man: who he might be and what he might look like, might *be* like.

Liana's mother had spent all Monday supervising the baking of *baklava*, *kadayif*, lemon cakes, and sugar-dusted cookies. Even with only one or two mothers of sons, it was necessary to have a well-stocked larder. And, of course, there would be others, but who knew how many? And how many would be mothers of sons? But now, on Tuesday morning, Theodora seemed even more apprehensive, as though she imagined that Liana had forgotten everything she'd been told. "Liana, look at your skirt, already wrinkled," Theodora admonished. "You need to brush your hair again. And remember your needlework. And for heaven's sake, don't forget . . ."

Liana nodded, letting her mother's voice pass by, almost unheard. She would not let this worry her; she would not be one of those pitiful girls so desperate for approval that she made herself sick. In past years she had watched her sisters go through this time. Plump Christina, who everyone agreed was the beauty of the family, with a pale complexion and charming dimples—all her parents had had to do was decide among the offers. After Christina had come Sophia, with the good full hips and large breasts that promised healthy babies. Sophie had not had as many offers as Christina, but she had made an excellent marriage. The third sister, Eleni, was as lovely as Christina, but while Christina's looks were the robust beauty of good health, Eleni's were more fragile. Nevertheless, a good match for Eleni had been found with ease, and by then the reputation of the Demirgis daughters was such that it seemed quite likely that most of the mothers of eligible sons were looking with great anticipation for Liana, the last of the four Demirgis sisters.

Sometimes Liana thought she must have been a disappointment. All her life Theodora had been urging her to eat, but no matter how much she managed to put into her mouth at mealtime, her mother never seemed satisfied. *Liana, you're so thin!* her mother would say. *Do you feel ill? Shall I send for the doctor? . . . Another piece of* baklava, *Liana? . . . Look how thin your face is . . . Don't eat so much salad, Liana—vinegar makes a person thin . . . You don't eat enough bread, child. Don't you want to be healthy?* For the first six years of her life, it seemed now, Theodora had spent every waking moment spooning food into Liana's mouth. Even between meals Theodora had followed her around with a plate in one hand and a spoon in the other, trying to put just one more bite into her.

"Leave her alone," Liana's father used to say. "Her appetite's healthy enough."

"Emmanuel!" Theodora would respond. "How can you say that? Look how thin she is! She'll blow away with the first *imbat*!"

"It's her nature to be thin. Don't worry so much about it."

"It's not healthy to be thin."

"It never hurt me."

"I don't have to worry about finding a husband for you, Emmanuel!"

"That's a long time away."

"It'll be here sooner than you think," Theodora would shoot back.

"You worried about Christina too, and how did she turn out?"

"Yes, but then I didn't know better. Now, after three daughters, I guess I know what the problems are. Liana will be a problem."

"Liana is a sweet, good child."

"Sweet and good don't buy husbands."

"They bought me."

"Don't be foolish, Emmanuel. This is serious business."

"Dora," he would say, wrapping his arms around her, "we have four lovely daughters. For heaven's sake, don't borrow trouble."

Now Liana stood gazing out the window of her little bedroom, the room she'd shared with Eleni until Eleni had married and moved into her own home. Over the years, her father had always smiled conspiratorially at her, as if they shared some special secret. *It doesn't matter*, she told herself now. *Someone will come.* And even if no one did, would it be so bad to spend the rest of her life here, with her mama and papa?

Just then, Theodora bustled up behind her, straightening the rose-colored ribbon in her hair and flouncing out her skirt. "Liana—"

"Mama, don't worry."

"You'll stay in here for a few moments. Don't let them think we're anxious."

"Yes, Mama, I know—"

"I'll call you. I'll say, 'Liana, won't you come and meet' . . . whoever it is. Then you will know it's time."

"Mama—"

"Remember to pinch your cheeks just before you come. Oh, dear, I wish Eleni would get here. And you'll bring your embroidery with you, and you'll sit there and be quiet, unless someone speaks to you."

Liana nodded as if she hadn't already been told these things dozens of times.

Sudden tears sprang to Theodora's eyes. Flustered, she embraced her daughter and kissed her on each cheek. Then, to calm herself, she rearranged Liana's hair one last time.

Liana clasped her mother's hands with her own. "Don't worry, Mama. You won't be ashamed of me."

Theodora stopped as if struck. "Ashamed? No, of course not! But Liana, a mother wants the best for her child. Always, that is what a mother wants."

"It will be fine, Mama. Whatever happens, it will be fine."

Theodora smiled, nodding. "It will. Of course it will." And she hurried away down the hall, the heels of her shoes clattering on the polished oak floor.

Minutes passed and Liana, restless, paced back and forth, sat down on her bed—and immediately jumped up with the realization that she was almost certainly wrinkling her skirt. She leaned out the window and watched a bird hop across the garden below. She could hear the distant sounds of the street: the *bahchevans* calling their wares, the clatter of carriage wheels on cobbled streets, and the farther away sound of a departing boat's horn coming from the harbor. Finally, from the front of the house, she heard the muffled raps of the doorknocker.

She rushed out of her room and down the hall as far as she dared, and now she could hear the voices more clearly: "Why, Anna, I'm so pleased you came!"

"Am I late? Are the others here?"

"Not yet," Theodora answered cheerily. "You're the first one."

"There *are* others coming?" Anna Hadjioglou asked rudely.

"Of course, dear. Come in, come in! Will you have a sweet?" Liana imagined her mother gesturing toward a table laden with goodies.

"Oh, I don't know . . ."

"Please do. One piece, surely. What a pretty dress!"

"Do you like it? I wasn't certain if I did or not. The fabric is French, though, and . . ." Their voices trailed off as Theodora led the way into the parlor.

Liana leaned against the wall. She would not be worried about Anna Hadjioglou. Everyone said that Anna was milking her son's availability by going to the homes of all the eligible girls in order to sample the sweets on offer there. No doubt Anna was more attracted to Theodora's cakes than she was to Theodora's daughter. Liana closed her eyes and envisioned chubby, baby-faced Panos Hadjioglou, and she was glad Anna wasn't actually interested in her. She thought of the other young men she knew even slightly, sons of her parents' friends or ones she had seen in church—the good-looking ones, the spoiled ones, the shy and serious ones—and she suddenly realized that she actually knew very few by name. Of all the Greeks in Smyrna and the surrounding towns, the people she knew best were all family members.

"Liana! *Liana!*" Her mother's voice broke into her thoughts. Guiltily, she wondered how long Theodora had been calling.

"Yes, Mama!" she replied.

"Come and meet *Kyria* Hadjioglou. She's here to call."

"Yes, Mama." She started down the stairway, patting her cheeks to bring out the color as she went. Then she stopped, remembering that she had forgotten her embroidery, and she dashed back to her room to get it.

"Here she is, my daughter Liana!" Theodora said brightly when Liana finally appeared. "Dear, you know *Kyria* Hadjioglou, don't you?"

Anna Hadjioglou held out a plump hand and Liana took it in her slim one, curtsying demurely. "May I get you a coffee, *Kyria*?"

"Oh!" Anna Hadjioglou feigned surprise. "Please, don't bother."

"Oh no, I insist!" Liana urged.

"Really, I'm quite fine without it."

"Wouldn't you like just one little cup?"

"Well . . . yes, that would be nice."

"And how do you like it?"

"Medium. But . . . perhaps just a shade sweet."

"And for you, Mother?"

"Yes, my darling. Sweet for me too, if you please."

In the kitchen Liana put the proper amounts of coffee, sugar, and water into the *jezveh* and held it carefully over the coal oil burner. She was aware of Despinise, the maid, standing back against the wall, arms folded across her chest, nodding judiciously. This was Liana's job, they both knew, because, as the saying went, *There are two ways to a man's heart—through his eyes and through his stomach.* Anna Hadjioglou, and any other mother of a son who came, would want to know that Liana could at least make a decent cup of coffee.

Liana watched the liquid as it heated and small bubbles began to roil up at the sides of the long-handled pot, then watched more carefully as the coffee, now boiling, foamed inward, a slowly growing circle. She smelled the sweet-sharp aroma as the coffee brewed, knowing it was the smell as well as the appearance that told a good cook exactly when the coffee was ready. Just as the ring of foam was about to close over the center of the liquid, she deftly lifted the *jezveh* away from the heat until the foam had subsided, then she placed it down closer to the flame again. Twice more she watched the ring of foam grow toward the center, and twice more she lifted it just as the ring was about to close. Finally, she poured the finished coffee into a tiny cup for her mother, the coffee rising exactly to the rim of the cup. Then she quickly rinsed out the *jezveh* and began the whole process again for *Kyria* Hadjioglou.

With a careful eye on the coffee, she thought once more of the steps she would have to go through. She would carry the two cups and saucers, both cups filled to the brim, walking carefully so as not to spill a drop—that was for grace. She would hand *Kyria* Hadjioglou her cup, bending over the seated guest as she did so, and at exactly the right moment, Anna Hadjioglou would ask her a question, and, still bending close, Liana would answer—that was for sweet breath. Then she would give the other coffee to her mother and retire to her proper place on the divan. Finally, *Kyria* Hadjioglou would casually take a sip of the coffee, and that would be the last part of the test—culinary ability. Of course, since Anna Hadjioglou was unlikely to be seriously considering Liana, this was really only another kind of practice, like the ones she had been going through with her mother and sisters for the last several weeks. Nevertheless, this *was* a boy's mother, and she *was* a visitor, and that made it something more than just another rehearsal.

Liana poured *Kyria* Hadjioglou's coffee very carefully, letting the last drops of foam mound up even higher than the rim of the cup. Then, with great care and as much grace as she could manage, she carried the two cups and saucers into the parlor.

"*Kyria*," Liana said, coming into the room, not pausing even for a moment at the threshold. (Christina had told her that would be impressive.) She walked toward the woman with the kind of smooth, sure step that Eleni had assured her would best show off grace and decorum, then she bent slightly to offer *Kyria* Hadjioglou her cup.

At that exact moment, *Kyria* Hadjioglou asked, "Liana, how does it feel to be the last of the famous Demirgis daughters?"

Liana blushed but remained leaning close to the woman's face, as she was required to do. "It's . . . I think it's a very great responsibility to keep the honor of my family."

Anna Hadjioglou smiled and nodded smugly.

Liana straightened. "*Bon appétit*." She used the French phrase because there was no comparable one in Greek, and on such an important occasion it would have been inappropriate to use the Turkish *Afiyet olsun*.

"Thank you," Anna Hadjioglou murmured, and she took a sip of the coffee.

Liana served her mother the other cup and retreated to her place on the divan.

Smiling and raising her cup slightly, Anna Hadjioglou said, "*Elinize saglik*," because even in French there was no phrase that was quite so apt: "Long life to your hand," the ultimate compliment to the cook.

Liana blushed and looked down at her handwork, murmuring, "*Efcharisto*," and smiled with relief. The dress rehearsal was over, and she had done just fine.

Only moments later Sophie and Eleni arrived, full of apologies for their lateness and carrying Eleni's two young daughters. Although Sophie was older and therefore had been married longer, she still had no children, a source of constant humiliation to her and a great disappointment for her mother. The arrival of these new visitors brought a flurry of activity, as Theodora called to Despinise to make more coffee. Eleni's older daughter, Marina, hugged Theodora, burying her face in her grandmother's bosom, but she shyly refused to greet Anna Hadjioglou.

"Never mind," Anna trilled. "She's such a darling child! Theodora, how lucky you are!"

Liana glanced at her mother, guessing that Theodora was imagining Anna storing up the incident to repeat to all her friends: how Theodora's grandchildren were such little barbarians.

Seven-month-old Doroush was passed from arm to arm. "How fortunate! Two granddaughters! How envious I am!" Anna Hadjioglou gushed.

Theodora stiffened. "I have two grandsons as well, you know."

Anna nodded politely and turned toward Liana, who was

now offering her a tray of sweets as a distraction. "Oh, no! No more for me, dear, thank you," Anna said, her eye seemingly caught by a mound of *baklava*, just as a child's would be.

"Really, you don't mean that, *Kyria*!" Liana urged. "Not any at all?"

"Well, perhaps just one."

"And more coffee as well?"

"Maybe just a bit."

After Liana had brought more coffee for *Kyria* Hadjioglou, she settled herself again on the divan. Sophie sat across the room, holding her four-year-old niece, Marina, on her lap and smiling encouragingly at Liana. Eleni, on the other side of Theodora, gently rocked the baby, who had fallen asleep sucking on Eleni's honey-dipped finger.

Soon a few of Theodora's friends dropped in, greeting Anna and giving hugs to Theodora's daughters, and the feminine conversation drifted back and forth across the room. Liana was not necessarily expected to contribute: She had done all that was required of her—at least until another mother of an eligible son arrived—and if she chose to remain quiet now, as she was doing, it was of no particular concern to anyone. It seemed almost as if she'd been forgotten. She would have loved to sit down on the floor with Marina and play with her niece's doll, but that would probably have been unseemly, so she took up her handwork again, and her mother smiled at her approvingly.

The women talked about the sudden fever Christina's children had developed, the new doctor in the Greek Quarter, the sudden and unexplained closing of one of their favorite shops. If their husbands had been together, they might have talked about business conditions, the newest regulations passed down from Constantinople, the high taxes, and, perhaps most of all, the agitation of the Young Turks for the sultan to restore the Constitution and what such a move would mean for the Greeks living in the Ottoman Empire. But since they were women, they didn't concern themselves with such things.

And all the time Theodora worried. Of all the possible mothers of sons, only Anna had come, and now Anna was beginning to glance at Liana with the knowing look of a mother of a son who knew that no one was interested in this particular girl. Beside her mother on the divan, Liana sat quietly, doing her handwork, as if oblivious to the conversations, as if she hadn't a concern in the world, as if her whole future didn't hang on the match her parents could find for her.

When the doorknocker sounded, Theodora nearly jumped up with surprise and relief, but she remained seated at least five seconds after the last tap was heard. Purposefully finishing her sentence, she counted slowly to herself. Then, casually, she rose from the sofa and walked unhurriedly to the foyer and opened the door.

The woman standing there was tall and thin—imperious looking—with a long nose. Theodora tried to keep herself from gushing too noticeably. "Why, Vaia! How nice to see you!"

"You received my message, no doubt?"

"Yes, of course. Come in, come in!"

Triumphantly Theodora led Vaia Melopoulos into the parlor, pausing to introduce the newcomer to her guests and to her daughters, and then showed her to a comfortable chair.

When Vaia Melopoulos entered, Liana gazed at the newcomer. She had never seen the woman before, and she wondered what her son was like, what his name was. Putting down her embroidery, she rose even before the guest was fully settled into her chair. "May I bring you a coffee, *Kyria*?"

"Oh, no, child. I've only come for just a moment."

Theodora's face fell, but Liana simply said, "Please, *Kyria* Melopoulos, it's no trouble at all."

Vaia stared at her, as if seeing her for the first time. "Well . . . yes, then," she said finally. "A coffee would be pleasant."

"And how do you like it?"

"Medium, please."

Theodora recovered her smile.

CHAPTER 3

"LIANA DEMIRGIS," VAIA MELOPOULOS SAID.

"What?" Dimitri asked. He had only barely heard his wife speak, his attention having already been captured by a phaeton rolling by, drawn by a smart pair of grays. They were sitting on their broad front veranda in suburban Bournabat. It was a late spring evening, and the perfume of roses and jasmine hung on the air. Somewhere, a street or two away, a group of young men sang a raucous love song.

"Liana Demirgis," Vaia repeated firmly.

"Who on earth is she?" he asked.

"The daughter of Emmanuel Demirgis."

"Never heard of him."

"I suggest you find out about him."

"May I ask why?"

"Because she's the one I want for Vasili."

Dimitri turned in surprise, almost spilling his drink. He was paying attention now. "Where have you seen this—this—what is her name?"

"Liana Demirgis, the daughter of Emmanuel and Theodora Demirgis. I saw her some time ago at the baths. And I went to her home to call two weeks ago."

"Two weeks ago? And you're just now saying . . . ?"

"I had to think on it a while. And I had to give them time as well."

Dimitri's eyes narrowed. "Give them time for what?"

"To find out that there will not be so many suitors for their precious daughter. To learn to be a little realistic about her." Vaia smoothed her hair and patted the thick braid coiled at the back of her head.

Dimitri cleared his throat, stood up, and walked to the edge of the veranda, where he spat over the side into a bed of roses. He took a deep breath, enjoying the scent of the flowers, before turning back to his wife sitting smugly in her rattan chair, and he could tell she had already decided on this Liana Demirgis.

"Have you said anything about this to Vasili?"

"Of course not. Not without your agreement first."

Dimitri laughed. That Vaia should wait for his agreement about anything was a joke. "All right, then. Tell me about her. Why should we want her for Vasili?"

Vaia held out her hand to her husband. "Sit down and I'll tell you." She waited, her hand outstretched, until he shrugged and sat back down beside her. "She's the fourth daughter. No sons. The other daughters are beauties, the first especially so. Good reputations, good wives—they made very good marriages. She's the last one and, from what I hear, her father's favorite. So, because of all this—and because she has few if any suitors—they'll put a good dowry on her."

"She's ugly, then?"

"No. Actually, no. She has lovely eyes, beautiful hair, good skin. She would have a pretty face, but she's on the slim side. She's . . . attractive in the European sense, not the Greek."

Dimitri smiled ironically. His wife had pretensions. And, in fact, Vaia herself was slim and always had been. "Pretty, and yet not pretty. But at least not ugly." He stared for a moment at the roses. "On the other hand," he added, "you must remember that Vasili will see her with Greek eyes, not European—as will I and everyone else."

Vaia nodded. "Nevertheless, she comes from good stock; they'll put a good dowry on her. And . . ." she paused for emphasis. "The Demirgis girls have good reputations. They run good homes, and they are respectful, obedient wives."

Dimitri drank the last of his brandy and immediately poured himself more. "Vasili should cheer you," he said, raising his glass to her.

"You'll speak to him about her?"

"Why? I haven't even laid eyes on the girl."

"Because it's proper."

"Proper be damned. What do I know about her? What do I know about choosing a wife, anyway?"

Vaia let out an impatient breath. "One would hope you would take an opportunity to find out about the family before you mention it to him."

"You've already done all that, Vaia. Why involve me at all?"

"Because you're the father!"

He turned away and took a long sip.

"Dimitri." Her voice was softer, cajoling. "I was only doing my duty as a mother. If you know of someone better, fine, we can discuss her. It doesn't have to be this girl. It can be another."

"What's wrong with the Garrifallow girl?"

"Too much of a flirt."

"What's wrong with a flirt? Might be nice."

"Don't be ridiculous!" Vaia snorted. "You play games with a girl like Litsa Garrifallow, but you don't marry your son to her."

"Tassos Giorgiano's daughter, then?"

"Engaged last month."

"Really? Well, still, of all the families in Smyrna, Vaia, I should think there must be plenty of desirable girls."

"The problem is not the number of desirable girls, Dimitri. It's that we'll never get the most desirable, and you know why," she said bitterly. "At any rate, there is no such thing as perfection. One has to set certain priorities and then see who most closely fits them. It's my opinion that Liana Demirgis fits ours. If you have another opinion, feel free to make other arrangements."

Dimitri drained his glass again and reached for the bottle to pour more. "And what, may I ask, are our priorities?"

"What I told you. Good dowry. Good family. Good in the home. Good enough looks. In that order."

"Is there any point in asking Vasili for his priorities?"

Vaia shrugged. "We can ask him. I'm sure his would be the same as ours."

"I'm sure they would." He spoke without a trace of irony.

"You'll tell him, then?"

Dimitri turned the bottle upside down and watched the last drops dribble into the glass. Then he lifted the glass to his lips. "If that's what you want," he said.

CHAPTER 4

VASILI MELOPOULOS'S HEIGHT CAME FROM HIS MOTHER'S SIDE of the family, and he had his mother's triangular face—wide at the eyes and narrow at the chin, with a long, thin, aristocratic nose. What appeared haughty in Vaia seemed more ascetic in her son. He had her fair skin and her long slim fingers. But that was where the similarity stopped.

Vasili was twenty-seven years old and he worked in his father's tobacco shop. When he graduated from the Evangeliki School, his mother had wanted him to go into medicine, but for the first time in his life, Vasili had defied Vaia's wishes. Instead, he chose to work with his father in the kind of silent companionship that is bred into men who are dominated by the same woman. If Vasili could not be what he most wished to be—a farmer—then he was certainly not going to be what his mother most wished him to be. Because it had seemed the only alternative at the time, he had chosen to go into his father's business. In fact, most of his companions had done the same thing, if for various other reasons.

There had been money once in the Melopoulos family, which accounted for the house in Bournabat. But Dimitri's father had spent much of his life trying to run the family's tobacco exporting business in a brandy-soaked haze that had succeeded only in bringing it to bankruptcy. Dimitri had married Vaia back in the days when the family was still a social force in the Smyrniot Greek community. Vaia, whose father had owned a small bedding shop in the city, had thought she was making a good marriage until she got into the family and discovered how precarious their position had already become. And when she learned, early on, that she had married a man who would actually rather be growing the tobacco than shipping it, she immediately envisioned herself the wife of a wealthy planter, and, liking the vision, she had replied, "Fine. We'll sell the business and buy land."

But there was no longer enough of the business to sell, and although Vaia's hopes were dashed, Dimitri's were not. He wasn't interested in owning a tobacco farm anyway; what he wanted was to do the farming. He suggested hiring himself out as an overseer, but Vaia was shocked at the idea. She hadn't married into what she had thought was one of the moneyed families of Smyrna just to find herself the wife of a farm manager. Dimitri urged. She refused. Dimitri pleaded. She turned a deaf ear. And, finally, Dimitri relented, and thus began the pattern of their marriage. When eventually Dimitri's father died in an alcoholic stupor, his creditors took everything except the house in Bournabat, and Dimitri borrowed enough from a relative to open a tobacco shop.

It pleased neither Dimitri nor Vaia that the family had turned into shopkeepers, but tobacco was all he knew, and while Vaia kept silent, she still clung to the hope that the business would grow and flourish and someday they could be in the export trade once again.

Dimitri was disappointed in the shop as well, not because he felt it was beneath him, but because it was even more confining than the tobacco warehouse had been. For a man who felt at home only in the broad cotton and tobacco fields and fig orchards of Aegean Anatolia, it was a difficult adjustment.

By the time Vasili, Vaia and Dimitri's only child, was old enough to hold opinions, Vaia had so dominated their lives that Vasili had grown accustomed to it, and he assumed all homes were run in such a way. Never confessing his ruined dreams to his son, Dimitri would take Vasili into the countryside for long walks in the fields and along the roadsides, and Vasili, never realizing what his father's dream had been, began to dream his own dream of his own fields and his own tobacco growing in the hot summer sun. They would walk side by side, communing by company rather than words, each dreaming a dream of fields and tobacco plants that the other unknowingly shared.

Vasili walked now with his father along a lane at the edge of town, breathing in the springtime perfumes: the last, lingering blossoms on the almond trees and the new leaves of the laurel. The sky was deep blue, and yellow-and-white chamomile daisies clustered among south-facing rocks, pressing their little faces toward the sun. Swallows swooped from tree to tree, chattering as they landed, and taking off again without even folding their wings. Across the tobacco fields, peasant women squatted, transplanting seedlings.

". . . Such a time comes, Vasili," Dimitri said, and Vasili realized that his mind had been wandering.

"Yes, of course," he responded, wondering what his father had been saying.

"Have you anyone in mind?"

Vasili looked blankly at his father.

"Any young ladies?" Dimitri added delicately.

Vasili's eyes quickly fell away from his father's face and drifted to a stone in the path that he kicked into the weeds. Of course he had been looking at the girls, but there was no one he was anxious to declare himself ready to marry.

"Well?" Dimitri asked, and Vasili knew he would have to answer.

"No, Father." His voice sounded suddenly husky. "I . . . no one I ever thought seriously about."

"But you don't deny it's time?"

"No, of course not."

"Hmmmm."

They walked on in silence.

Dimitri tried another tack. "If you've not seen anyone, perhaps you'd like us to start looking."

Vasili laughed, embarrassed. "If I know Mother, she already has."

Dimitri didn't respond.

The truth dawning, Vasili turned to his father. "She has, hasn't she?"

Dimitri tilted his head back and forth, noncommittally.

"Well?"

Dimitri shrugged and looked away.

Vasili stopped and faced his father. "She's found someone?"

"She'll find someone if you don't," Dimitri hedged.

"I'll not marry someone of her choice."

"You don't have to."

Vasili walked on silently for a time. "Who is it?" he finally asked.

"Someone you probably don't know."

"Who?"

"I think I've forgotten the name."

Vasili stopped dead still. "*Who?*"

"Let me think now." But Dimitri realized he was not going to get away with having forgotten the name. "Some girl named . . . ahhh . . . Demirgis."

"I don't recall any Demirgis girl."

"Liana Demirgis."

Liana. A pretty name—which probably meant she was as ugly as a camel. "Have you seen her?" Vasili asked.

"Yes, once."

"Well?"

"What does she look like? She's tall—not as tall as you, of course. Very black hair, pretty hair. Nice eyes, good complexion, a sweet girl, they say. Perhaps"—Dimitri shrugged—"perhaps a little thin."

"Is that all? You must not be telling me something. She must have some bad points."

"You think so? Why should she?"

Vasili shrugged. There was more to this than his father was telling him. There was something he was holding back.

"Have you spoken with her parents?"

"Of course not. We thought you would want to see her first."

Vasili felt an unexpected fullness in his chest.

"Her father has a silversmithing business in the *charsha*," Dimitri offered. "He has a reputation for fine filigree work. There are two or three employees. There's money there; not a fortune, but some."

Liana. Vasili kept saying the name over and over to himself. *Liana. Pretty eyes, pretty hair, good skin. And perhaps a little thin*—what did that mean? Why did this girl, whom he had never seen or even heard of until a moment ago, make him feel more excited than any of the girls he knew?

"I want to see her," he said at last.

LIANA PLACED AN AMBER BEESWAX CANDLE INTO AN EMPTY SOCKET of the large circular silver candelabra at the back of the church and crossed herself three times. Then she bowed over the icon stand and prayed. Her murmured words reflected the confusion she had come to feel—the fear that, unmarried, she would become a burden to her family, and the hope now that she could have a husband and children of her own. As she prayed, her head bobbed up and down, kissing again and again the delicate silver filigree that surrounded the icon's face.

She crossed herself again three times and backed away toward her waiting mother. For a moment Liana's eyes held on the candle she had lit, willing her prayer onto it, that it might serve to repeat her prayer for as long as it burned. Then she turned back to her mother, and the two walked together toward the front of the church.

In the dim candlelight, the priest sang the service and incense hung on the air. Liana's thoughts, mesmerized by the rhythm of the priestly voice and the heavy odor of the incense, drifted to the back of the church, to where one candle among many was burning with her prayer. *Please*, she thought, *someone I can learn to love.*

Four weeks of going to the baths; four weeks of serving coffee to women who came and looked and talked and admired her embroidery—and who drank the coffee and ate the sweets; four weeks of meeting women, of seeing one or two, perhaps, again, of furtive questions and cautious responses. Four weeks of tentative smiles and tentative hopes and finally tentative goodbyes from cagey women who never made any offers.

"It's still quite early," Theodora kept reassuring her. "Why, only Christina had the arrangements made so quickly." But Liana saw her mother looking sidelong at her when Theodora thought she didn't notice, and her sisters stayed too cheery and too casual, and her father smiled too indulgently, and Liana knew everyone was worried. *Please*, she thought, *I only ask that he be a good man.* The priest continued praying, bowing his head sometimes and raising his arms at other times. *God can do anything,* Liana thought. *Was it too much to ask God to send someone?*

She felt a kind of pressure on her head, not like the touch of a hand or the breath of air that might be felt if a door had suddenly been opened, but a gentle feeling as if something were there but not quite there. Unthinking, she put her hand to her head but felt nothing. The sensation left, but then it returned almost as fast as it had gone, so delicate and ephemeral that she was no longer sure she even felt it. She turned and looked behind her. A small crowd of men was clustered together in the back of the church, and for an instant she caught a pair of eyes. But then they looked away and she turned back. *Had he been staring at her?* She considered this; she had never seen him before. She turned again, and once more it seemed he looked away, but this time so fast that she couldn't quite be sure.

She leaned toward her mother and said something, and when she had finished whispering she didn't turn back. She could see him now out of the corner of her eye, and he *was* staring at her. She felt her face flush under his gaze, and, embarrassed, she turned away. The priest and the service were almost forgotten; the man staring at her across the church filled her mind. Who was he? The son of some woman who had come? Now he no longer even looked away, no longer even pretended not to be looking at her, and she blushed more fully. Surely he knew that she'd been aware of him watching her.

As the service ended, Theodora turned to speak with friends, and Liana turned too, as if looking for someone, but he was no longer staring at her. Talking with a man at his side, he seemed completely unaware of her. Her stomach suddenly felt tight with disappointment; she had been mistaken. He had only been gazing into space and she had simply been a part of that space; he had not noticed her at all. She turned back to her mother in dismay. *It is not as easy as that to find a husband,* she told herself. But her mother was still talking, and she turned away once again, and now she saw him across the heads of other people. His eyes were on her again, and this time she was sure: He really was watching her.

"Liana," her mother said now, pulling her away. "We must be going. Your sisters will be home before we get there!" She held Liana's elbow with her hand, guiding her out through the dispersing crowd. Frantically, Liana's eyes sought the man. He had been there only moments ago, but now he was gone.

Disappointed, she walked with her mother from the dim church into the bright sun of the outside. For a moment her eye caught on someone ahead of her, but then the man turned to his left and hurried off and she saw it was someone else. The man she had been so sure was staring at her was gone.

Back in the church, the candle still burned, carrying her prayer heavenward.

"WELL?" ARA FAYROYIAN SAID, DODGING A BOY RUNNING ALONG the street with a tray of tea glasses. They were walking toward the seafront. Already, one could hear the clank of camel bells and, in the farther distance, the deep-throated bellow of ships' horns.

"What do *you* think?" Vasili asked.

"It's not up to me," Ara said. And then he added, "But if it were . . . She's not bad."

Vasili grinned. "She's beautiful."

"She's *pretty,*" Ara corrected.

"She's beautiful."

"Maria Hagopian is beautiful. This one is pretty."

Vasili said nothing, trying to picture her again in his mind's eye.

"Your mother chose her," Ara pointed out.

Vasili chuckled. "You know, I told my father I wouldn't take someone of her choosing. But, my God, you have to admit, she's not bad."

"You haven't even met her. She could stink to high heaven as far as you know; she could have a voice to call pigs with; she could not have a brain in her head; she could—" Just then Vasili shoved him out of the path of a handsome matched pair of chestnuts, pulling an enclosed carriage. Ara stared at the banners flying from the carriage. "Those shits! Think they own the place!"

"They do."

Ara stared at him. "That's the problem. That's exactly the problem. *You bastards!*" he yelled after the departing carriage. "*You fucking bastards!*"

"Ara."

"What?"

"It doesn't do any good, you know."

Ara laughed. "It does me a world of good, actually. Yelling is better than keeping it all inside."

"You know what I mean."

"Actually, Vasili, it wouldn't be hard to really do something."

"Really do what?"

Ara shrugged.

"You're not serious."

"Why not? Shake them up, put them on notice."

"You'd never get away with it."

"A person might. If you watch long enough, there might be a routine. You could be on the route, have a gun, throw a bomb."

"Where would you get a bomb?"

"A person could make one, Vasili. It's probably not that hard."

"You'd never get away with it," Vasili repeated.

"A person might. And think what a glorious act it would be."

Vasili punched him lightly on the arm. "You never change, do you, Ara?"

"Nor do you," Ara responded, suddenly serious. "But you should."

Vasili gazed into the distance. They were close enough now to the sea to smell it, to glimpse the water between buildings.

"You have too comfortable a life here," Ara prodded.

"We always have. It's always been this way," Vasili responded. "Yours is comfortable too."

"And so you think it always will be so. It won't."

"Why should it change?"

"Vasili. Something always happens. The world always changes. Nothing is forever."

"Well then, at least you don't have to start it."

"It's already been started."

"Stories. How do we even know they're true?"

Ara stopped and turned toward Vasili. "I know," he said quietly. "In my gut, I know."

CHAPTER 5

LIANA LAID DOWN HER EMBROIDERY AND TOOK A DEEP BREATH. With her hand, she absently smoothed it, the rose-and-leaf pattern coming alive with the movement. Her head was a muddle. For as long as she could remember, she had looked forward to being married, to having a home, family, children. She had imagined children running boisterously through the house, crowding around the table with her as they helped make *keftethes*, or carefully rolling cabbage leaves into *lahano dolmathes*, their hands messy with the task but their faces grinning with enjoyment. Or playing games in the garden, drinking lemonade on hot summer days, telling stories at bedtime.

But she had never imagined a husband, a father for those children. In her sheltered life, she had known so few men—her father, her brothers-in-law, sons of her mother's friends that she had seen sometimes at Aghios Giorgios, none of them close enough to her age to imagine marriage with them. In the past weeks, no one she knew seemed to fit what she might have imagined. Someone as loving as her father, she thought now. And, with a smile, someone as handsome and charming as Sophie's husband, Themo. Someone who would be a good husband and father—yes, that, whatever that might mean.

She rose and looked out into the garden. And then she walked out, bending to smell the roses, to gently touch their satin petals. Could there ever be a man who could give her the kind of life she already had? Might it not be just as well to remain as she was, living in this house with her parents and this lovely garden, close enough to her sisters' homes that she could walk to visit them and to play with their children, close enough to the harbor that she could sometimes hear the bellow of the ships' horns? What more could she ask for?

What would her parents say to that? Her father would frown: *But don't you want your own family?* he would ask. *What would you do when your mama and I grew old and died?*

Her mother would laugh at that, and then she would become serious. *Don't you want your own family, your own husband and children?* she would echo.

But in this whole city, Liana thought, *with its thousands—tens of thousands—of Greeks, how could one find the right person? And even if one found him, how would one know he really was the one?*

"Liana"—her mother's voice came to her as from a long distance—"child, you should be working on your *proika*. Don't you want to have a trunk full of things to bring to the marriage?"

Liana laughed. *What marriage?* she thought. "There's plenty of time," she said.

"One never knows," her mother responded.

But Liana only smiled at her and walked back toward the house. *It would not be a bad thing at all,* she thought, *to spend the whole rest of my life right where I am.*

"They say his father drinks," Emmanuel Demirgis told his wife.

"I know what they say," Theodora retorted.

"His grandfather died of drink. Lost the family business from drink."

"We're discussing the boy, not his grandfather."

"Like father, like son."

"With a wife like Vaia, you would drink too."

"And that's another thing."

"Mano, he's a good boy. Everyone says so."

"If he's so good, then why—"

"Why what?"

"Nothing," Emmanuel said, turning away.

"Why do they want our Liana? you're asking." Theodora's voice was accusatory. She shook out her hair and began brushing it with sharp, agitated strokes. Already in bed, her husband watched. Despite four pregnancies, Theodora's hair was still as thick as when she was seventeen, and it still gleamed like moonlight on the black waters of Smyrna Bay. She washed it every week with a goose egg dissolved in beer, and she had recently taken to plucking out any gray hairs that dared appear.

"I have not noticed," Emmanuel said, choosing his words carefully, "that many people have been aware of Liana's very special gifts."

Theodora turned toward him. "In other words, they compare her with her sisters."

"She is our smartest and our most independent . . ."

Theodora shook her brush at him. "Yes, and she needs to hide that. Men don't want too much independence in a wife."

"I doubt that Vaia Melopoulos would want it at all. I wonder why she's interested."

"Vaia's not aware, obviously. We should keep it that way." Theodora turned back to the mirror, mentally counting the strokes of the brush as she spoke.

"No, I disagree."

Theodora stopped brushing and turned again to face her husband. "Mano, it's all lost if she finds out."

"If she's that hard to live with, then better for Liana that she does find out and loses interest. We married the other three off happily and we'll do the same for Liana, or not at all."

"Are you really ready for that? For the not at all?"

"Someone will come. It's only been a few weeks."

"Four! Four weeks, and this is the first solid possibility."

"You don't jump at the first chance."

"You do if it's the only chance there is."

"You really think our Liana is such a bad catch?"

Theodora moved to the bed and sat down on the edge of it. "I want her happiness too. If you knew how ashamed she feels!"

"And who makes her feel ashamed? What is there about Liana to be ashamed of? She's the sweetest of them all."

Theodora chuckled and leaned over to her husband, running the backs of her fingers along the side of his face. "You are so transparent, Mano. You love her best, don't you?"

Emmanuel caught her hand and held it to his lips. "They are all precious—four lovely daughters. And Liana is every bit as precious as the others."

Theodora leaned her forehead on his chest. "It would have been fine to have had a son."

"I've never regretted any of our daughters, never wished any one of them was a son."

"But a man wants sons."

"Dora, God gave you four beautiful daughters, whole and perfect. Why should you wish for a son?"

Theodora didn't respond.

"Come now, put the brush away and come to bed."

Theodora rose and walked to her dressing table, laying the brush beside its matching hand mirror. Then she turned down the wick of the lamp, and in its glow, before the light faded completely, she moved back to the bed.

"I only want for my family to be happy," she said. "For you to be happy, and for all of our daughters as well."

"I am the happiest of men," Emmanuel whispered, putting his arm around her.

Theodora giggled. "I remember when I first saw you, how frightened I was!"

"And I. I was frightened too."

"You, Mano! Really?"

"Really. I hadn't the faintest idea of how to treat a woman. Sisters, yes. My mother, of course. But a wife? I was terrified."

Theodora chuckled. "We were both terrified."

"At least our daughters knew the men they were going to marry."

"And Liana?"

"Liana too. She'll not marry anyone unless she chooses to."

"They say he's a nice boy." Theodora's voice was hopeful.

"From what I hear, the problem will not be with him. It will be with his mother."

VAIA MELOPOULOS PULLED HEAVY DAMASK DRAPES AGAINST THE afternoon sun, and the warm golds and reds of the Ghiordes rug on the dining-room floor darkened. "I'm not entirely in favor of it," she said.

Her husband leaned back in his chair and sipped his brandy without responding.

"Where is Vasili now, anyway?" Vaia asked suddenly. She sat back down at the table and began restlessly drumming her fingers. Without waiting for a response, she added, "He's probably off with Ara again. I just wish he'd . . ." Her voice trailed off, which was unusual for Vaia, who always knew exactly what she thought about everything.

"Ara's a nice boy."

"Dimitri, look at him. Anyone can tell what he is without even half looking."

Dimitri said nothing.

"I don't know what he was doing at the Evangeliki School anyway. It should only be for Greeks."

"The Fayroyians are Christians."

"Armenians are not Greeks. They don't have behind them what we do. Where's their Socrates? Where's their Plato? What have they ever done in the world?"

"Ara's a nice boy. He comes from a good family."

"Ara's trouble. He was always getting into mischief as a boy. And if you look at him closely you can tell it's still in him. Well, thank God, at least they managed to marry off their daughter without coming to us for Vasili."

"Why would they have done that? We barely know their family."

She shrugged. "People do that. If they think it's to their benefit." She let out a long, impatient breath. "I just don't know what things are coming to these days."

"Vasili's a grown man, Vaia. He doesn't have to report to us."

"He's being difficult in this. And they are. And *you* are. One would think such a thing could be easily arranged, but no. First he has to see her. All right, that's arranged. Next thing you know, he wants to meet her, and now they say they want *her* to meet *him*!"

Dimitri held up his hands as if in defense. "So what? That's not unusual. We met before."

"Of course they can meet. But *after* the arrangements are made, not like this. Not Vasili insisting on meeting her before he agrees; and—worse—*her* wanting to meet *him* first. As if we parents are nothing! *And you seem to think there's nothing wrong with any of it!*"

"Times change, Vaia. Why not let them have a say?"

"Yes, of course, they can have a say. I wouldn't dream of not considering their wishes. But this is ridiculous! A silly seventeen-year-old girl—what does *she* know about a husband? And Vasili, he's older, but it hardly makes any difference. What does he know of marriage anyway?"

Her husband sipped his drink in silence.

"And you, Dimitri, *you think it's just fine!*"

"You chose her, Vaia. They would never have even known about each other if it hadn't been for you."

"What if she takes it into her head that she doesn't like him, what then? How will that look?"

"What if he doesn't like her?"

Vaia dismissed the possibility with a wave of her hand. "I hope I know my own son."

"Perhaps you need to keep looking. I'm sure there are other girls."

She sat stiffly in her chair for a long moment. "No," she said finally, "everyone says she's a very obedient and well-brought-up child." And that, she had known all along, ought also to make her a very compliant one.

CHAPTER 6

SOPHIE'S HOUSE WAS SMALL AND COOL AND PERFECTLY SERENE, even on this day, so warm already for late May, and despite all the party arrangements. Liana placed her armload of carefully wrapped packages on the worktable in the kitchen—scrubbed to gleaming as always—and wandered into Sophie's parlor. The shutters were closed and the draperies drawn, keeping the morning cool inside against the heat of midday. It was Liana's favorite room in all the world. Lace antimacassars that Sophie had crocheted covered the backs and arms of the heavy furniture, and embroidered pillows lay in studied arrangement on the sofa. On the wall were three small paintings Sophie had done as well, each of a quiet country scene. A pair of pale green faience vases stood on the mantelpiece, each filled with pink and white roses from Sophie's own exquisite garden, and the polished floor was covered with the finest rugs from the best rug dealer in all of Smyrna.

If I had a house of my own, Liana thought, *I would want it to be just like this.* But in the next moment, she knew that was not quite true, for despite all its treasures, Sophie's house was missing the one thing she held most dear: the sound of children to enliven the quiet house. After six years of marriage, Sophie and Themo were still childless.

Themo worked for his uncle, Constantine Panayotis, who was in the rug business. Constantine's "factory" was really only a warehouse in which he stored the carpets made for him by cottage labor in the villages. Because of Themo's widowed and childless uncle, it had fallen to Sophie to arrange a name-day party on May 21, the patron day of Saints Eleni and Constantine. Honored guests were Sophie's sister Eleni, her nephew Constantine—the son of her sister Christina—and of course her husband's uncle. Naturally Sophie had invited her own immediate family to attend, and to honor Uncle Constantine, she'd invited some of his old friends, including the family of Dimitri Melopoulos, who had been a good friend of Constantine Panayotis back in the days when the Melopoulos tobacco warehouse had been right next to the Panayotis rug factory.

Because of the size of Sophie's house, it was fortunate that the name day came at a time of year that the party could be held outdoors in the garden. Theodora had offered to help her daughter by preparing some of the food in her own kitchen, and she and Liana had come early to assist in arranging the tables in the garden, to place bouquets of flowers, and to perform whatever other last-minute chores needed doing. Knowing that she would be helping in the kitchen and perhaps serving some of the food, Liana chose to wear a nice serviceable dress of dark brown with narrow pink stripes.

But when Theodora had seen her, she'd said, "Oh, Liana! Don't wear that dress! Wear something prettier. It's a party, after all! Why not wear your shirtwaist with the yellow roses?"

"But Mama, I'll be helping. It's bound to get messy."

But her mother had ignored her. "And your hair, don't wear it in braids like that around your head. Wear it down today; it's so much nicer that way."

"This party isn't for me," Liana had said. "No one's going to notice what I'm wearing."

Theodora had gazed at her for a long moment. "Well then," she'd finally said. "You keep this dress on, but let's bring the other. Then, just before the guests come, you can change. But Liana, do go and fix your hair some other way."

"I don't understand what all the fuss is about. No one will even be paying attention to me. It's Eleni and little Dino and Sophie's Uncle Constantine they'll be seeing, not me. Unless—"

"Unless what?"

Liana laughed uneasily. "Unless you've gotten so desperate for me that you want to impress an old man like Sophie's Uncle Constantine."

Theodora had stood for a moment with her mouth hanging open. Then she'd said briskly, "Don't be ridiculous! Now run along and do as I say. Look pretty, Liana, you never know whom you're going to see."

Now, in Sophie's parlor, Liana heard her sister's distant voice calling her. "Liana! Come out to the garden. Tell me what you think."

Liana turned abruptly to leave the room and nearly walked right into Themo, who'd been standing less than an arm's length behind her. *How long has he been there? Why hadn't I heard him?* she wondered.

"You're looking especially pretty today, Liana," he said. He reached out a hand and with his fingertips brushed a strand of hair back from her face.

Suddenly flushing, she looked away. She'd had a crush on Themo in the first years of Sophie's marriage; she supposed he still remembered that.

Now his gaze swept slowly over her, from the top of her head to the pointed toes of her shoes. "The last of the Demirgis girls," he said softly. "Your mother must be very proud." Then he stepped aside that she might pass. And as she did so, he put a hand lightly on her back, as if to guide her. It was a casual move, and it lasted for only a moment, but the feel of it lingered much longer. Since she had turned thirteen, no man other than her father had ever intentionally touched her.

She found her mother and Sophie in the midst of the garden. Lace-covered tables had been set up between the flowers, and Liana clasped her hands in delight. "Oh, it's absolutely beautiful!"

"Sophie, you do have a way with roses!" Theodora exclaimed.

"Mmmmm, smell them," Liana said, her eyes closed as she breathed in a rainbow of fragrances.

"Do you think the tables are all right the way they are?" Sophie asked uncertainly.

"Of course, darling. Everything looks perfect."

"Do you think it'll rain?" Sophie asked.

Liana and her mother both looked up into a cloudless sky. "Sophie, really." Theodora laughed, turning back toward the house.

"Liana—" Sophie stepped closer and placed her hand on her sister's arm. She took a deep breath, as if she were going to say something important, but she simply said, "You're looking so pretty these days."

It was not, Liana realized, what her sister had started to say. "Mama made me bring another dress to change into. Can you imagine anything so silly?"

Sophie smiled broadly. "It's the way mothers are. Don't think anything about it."

"I accused her of going after your Uncle Constantine."

Sophie laughed outrageously at that. "He's old enough to be your grandfather, child!"

"I'm glad to hear you laugh. From the way Mother acted, I was beginning to think there might be some truth to it."

"Oh, no, no, Liana! Don't worry so much."

"That's all anyone says to me these days: Liana, don't worry."

"It's just our way of saying 'be yourself.'"

"What else would I be?"

"My precious sister." Sophie took both Liana's slim hands in her own plump ones. "We all love you dearly, you know that?"

Liana nodded gravely.

"Then forget everything else. Today is going to be a party! Forget everything else and have a good time."

"Auntie Liana." A small hand tugged at Liana's skirt. Turning, she smiled at Christina's daughter and knelt to the four-year-old's level.

"Yes, Soula. What is it?"

"Naso says I mayn't have any more to eat."

Liana took Soula's tiny hands into her own, disregarding their stickiness, a remnant of the syrup-soaked cakes Soula had already eaten. "Have you had so much, then?"

"No. Hardly anything."

"And big brother is bossing you around?"

"Yes."

Liana gently squeezed the little hands in her own. "I know how it is to be the youngest. Never mind, Soula. It's a party. You can have as much as you like."

Soula's serious eyes gazed into Liana's. "I'm not the youngest, Auntie."

"Of course not. Do you think Baby Constantine likes his party?"

"Liana." It was Themo's voice, and Liana turned in surprise. Her eyes darted up the two pairs of pantlegs that were standing next to her now and she saw Themo, and with him was another man, someone she had never seen before.

"Liana," Themo repeated as she sprang to her feet. "I'd like you to meet a friend of mine."

Liana's eyes moved from Themo's face to that of the stranger, but now a chill ran down the backs of her arms as she realized she had seen him before. In church, across the heads of other worshippers, these had been the eyes that had stared at her. In that instant, with the chatter of the party surrounding her, with the sweet smells of jasmine and roses and honey hanging in the air, with the quick dart of Soula away from her, searching out yet another sweetcake to pop into her mouth, with the blue, blue sky hanging above the garden, Liana knew what was happening.

"He's the son of our good friend Dimitri Melopoulos—his name is Vasili."

Liana felt the crimson flood into her cheeks, and she was suddenly aware that the loud chatter of the party was now suppressed as all the others, literally and figuratively, held their breaths. Vaia Melopoulos had come only once, Liana thought with a kind of panic, and no one had said anything at the time about it. Now it was obvious that Liana had won at least one mother of a son.

"I'm very pleased to meet you, Liana." Vasili Melopoulos's eyes were serious, and he made a curt little bow as he spoke.

"And I to meet you," she whispered. *What do I do?* she wondered desperately. She made a small quick movement with her hand, then thought better of it, but Vasili had seen the move and extended his own hand. Now there was nothing to do but let him take hers, but the instant he clasped her hand she knew it had been a mistake. The flush deepened and her head lowered in embarrassment. As their hands touched, they both felt the syrupy stickiness that had come to Liana from little Soula's fingers.

Her first reaction was to pull her hand away, but he held it firmly in his own and made another little bow over it. And he laughed.

"It—it was . . ." she stammered.

"From the child, I suppose."

"I should have washed. I didn't think."

"Now we shall both have to wash."

Only then did he release her hand, and only then did she dare to look him in the face once again. His mouth was smiling, but his eyes still looked at her seriously, as they had done in church, with great concentration and as if from very far away.

Theodora had watched her son-in-law introduce Vasili Melopoulos to Liana, and she bit her lip in nervous anticipation as Liana looked for the first time at Vasili. Theodora caught the quick movement of Liana's hand as she hesitated, uncertain whether or not to extend it, and she tried to will the proper response toward Liana. But then she saw the two join hands, Liana's sudden, embarrassed downturn of face, and Vasili's quick laugh. "What happened?" she whispered to her husband, who stood beside her, watching the youngsters.

Emmanuel didn't respond, but his gaze still held on Liana and Vasili. Theodora's eyes narrowed in concern as she noticed that Vasili still held her daughter's hand. Unseemly, to say the least.

Then Liana turned abruptly from Vasili and ran toward the house. Theodora grasped Emmanuel's arm in alarm. "*What happened?* I'm going to her!"

But Emmanuel held her with a quick move of his hand. "Leave her be."

"But Mano, you can see something's wrong!"

"Leave it alone. It'll be all right."

Theodora looked anxiously about to see who else had noticed. Of course Vaia had, standing a few feet off, looking horrified at Liana's bad manners.

Indignantly Theodora thought: *And what about your own son's manners? The way he held her hand for so long, no wonder she was frightened.* Vaia, with her superior ways, probably hadn't even noticed what her precious son had done. It was a good thing Sophie had had this party after all. Liana was not so desperate that she needed to marry the bad-mannered son of haughty Vaia Melopoulos.

But then Liana emerged from the house, carrying a damp kitchen towel, and Theodora watched curiously as her daughter crossed the garden once again and gave the towel to Vasili. He took it, saying a few words to Liana as he wiped his hands clean. Then he chuckled, still holding the towel as Liana tried to take it from him, and the two of them moved off toward the back of the garden, where they sat down together on a wide stone bench.

"What was it?" Theodora asked, her face full of concern.

"It doesn't matter, she evidently handled it," Emmanuel answered.

"Did you see the way he held her hand?"

"Now Dora, leave them alone."

But Theodora looked back toward Vaia, who was gazing absently at the youngsters. *She doesn't like it*, Theodora thought. *And that makes two of us.*

"It's a lovely garden," Vasili said.

Liana smiled, delighted that he too appreciated Sophie's flowers.

"Do you like to garden?" he asked.

"Yes. But of course I'm not nearly as good as Sophie."

"But then, she's had more practice, probably."

"Still, she's very good with plants and things." She felt much more comfortable talking about Sophie. She had never before spoken alone to a man who was not a relative.

"I'd like to have a garden, only bigger than this. In fact, I'd like to live in the country."

"Where do you live?"

"In Bournabat."

"But Vasili, that *is* in the country!"

"I mean really in the country. With fields all around."

"Oh."

"I suppose I never really will," he hastened to add, realizing that she probably wouldn't think much of the idea. He cleared his throat. "You seem to think very highly of your sister." A safer subject.

"Of all my sisters. I have three." She felt more comfortable now, talking about her family. He nodded, and it occurred to her that he probably already knew that. And that she knew nothing about him. "How many sisters and brothers do you have?" she asked.

"None."

She looked nervously about. What should she say? What does a person say at a time like this? "I can't imagine what it must be like not having any brothers or sisters," she ventured.

"And I can't imagine what it would be like to have had any."

"Oh Vasili, it's so much fun! We always have such good times together! You would have loved to have had brothers and sisters, I should think." Her eyes glowed with the memories that tumbled into her mind. "We always laugh—and we talk all the time—and of course we always eat way too much!"

"They say your father loves his daughters very much."

She wondered if there was something wrong with that, if

Vasili would prefer that her father didn't care so much about her. But how could a father not love his children? She couldn't imagine that.

"And I can tell you love your family too," he added. He looked about, and then he cleared his throat again. "Liana, I want you to know that I would never make you leave them. We wouldn't have to live in Bournabat. Or in the country. If you prefer, we could live in the city, near your family."

Her breath caught in her throat, and "Thank you" was all she said, her voice calm and even, as if he had offered her something simple, like a rose or a piece of candy. But inside, her heart was singing.

CHAPTER 7

Emmanuel Demirgis sat alone at a small table against the wall, coffeehouse sounds surrounding him—the hard slap of *tavli* pieces moved aggressively and the clatter of dice, the rise and fall of political argument, the soft click of worry beads moving through restless fingers, the gentle bubble of *narghiles*. He held a newspaper open before him, but he was no longer reading. He saw the boy then—no, he corrected himself: This is a man—pausing at the open door. Emmanuel did not signal, but he held the paper before him as if engrossed, while in reality he watched over the top of the pages.

Vasili caught sight of him finally and moved toward the table where Emmanuel sat. *He is good looking*, Emmanuel thought. *It's no wonder Liana is taken with him. But I should hope there's more to him than that.* In this first meeting of the two of them alone, he would begin to learn whether in fact there was more.

Vasili stood before him now, and Emmanuel slowly folded the newspaper and touched it deliberately against the back of the chair opposite him. Vasili, acknowledging the invitation, drew out the chair and sat down.

"I appreciate your coming," Emmanuel said.

"It was nothing."

"Coffee?"

"If you please."

Emmanuel snapped his fingers, and when a boy appeared, he ordered two coffees and then turned again to Vasili. "It was not difficult for you to get away, I hope."

Vasili stared at him for a brief moment, then half smiled. "It's a good time of day. My parents are still having their afternoon rest. They'll think I've gone to open the shop, but it won't hurt if it opens a little late instead."

Emmanuel nodded approvingly. The boy was perceptive. He had responded better than Emmanuel had feared. Emmanuel had to keep reminding himself that this person who would marry his child was truly a man. And Liana was nearly a woman. For her, they would have to join forces.

"I wouldn't want you to deceive your parents," Emmanuel said cautiously.

"Of course not."

"I asked you here because I have concerns for my daughter."

Vasili looked down at his hands. When he looked up again, his eyes were clear and direct. "I think we would both want whatever would please her."

Emmanuel said nothing, and finally Vasili went on. "I have already told her that we would live wherever she chooses. I know her family is important to her."

"You discussed it?"

"Yes. That day, when we met."

Emmanuel cleared his throat, surprised. "My daughter will expect such a promise to be kept," he said stiffly.

"Of course."

Emmanuel saw no vacillation in the dark eyes. The boy really meant it, then. He leaned forward. "Vasili, how can you make such a promise?"

"For your daughter, I already have."

"But how will you keep it?"

The coffee came, mounded with foam, the sweet-acrid smell of it rising from the cups. Vasili took a few moments for a sip, then he set the cup down. "We shall be honest with each other. I know what you're thinking. You are concerned about this. You worry about my mother, about whether she will run our lives, and how that would be for your daughter. You worry about me, if I am good enough for your Liana, how I will treat her. Maybe you even worry about how many women I have already known, and how I will be after the wedding, whether I will continue with them. What you can't know is what I am like, how I have been brought up, or what expectations I have for a wife—for marriage." Vasili flicked an imaginary crumb off the table, and then his eyes returned to Emmanuel. "Well. You look at my parents and you have a right to be concerned. My mother has dominated me all my life, that's true, but not without my being aware. She will not dominate my marriage, I will promise you that. Liana is quite different from her. She doesn't demand, does she, and therefore what I give to her will be of my own giving, and not of her taking. For that reason she will come first for me, in all ways. I will keep my promises to her."

"Do your parents know about the promise you've already made?"

"No."

"A young couple generally lives near the husband's family. Surely they are expecting that, for you to live in Bournabat."

"My mother is no doubt expecting us to live *with* them. It's a big house."

Emmanuel raised his eyebrows.

Vasili saw and went on. "I am not saying it will be easy, but that is no reason to give in. One must be willing to work for what one wants. Liana loves her family. I know it would hurt her to be separated from you. She has a feeling for family that I've never had, but I would like to. It's what I would like for my children, as well as for Liana and me. You're her father—the head of her family. You must know how to make this feeling. You could help us."

"Do you know what you are asking?"

"Yes, of course."

"It's very strange for a man in your position to say these things to his future father-in-law."

"If I must choose, you can see what I would choose."

Emmanuel picked up the folded newspaper and tapped it on the table, lost in thought. Finally he said, "Vasili, what have your parents said concerning a dowry?"

"Only that it should be a good one . . . because Liana is a well-loved child . . . and you will want to marry her off properly. Naturally, they know you have your own business."

Emmanuel nodded absently, still tapping the newspaper on the table. Then he stopped, laid it down deliberately, and ran his fingers along the folded edges, as if the creases weren't sharp enough to suit him. At last he leaned back and smiled broadly. "In that case," he said, "perhaps we can work out a way to buy them both for you."

Vasili frowned. "Both?"

"Yes, both. Not only my daughter, but also freedom from your mother."

CHAPTER 8

LIANA SAT STIFFLY IN HER CHAIR, LOOKING DOWN AT HER HANDS. The table had been set with her mother's best linen tablecloth, embroidered with elegant designs in white silk thread. Three white candles burned low in three silver candlesticks. The meal had already been served: *kayit kebab* and *itch pilav*, the rice so fluffy that if one blew on one's fork the grains would fly off one by one. "Liana is such a good cook!" Theodora had exclaimed, as if anyone actually believed that Liana had done it all herself. The *tulumba tatlisi* had been eaten and commented upon. "Liana is the best cook of all my daughters," Theodora had said. The coffee had been passed and the *lokum* sampled. "I'm sure I don't know," Theodora had added, "how Liana has managed to learn so much at such a young age." And the brandy had been poured for the men.

Finally, Emmanuel had grinned expansively and pushed his chair back. "Shall we go into the parlor?" he'd asked Theodora.

And she'd smiled and looked at Vaia Melopoulos and at Vaia's husband, Dimitri, and then had said, "Certainly."

They'd all risen then, Vasili with his hand on his mother's chair to help her, Liana still barely daring to look straight at him, and Emmanuel had led the way into the sitting room, where Theodora asked if anyone cared for more coffee.

Vaia had said, "No thank you, the dinner has been delicious but we've had quite enough," and Dimitri had held out his glass for a bit more brandy, and Emmanuel had poured him half an inch and smiled and offered the rest to Vasili. Liana had stood in the arch of the doorway until everyone else was seated—Vaia having taken the most prominent chair—and then Liana settled herself into a divan next to her mother. She wished she could be anywhere but where she was.

"Vasili is quite well situated," Vaia stated. "An only son. The house in Bournabat will be his, of course, and of course also his father's business." She frowned at Dimitri.

Dimitri cleared his throat. "Quite true," he said, "quite true."

No one else said anything.

"The tobacco business," Dimitri said at last. "Of course, it's a very good business. And we deal only in the very best quality. The world comes to our doorstep. All the best blends include our own choice Turkish tobacco."

Vaia looked at Emmanuel, and Dimitri looked at him as well.

Liana pressed her thumbs together.

Emmanuel cleared his throat, and Liana imagined he sat straighter in his chair, but she didn't look up from her lap.

"I have four daughters," Emmanuel began. He cleared his throat again. "I have been very well blessed, thanks to God. But I have no sons."

Liana pressed a thumbnail into the palm of her hand.

"And . . ." There was a pause, and Liana imagined a shrug of her father's shoulders. "And I no longer expect any."

Theodora murmured something, but no one caught her words.

"So . . ." Emmanuel said, ignoring his wife. "So I have come to realize that no son will inherit the business."

Liana felt a sudden stillness in the room.

"Business is quite good. We enjoy a good location—the only silversmith on a street of gold artisans. Some of the wealthiest of Smyrna's citizens come to my shop, from all quarters of the city. Greeks and Turks and Armenians and Jews. And of course the Levantines and the Europeans."

Liana was listening intently now, staring at her hands folded in her lap.

"The shop brings in enough to easily support two families, as well as the families of my assistants."

Liana held her breath.

"And I am not getting any younger."

She stole a look at her father; his face was serious—sour even, as if he'd just eaten three lemons, though in fact he'd had the same meal as the rest of them.

"And I've grown tired of dealing with the public. What I need is someone who will take care of that, so that I can concentrate on what I do best."

Across the room, Vaia's skirts rustled. "I'm not sure—" she began, but Emmanuel interrupted her.

"What I need is a partner." Emmanuel paused. "Actually, more than a partner. What I need is someone who can take over the business. A new owner, so to speak."

Liana looked at him in surprise.

Emmanuel waved his hand vaguely in the air. "Fresh ideas. New blood."

Liana glanced at Vaia, who was staring at Emmanuel as if she thought he might have lost his mind.

"What do you think?" Emmanuel asked.

"The business?" Vaia asked.

"The business," Emmanuel said firmly. Beside Liana, Theodora fluttered her eyelids, and for a moment Liana thought her mother might faint.

"Who would help *me*?" Dimitri Melopoulos asked.

Vaia didn't even glance at him. "Exactly what terms?" she asked Emmanuel.

"In his name, of course. He runs it."

She narrowed her eyes. "A partnership of sorts?"

Emmanuel stared at her for a long moment, and Liana saw Vaia's mouth form into a thin, self-satisfied line.

"No," Emmanuel said finally. "In his name. Only his. I relinquish all rights."

"You will—"

"I will become his employee." He chuckled softly. "Pray God he pays me well enough to support my wife and myself."

Vaia's eyes moved from Emmanuel to Vasili, who sat across from her, next to Emmanuel. "You are offering the business," she said, still looking at Vasili.

Emmanuel uncrossed his legs and slowly recrossed them. Vaia's eyes returned to him. "I am," he said at last.

Dimitri looked down into the empty brandy glass in his hand.

A smile edged its way onto Vaia's mouth. "The business," she said again.

"The business."

Vaia looked at Vasili again. "That sounds satisfactory."

Vasili nodded.

"Fine," Emmanuel said. "Then there is only the matter of drawing up the papers."

"We haven't discussed the furnishings."

"But of course, I thought it went without saying," Emmanuel said hastily. "The house and the furnishings, of course."

"The house?" Vaia said.

"The bride always brings the house and its furnishings, does she not?" Emmanuel asked.

Theodora put her hand on his sleeve. "Mano—" she whispered, but he waved her off.

"It's still customary, isn't it?"

"But of course we already have a house, large enough for Vasili and his bride," Vaia said.

"Plenty large," Dimitri said loudly.

Emmanuel leaned forward. "But perhaps . . ." He stared fully at Vaia. "My shop is in Eski Buyuk Pazar, close to an hour by train and horse tram from Bournabat. Too far for Vasili to travel if he lives out there."

Dimitri straightened in his chair. "I make the trip every day."

"And come home for dinner at noon every day?" Emmanuel challenged.

"I do."

Emmanuel gazed at him, as if measuring him. "But of course, a tobacco shop. I imagine sometimes it's a little late in opening in the afternoon?"

"Well . . ." Dimitri allowed.

"Yes, well. And of course your shop sells superior tobacco. If it's not open when someone comes, well, a customer will come back, won't he? But it's different with me, I'm afraid. The whole street is jewelers. If the store isn't open, the customers will just go next door, won't they? Vasili would not have the luxury of closing for so long."

"It's not necessary to come home for dinner every single day," Vaia said.

An indignant look passed Emmanuel's face. "For my daughter, I would want her husband to eat dinner at home. Every single day."

"It's not necessary," Vaia repeated.

"It is for me." Emmanuel straightened his coat, as if he felt the interview was nearly over, as if he expected to leave, even though it was his own house. "That's what I want for my Liana. My other daughters have that—their husbands coming home midday—and Liana will have it as well." His chin rose decisively on those last words. "Unless . . . unless you want to rethink . . ."

Vaia's eyes flickered to Vasili and back to Emmanuel. "What kind of house do you intend to provide?"

"One suitable for them. As I have done for my other daughters. And the furnishings, of course. But perhaps we should ask Vasili if such an arrangement is agreeable . . ."

Vaia turned her attention to Liana for the first time since the group had settled itself into the parlor. Liana's eyes dropped to her lap. She was afraid that if she looked at Vaia straight on she would reveal how much she had understood.

"Very well," Vaia said at last.

"This is an agreement?" Emmanuel asked formally.

"Yes."

There was silence, and then Dimitri said, "Yes."

And then Vasili's voice: "Yes." He had never looked at her, not once, and through everything his face had remained impassive, as frozen in seriousness as her papa's was, and that had been how Liana had understood. Vaia had been surprised, and Dimitri had been surprised, and Liana could imagine the thoughts that were dancing in their heads. Even her mother had been surprised. But Vasili had not been at all surprised, and that was how she knew that she was fortunate to have two such men love her.

CHAPTER 9

THE WEDDING OF LIANA DEMIRGIS AND VASILI MELOPOULOS was celebrated in August, on the hottest day of the summer. The *bahchevans* had started even earlier than usual that day and had covered the fruits and vegetables on their carts with wet gunny sacks in hopes of keeping them from wilting in the heat. Carriage drivers stowed buckets of water under their seats to refresh the horses, who stood with necks drooping. Alley cats found shaded corners and stretched full-length against stone walls to absorb whatever meager comfort the once-cool stones still held. Even in the church, whose small high windows admitted even less heat than light, the walls felt warm to the touch and the candles drooped limply in their candelabrum.

Sweat ran down the priest's face and dripped from his jowls. Emmanuel Demirgis mopped his forehead and immediately mopped it again. Theodora, standing beside him, discreetly sprinkled her hands with lemon water from a vial and daintily patted her forehead and neck. Dimitri Melopoulos, fortified with brandy, smiled beatifically, as if unaware of the heat. Vaia wore a high-necked, long-sleeved gown from Paris without a sign of discomfort.

Liana, her face already flushed with the heat, tried holding her breath to keep from being overcome by the oppressive odor of the priest as he stepped near. Raising his arms, he held the wedding wreaths, linked by a white satin ribbon, over her head and Vasili's. It would not do to faint. Something like that would displease Vaia Melopoulos immensely, and it would certainly be a bad omen. Standing so near that even in the dim candlelight Liana could see the pores of his skin, the priest intoned the words of the ceremony as he crossed and uncrossed his arms, switching the wreaths back and forth over their heads. Beside her, Vasili, in a barely perceptible move, stepped close enough that his arm was against her shoulder. It was the first time they had ever stood so close that their bodies touched. Liana knew that if Vaia had seen the move, she would be outraged. But it no longer mattered. Liana was going to be his wife and he was doing this now for her. Knowing that, she had the strength to stand beneath the priest's upraised arms, nearly overwhelmed by the suffocating stench of him.

Finally, the priest laid the wreaths on their heads, stepped back, and grasped Liana's hand to lead the couple in the Dance of Isaiah, three times around the altar—three times for love, swearing themselves to each other for life. She followed the black-robed figure obediently, Vasili behind her. She had been to weddings before and she knew the rituals. The priest would bring them back to the starting point at last. There would be more words, and the priest would hold the gold-encrusted Bible over her and Vasili's heads for a final prayer; she would kiss the Bible then, and Vasili would, as a sign of respect for God's word, and it would be over. Soula, dressed in pink and white and hopping impatiently from one foot to the other, would finally have her chance to help distribute the Jordan almonds, and everyone would congratulate them and they would be married. Then the whole assemblage would pile into the hired carriages already standing in the street outside and go to the little house only five minutes from her parents' home. It would be the first time that she and Vasili had been at the house together, though she knew he had seen it with his parents. She knew also that Vaia had said it was too small. Vaia was already trying to renege on the agreement about Vasili's living in town.

There would be food and drink and dancing at the house, and after a while everyone else would go home and at last Liana and Vasili would be alone for the very first time. Then, Liana understood, they would really be a married couple.

BY THE TIME LIANA AND VASILI'S CARRIAGE ARRIVED AT THE house, it was already filling with guests. Theodora bustled about, perspiration running down the sides of her face as she rearranged the serving platters one last time. Christina and Eleni were doing their best to calm their mother and greet the guests at the same time. The sisters' husbands, standing near the door, added hearty voices to the general confusion as they called greetings to everyone who arrived.

In the garden at the back of the house the *politakia* musicians had already begun—two mandolins, a zither, and a guitar. Their music could be heard from the street, the bright, tinkling notes undergirded with the fine, full chords that Liana loved. When she and Vasili arrived they were playing one of her favorites—"The Lemon Grove." She broke into a wide smile, astonished still at her good fortune. A handsome and attentive husband, a beautiful wedding, and now this party. This was going to be the most wonderful evening. There would be dancing: Vasili and the men in the groom's dance; she and the women in the bride's dance; everyone together; and later, when spirits were mellowed by the brandy, she and Vasili together in the wedding dance, a dance so elegantly sensual it had always taken her breath away, even as a child.

But now the young people were clamoring for the butcher's dance—the long, sinuous line dance, where a skilled leader could show off in a series of intricate steps and high leaps. Ara Fayroyian, Vasili's best friend from childhood, was demanding to be the leader. Someone shoved Liana and Vasili to the head of the line and Liana took her place between Ara and Vasili, holding the other end of Ara's white linen handkerchief high as he proudly began the steps.

Vaia, alone and aloof in the most prominent corner of the garden, surveyed the scene disdainfully. She had never cared for Ara. And the house was not a suitable one for Vasili. It was much too small, even if it was only three streets away from Sultanie Street, one of the finest streets in the Greek Quarter. If Vasili must live in the city, she had hoped at least for a neighborhood like Karatass. Somehow, this whole thing had gotten out of hand. Nothing had gone the way she had wanted. The girl had not been as pliable as she had assumed, and Vasili was being impossible. If it had not been for the ownership of the business, there would be nothing at all worthwhile about this marriage. But, on the other hand, this was only the beginning, and they were still young. When the wedding festivities were over there would be plenty of time to rearrange things.

Theodora, as hostess, had hardly a moment to reflect. This was the last wedding for her as mother of the bride. As with all the others, in the weeks to come friends and relatives would exclaim over the beauty of the house and its furnishings, the magnificence of the serving table, the abundance and flavor of the brandy, the excellence of the musicians. In order to hear that future praise, she must earn it now. On top of everything else, they'd had the heat to contend with. Thank God the house was not so far from the sea that it had no hope of catching a breeze. Already an *imbat* was blowing off the water. With luck, the house would soon be bearable. There was no point in worrying—there was too much to do. She would have plenty of time to relax tomorrow.

Emmanuel Demirgis poured another glass of brandy for his good friend and neighbor Giorgi Econopoulos. "Yes, of course it's a good match," he agreed. "He's tall enough for her and he'll be smart enough for the business."

Giorgi raised his eyebrows. "The son you never had, Emmanuel?"

Emmanuel shrugged. "Perhaps" was all he would say. But his hopes were high. He liked Vasili very much and thought he would indeed make a good partner for the business. But there was no point in pushing it. There would be plenty of time to see how close Vasili would come to being like a real son.

There will be plenty of time to drink another day, Vaia had warned. Rarely did she say anything. It was part of the bad bargain she'd gotten, Dimitri Melopoulos thought ruefully. *For Vasili's sake, if not mine,* she'd said, *don't drink at the party.* Well, he did want a good wedding for Vasili. One or two drinks wouldn't hurt, but he would definitely stop there. She was right: There would be plenty of time to drink another day.

"Vasili! Don't you think it's time?" Ara finally called out, only slightly drunk. Ara raised his glass, toasting Vasili across the crowd that separated them. But his voice was barely heard above the clamor. *"Yes, Vasili, it's time!" "Take her, Vasili!" "Now, Vasili!"* It was after midnight. Some of the older folks had already left. Vasili turned to Liana, his face darkening in embarrassment. "Liana?" he said softly.

The *politakia* changed quickly to a delicately haunting melody. The crowd melted back into a circle surrounding them, and Liana found herself alone in the center with Vasili. He drew a clean, white linen handkerchief from his pocket, twisted it into a straight cord, and held out one end to her. She took it and they began the dance. It was the way she had always dreamed the bride's dance would be: she dancing for him and he dancing for her, joined only by the white handkerchief, dancing their own steps in counterpoint. It was all of marriage re-created in the dance—he doing his part, she doing hers— joined, but still separate, turning and dipping, the music weaving around them, closer and closer, until it was only she and Vasili and the music. Nothing else.

The dance ended, as she knew it must, amid applause and cheers. Liana stood with Vasili, each still holding an end of the handkerchief. *It's over*, Liana thought. *This wonderful party is over.* Christina rushed up and enfolded Liana in her arms. "It was beautiful," Christina said, her voice breaking with emotion. "And you and Vasili are going to be so very happy."

Then suddenly she was surrounded by friends and family, all hugging her and wishing her a happy life. She caught a glimpse of Christina, now gathering the sleeping Soula into her arms. Eleni gave her a quick hug and then headed for the door. Sophie smiled broadly and kissed her. Even Themo came close and kissed her on each cheek. It was all so fast, Liana thought sadly. It was all ending so fast.

"Liana." Vasili's voice was at her ear, his hand on her elbow. She was his now; he could do this without risking disapproval. In the corner of the garden, Vaia still sat as straight as a tree, observing everything. *She will stay until the very end*, Liana thought, and then felt guilty for thinking such a thing. Her own parents were near the doorway to the house, saying goodbyes to departing guests, her mother kissing each woman in turn, her father shaking the hands of the men. Yet not everyone seemed to be leaving. Perhaps it would go on a little longer, she hoped.

"Liana." Vasili's voice was more urgent. "Liana, it's time for us to go."

"Vasili, it's not even over . . ." she began. But with his hand on her elbow he was already directing her toward the house.

At the doorway, Theodora reached out and cupped Liana's face in her hands. "My child," she said, weeping openly, "my littlest one."

"Mama, we're only a short distance away."

In response, Theodora enclosed Liana in her arms and held her tightly for a moment, and Liana breathed in the old familiar fragrance of lemon that had always meant her mother. Then Theodora let go, stepped back, and looked directly at Vasili. "Take care of her," she said sternly.

He nodded. "I will."

From the other side of Vasili, Emmanuel Demirgis spoke stiffly. "We have given you something more precious than all the gold in Smyrna."

"I know," Vasili said. "I know how precious she is."

Liana hugged her father then. "I love you, Papa," she whispered.

Emmanuel drew her back and held her at arm's length, looking at her. Without a word he gently moved her closer to Vasili and turned away. She went with Vasili then into the house, up the stairs, and into the bedroom. Once inside, Vasili closed the door quietly, deliberately, and turned to face her.

She stood uncertainly before him, still glowing from the heat and the dance. Some strands of hair had come loose with the exertion of the dancing, and as he gazed at her, she tried to push them back into place. *She's nervous*, he thought. *And she's very beautiful*. He took a step toward her and held out his arms.

Without a word she came to him and he wrapped his arms around her. She smelled like jasmine. Her hair was soft and cool against his skin, her neck smooth and warm. He kissed her neck, her cheek, her mouth, and she hesitated for a moment, then responded.

"Vasili," she whispered into his ear, and he found the buttons at the back of her dress and undid them, one by one, until the dress fell, with the shimmer of silk, to her feet. Her shoulders were damp with perspiration as he kissed them.

He ran his thumbs lightly along the bones of her shoulders, then down her sides to her waist. She was as slim and lithe as a boy. He drew her toward the bed. "Liana, you're very beautiful," he said.

Her eyes slid away from his, surprised, embarrassed.

He pulled the pins from her hair and watched as it fell in soft waves down her back. He gathered handfuls of it and buried his face in the jasmine smell of her. He gently moved her down onto the bed and she lay back, clad only in her chemise, and he leaned above her. She was all he ever wanted, the most beautiful woman he had ever seen.

And he could not believe what his body was doing to him.

Softly, hesitantly, he ran his fingertips along the edge of her chemise, feeling the rise of her breasts. He bent and kissed the skin at the edge of the lace, whispered her name again, and, almost as if unwilled, his finger slipped beneath the garment and felt there the small round breast with its tight high nipple. He whispered her name again and again as his hands explored her body—the smooth flat stomach, her long, pale legs, the warm, moist place between them. There was a question in her eyes, but no fear. Beneath his hands her body began to respond, uncertainly at first, then in a rhythm that drew him closer to her. She was all he had ever dreamed of, and he took his hands from her, sat up on the edge of the bed, and buried his face in his hands.

He felt the movement on the bed next to him before she touched his shoulder. "Vasili," she asked, "what's the matter? Did I do something wrong?" There was worry in her voice, and fear.

"No." He didn't take his hands from his face, but she gently pulled them away and turned his face toward hers.

"Vasili? What is it? Was I not supposed to . . . ?"

"No, it's not you," he said more curtly than he meant. "It's nothing you did. It's me."

"I'm sorry. I don't understand."

"It's I who should be sorry, Liana. I don't know what happened—it shouldn't be this way—but I can't do it."

"Do what?"

My God, he thought, *she doesn't know.* And then, in a panic: *Why wouldn't they have told her?* "Liana," he said gently, "what do you think the couple does at the end of the wedding party? What do you think the sheet is all about?"

"The sheet?"

"You've been to wedding parties before—yes?"

"Yes." She nodded.

"And at the end, what happens?"

"The couple dances together, and after that, everyone goes home."

"Liana, we danced. Then we came in here. You saw. Some people have gone home, but not everyone."

"But I always went home."

"You don't know what happens after? What married couples do?"

She frowned in uncertainty for a long moment, and finally he asked, "Do you know how babies come?"

"Of course! I have sisters; I'm not blind."

His eyes narrowed as he looked at her. "Do you know how babies get started? Did your mother ever tell you that?"

"Of course she did. When a man and woman love each other, a baby grows. It's proof of their love."

"That's it? That's what you know?"

"Yes . . ." Her voice was hesitant.

"Liana, you *must* know this: What does it mean to be a virgin?"

"That . . . you've never been with a man before. Alone." She searched his face now with uncertain eyes. "Isn't that right?"

Gently, he laid her hands in her lap and stood up. From beyond the shuttered window he could hear the muffled sounds of voices. *They will stay*, he thought with anguish. *And what will we do?*

"Vasili," she said, standing now and leaning toward him. She cupped his face in her hands. "What is it? What's the matter?"

He sighed, took her hands in his again, and touched them to his lips. "They love you very much, Liana. It's understandable they would want to protect you, but I can't understand why they would do this to you. Surely your sisters must have said something about the wedding night."

She flushed and looked at the floor. "You have to understand, Vasili. Everyone was afraid about me—before you, I mean. No one ever said it, but I knew they were worried. All they ever said was 'Don't worry.' And then, when the arrangements were made for you, we were all happy. You were exactly what I—just right for me. Everyone congratulated me and was happy for me. And then they all began saying it again. 'Don't worry, Liana,' they said. 'He'll be very gentle, Liana.' But . . . it never occurred to me that . . . ." She looked directly at him now. "Vasili, *please. What is it?*"

He put his arms around her and held her close without speaking for a long time. Then, finally, his voice sounding strange to his own ears, he said, "On the bed, when you were lying down and I was . . . touching you . . . did you feel something you've never felt before?"

Against his chest, he could feel her head nod, but she said nothing.

"When men and women are married . . . and touch each other in such ways . . . and feel such feelings . . ." It was impossible. If none of them could have explained it to her, how could he?

He tried again. "When a man and a woman love each other very much, there's something they do. Something the man does to the woman. And it is that . . . *something* . . . that makes a woman no longer a virgin. And what they are waiting for . . . down there in the garden . . . is the proof of that: that I brought you into this room a virgin. It's what will seal the agreement between our parents—that I got what my parents bargained for. And it will justify your parents—that they provided what they agreed to. It's why people are still here. They are waiting for the proof."

"Then why don't we do the thing?"

"Liana, *I can't*! A woman has it done to her. It can happen to her anytime. But a man's body has to . . . cooperate. And *mine isn't*. It's not that I can't—it's just that, for some reason, it's trying to embarrass me now, and it won't."

"Does it have to happen now? Can't we just wait?"

"*No! We can't!* They're waiting out there for us. After a while they'll begin to wonder."

She shrugged. "Let them wonder, then."

"Liana. Don't you know what they'll think? Not that *I* can't do it. No one ever thinks that. A man is always supposed to be aching to do it on his wedding night. What they'll think is that you're not a virgin. Your parents will be mortified."

"We can pretend we did it. They'll never know."

"We can't pretend. They would know."

"How would they know?"

"Listen, Liana. This is what is supposed to happen: We do the thing. Then we throw the sheet out. The blood on the sheet is proof we did it."

"You didn't say anything about blood."

He spoke with a forced calm, trying not to reveal the panic he was already feeling. "When you do it the first time—a woman bleeds. It's the proof she's a virgin. Those who are still here are waiting for that proof—the blood on the sheet. If we don't provide it, they won't believe you're a virgin. Nothing you or your family can say will make them believe it. Even if I were to walk out right now and tell everyone the truth—that *I* can't do it, that it's *my* fault and not yours—they probably wouldn't believe it. Your family would be crushed with embarrassment."

"But—*blood*? It must hurt, then."

"Maybe it does, a little. Really, Liana, it won't hurt a lot."

Liana moved away from him and stood for a moment, looking down at the bed. "How much blood does there have to be?"

"Not much."

"So, then, if they want to see blood on the sheet, why don't we give it to them?" She looked at him. "Do you have a knife?"

He gazed at her for a moment. "No, but I think . . ." He walked to the commode and turned again toward her, grinning, lifting the razor that lay neatly beside the water pitcher. "You can thank my mother. She would have done it, of course, so that I can shave in the morning. A proper husband."

"For a proper bride," Liana said.

He had to look at her again to make sure of her smile. "A proper *virgin* bride," he said, smiling too.

"Whatever in the world that means."

"Lianoush," he said tenderly, "you will learn."

"Lianoush?"

"No one ever called you that?"

"My parents," she said, laughing softly, "when I was little."

"Lianoush," he said firmly.

"Does it matter where on the sheet the blood goes?" she asked.

"In the middle will be fine."

"All right then, give me the razor."

"Give you? No, I'll do it."

"But Vasili, you said it's supposed to be my blood."

"Liana," he said, kneeling beside the bed, "they can't tell what caused the blood, and they won't be able to tell whose it is, either."

"But it's not supposed to be *your* blood."

"But it's my fault we have to do it this way." He leaned over the bed, his left arm extended and the razor in his right hand.

"Vasili," she whispered, touching his arm, "will it make a lot of blood?"

"Will you faint if it does?"

She giggled. "But maybe I should get a towel to wipe up the extra?"

"I hope not to commit suicide here—only to make a few drops. Why are you laughing?"

"I'm sorry. I shouldn't. You're going to have to cut yourself and everything. It's not funny, but it just seems so foolish."

He looked at his arms extended over the bed, and suddenly it did seem very, very foolish. Beside him she was still giggling, and he too began to laugh. "If you make me laugh," he said, trying to stop, "I'll probably cut my whole hand off!"

She attempted a serious face, but almost immediately broke into giggles.

He leaned his head against the bed, and the mattress shook

with his laughter. Her hand rested on the back of his neck, and now they were both laughing uncontrollably.

He lifted his head at last, his face serious finally, but tears of laughter still in his eyes. "No, Liana. We will do it, *then* we will laugh about it."

Composed at last, he pressed the razor against the inside of his wrist. As the first drop of red appeared, Liana caught her breath, and it fell onto the sheet, followed by another and another.

"Liana," he ordered, not looking at her, "spit on the blood."

"Why?"

"Don't ask why. Just do it."

She leaned over the bed and spat, or tried to. It took four attempts before she managed a meager trail of spittle.

"Again."

"Ladies don't spit," she apologized.

"Do it anyway."

This time she did it on the first try.

"Again," he said once more.

She spat again, the spittle falling directly onto the blood, diluting and smearing it slightly on the sheet. Liana watched, fascinated, as the sheet absorbed her spittle and Vasili's blood. "Again?" she asked.

He rose and leaned over the bed, looking at the effect they had created. Then he stepped toward the commode and pulled a towel from it. Holding it against his wrist, he looked again at the bed. "We should have wrinkled the sheets first," he commented.

"Will it work?"

He looked at her and then back at the sheet. "Yes. They want a bloodstain, and that's what they'll see." With a broad motion, he tore the sheet from the bed, crushed it into a rumpled heap, and walked to the window. He opened it, then the shutter, threw the sheet out, and closed the shutter again. "That's it," he said seriously. "You are now a proven virgin." From below, they could hear Ara's cheer and then the murmured voices of the others.

"Vasili." She held her arms out, and he came to her.

"I'm sorry it had to be like this," he said.

"It's very important, isn't it?"

"To some people."

"To you?"

"That you're a virgin? Or that I could do it?"

"Either."

"I never doubted that you were. Or, for that matter, that I could do it when I needed to. Or wanted to. A man wants to be a man on his wedding night."

She pulled him down onto the bed with her. "Another time we will," she whispered.

He held her closely, her jasmine scent enclosing them both.

"Vasili," she whispered after a time. "When we started, before we knew you couldn't . . . what you did . . . was I supposed to like it?"

He didn't answer for a while. Then he said, "You don't have to . . . But I guess it would be nice if you did. It would certainly be more enjoyable for us both—if you liked it."

She snuggled closer to him. "Good," she said.

The next night, with the quiet of an empty house surrounding them, Liana discovered what it meant to no longer be a virgin.

CHAPTER 10

LIANA LAY IN BED IN THE DARK, LISTENING TO THE SOUNDS OF the storm. Rain battered against the shutters; cold fingers of the wind reached through their slats and rattled the windows. She had gone out in the afternoon to Christina's, and along the seafront the wind had been whipping the waves above the quays and across the promenade of the Kordon. The storm had not let up since then—Vasili had come home soaked to the skin. She loved these winter storms. If she had not had a reason to go out—Christina's ailing mother-in-law—she would have invented one. *Someday,* she had always said to herself, *someday I'll have a home overlooking the sea and then I'll be able to watch the storms come up across the water, see the sky turn dark in the west down the long funnel of Smyrna Bay, watch the waves crash against the seawall, even stand on my own balcony and feel the salt spray driven across the road by the wind and the power of the sea.*

There was, of course, no immediate hope for that; she couldn't even imagine when they would be rich enough to own one of the big houses along the seafront. She snuggled deeper under the quilts and slipped her arm around the sleeping Vasili. She was rich enough the way it was. She had Vasili and now the baby coming. She had her father and mother only minutes away. She had her sisters and her nieces and nephews. She had a whole little world of love and caring, which was what made the storm rattling at the house sound so delicious. No storm—no matter how hard it blew—could batter down the house. The lamps would still be lit, the fires would still burn warmly in the coal-oil stoves, the rooms would still hold the aroma of orange peels drying on the stovetops. Nothing could break into this tight little world, shuttered and warm. She was, and always had been, safe in her world, and that was why the storm was so exciting— because she knew she had this safety. And she knew she was fortunate. The fishermen who had to go out to sea—their lives were not so safe. Nor were the lives of the beggars, without home or shelter, with no warm stove and no smell of oranges. It was a luxury, she told herself, to lie there in the night, cuddled close to Vasili, listening to the wind pounding at the door.

Pounding at the door? Could that be the wind? She pulled the quilt away from her ears and listened more closely to the sound. That was no wind lifting the doorknocker and slamming it home against its polished bronze rosette. Who was it, then? Who would be out on such a night? And at this time of night?

"Vasili," she whispered. He stirred, then settled back into sleep. "Vasili," she whispered more insistently. "Vasili, someone's at the door."

"It's the wind," he said sleepily.

"No, it's not. Listen. Someone's banging the doorknocker."

Vasili, awake now, pulled the quilt back and lifted his head. The sounds were clear and persistent—a fist pounding against the door and simultaneously a hand banging the knocker again and again.

"Who can it be?" she asked. In the pitch black of the room she couldn't see him, but she felt the movement as he threw the covers back, sat up, and fumbled at the bedside for his slippers. "Vasili, are you going? Do you think . . . ?" She didn't dare speak the dread that had occurred to her.

He felt on the bedside table for the lamp and a match. In the faint spurt of the match, he found the wick and turned it up slightly until the kerosene caught. Carrying the lamp, he padded across the floor, awkwardly managing with one hand to pull on the robe he'd taken from the foot of the bed. "Anyone out on a night like this—it must be an emergency."

"Maybe Christina's mother-in-law?"

"I doubt they would come out in this to tell us that." Immediately he wished he could take the words back. It was not really Christina's mother-in-law she was worried about. The glow of the lamp preceded him down the stairs as the pounding continued. The noise only stopped when whoever was on the outside heard him turning the latch.

Vasili opened the door slowly—even he had begun to fear the news that prompted such an unusual visit. In the lamplight he barely recognized the man before him, coat collar turned up against the cold and rain, wet hair disheveled and plastered against his forehead.

"Ara? For God's sake, Ara," he said, opening the door wider. He moved back as Ara Fayroyian stepped into the house, streams of water pouring from his clothes onto the terrazzo floor. "Good heavens, man," Vasili said, staring in astonishment, "you're soaked clear through. Let me get you dry clothes."

He turned away, but Ara reached out to stop him. "No, I'm not staying. I just wanted to come by and see you before I leave."

"Leave? In the middle of the night? Where are you going that's so important? And look at you—you're soaking wet."

"Listen, I came to say goodbye, and—"

"*Goodbye?* Where are you going at this time of night? Couldn't you have come round to see me in the morning?"

"I'm leaving at dawn. And Vasili," he said, taking his friend's hand, his face serious, "I don't know when I'll see you again."

"But you haven't said where you're going."

"It's better if you don't know."

Vasili stepped back, his face skeptical. "You're drunk."

Ara lifted his chin in disagreement. "With pride, yes."

Vasili took Ara's elbow and led him into the parlor. "Come in, sit down," he said. "Tell me what's going on. And, my God, what's the urgency?"

"Vasili, it's time to do something other than sit around and complain. Past time."

"What are you talking about? What have you—"

"You don't believe what they say, do you? Of all the Greeks in Smyrna, to have elected only two representatives—and we Armenians got none—while the Turks got ten? Who is in the majority in Smyrna, after all? This was supposed to be an honest vote. You don't believe it can be right, do you?"

"The Constitution is still new. We may have to work some things out . . ." Vasili conceded.

"And the taxes and the military service? Someday you might have sons: Would you want them to have to serve in the Turkish army? We never had to do that before. Why would we want this now?"

"But if we're going to be part of the nation—all of us—it's our army too."

"Nation? An Ottoman nation! If we're going to be nationals, Vasili, wouldn't you rather be a Greek national? Wouldn't I rather be an Armenian?"

"That's a foolish dream. You will never have an Armenian nation."

"You think not?" Ara had always been quick to anger, quick to a fight.

"You didn't come here in the middle of the night to argue politics."

Ara stepped closer, nodding, and when he spoke his voice was confidential. "No, I didn't. I came to say goodbye."

Vasili took Ara's hand in both of his. "Why can't you say where you're going?"

"Because this way, if they come here and ask for me, you won't have to lie when you say you don't know where I am."

"Why would they ask for you?" Then he felt a sudden chill. "What's happened?"

Ara pulled his hand from Vasili's. "Let's say I left them a farewell present."

"What are you talking about? What have you done?"

"Let's talk about what *they've* done."

Vasili jerked his head back, dismissing the intimation. "Rumors. And from so far away. How can you know what's true and what's not?"

"It's true, Vasili—a hundred or more men killed, and women and girls abducted into the mountains. God knows what's been done to them. It's starting all over again. The new Constitution means nothing—*nothing!*"

"You're going out there, aren't you? You're going to fight them?"

Ara said nothing.

Vasili frowned. "You won't win, you know."

"The Ottoman Empire is weak beyond belief. This is our chance. And we have right on our side. When we are mobilized—"

"They'll cut you down, one by one, if they have to. In the villages, in the towns—"

"Then you do believe the rumors," Ara interrupted.

"I believe they'll do what they have to do to make this government of theirs work."

"Then you'd better get out too, Vasili."

"We're safe here. Smyrna has always been Greek. They'll accommodate to us."

"First the Armenians and then the Greeks."

"Not in Smyrna, Ara. Here *we* are the majority."

"That's true, and yet you can see how much that means to them!"

"Nothing will happen if we don't start it."

Ara chuckled ruefully. "You don't really believe that. The only way to be safe is to draw the line first, before they cross it."

"How long will you be gone? What do you plan to do?"

"God knows."

"How are you going?"

"Never mind. By the time they come for me, I'll be long gone."

"Gone where?" Both men turned at the voice behind them. Liana stood in the doorway, wrapped in a quilt against the cold.

"Liana," Vasili said quietly, "go back to bed."

"Look at you!" Liana said to Ara. Then she turned on Vasili. "How can you let him stand there all wet like that? Go get—"

"Liana," Vasili interrupted. "We've already discussed it. Go back to bed."

Liana tossed her head back. "No one stands in my house like that. I will get him dry clothes, or you will, Vasili. And I'll put them on him, if he won't do it himself. But he will not leave here in those . . . *things*." She turned on her heel and left them staring after her.

Ara chuckled. "I thought you said—"

"Sweet and good and loving," Vasili said, nodding. "And with a mind of her own."

"Just like . . . ?"

"*No.* Not like her at all."

"I think I'd better leave before she gets back."

Vasili caught his arm. "Oh no, my friend. You'll stay now, and you'll take the dry clothes she brings, or I'll never hear the end of it. And you'll put them on, or she really will do it herself."

VASILI HAD JUST STARTED HIS SECOND GLASS OF MORNING TEA when the knock sounded at the door. Automatically, he rose from the table, then hesitated as he remembered.

Liana looked up at him. "What are you thinking?"

He looked at her vaguely and shook his head. Then he walked slowly toward the foyer. When he opened the door, he didn't even feel surprise at the two men standing there, gray woolen uniforms with black belts at the waist.

"Are you Vasili Melopoulos?" one of them asked in Turkish. Vasili nodded, and the man moved forward into the doorway, forcing Vasili to step back and allow them to enter. "And Ara Fayroyian is your friend?"

"What is this?" Vasili asked. "Why do you ask me about Ara?"

"Is he here?"

"Of course not. Why should he be? Why don't you look for him at his own home?"

The second policeman, the one who hadn't spoken, had moved past Vasili and farther into the house.

"Hey there," Vasili called after him. "You can't just come in like that. My wife—" He hurried after the man, who had paused at the dining-room doorway and looked in.

Liana, surprised, glanced up at Vasili, then she rose. "Who—"

"It's all right, Liana," Vasili said from behind the officer. "But you, sir, have no right—" Already the man had moved across the hall and walked into the kitchen. He looked around, opened a cupboard door, and then turned back toward the front of the house, Vasili following.

"You think he's here, is that it?" Vasili asked. "Why are you looking for him, anyway? What did he do?"

Wordlessly, the policeman went on, mounting the stairs, with Vasili right behind, and then the officer stopped. At the top of the stairs was a small stove, still putting out heat, though the fire had been turned down. And on a wooden rack close to the stove hung two sets of coats and pants, two shirts, two pairs of stockings, and two sets of underwear. On the other side of the stove, two pairs of men's shoes had been carefully placed, just close enough to dry without ruining the leather. At last, the policeman turned and faced Vasili.

"I can explain," Vasili said, "they are—"

Behind him, Liana laughed, and he felt her fingers lightly touch his shoulder. "I told you you'd catch pneumonia," she said.

He looked at her, and her smile was broad and her eyes danced as she went on, lovingly teasing him. "But I never thought it was against the law." She turned to the policeman, her eyes wide with indignation. "It was bad enough that he came home from work soaked to the skin, but then, later, he insisted on going out again and getting another whole set of clothes wet—to say nothing of himself. He thinks dry clothes grow on trees, I suppose. Can you imagine anything so foolish? I guess it ought to be against the law for a grown man to act so carelessly. He could have caught his death."

She had advanced on the policeman, backing him against the wall. She turned now, and her eyes lingered on Vasili before she faced the second officer, who had followed them up the stairs. "Can it really be against the law? For a man to go out on such a night as we had last night? Would you arrest him for that? But you shouldn't blame him entirely; you can see what condition I'm in. And if either of you is married, perhaps you understand what kind of strange cravings we women have when we are—you know. So last night, I made the mistake of telling him that I was dying for the taste of my mother's own pickles. She has a special recipe—would you like some? And of course, because it is the first child for us, and he does spoil me—" She glanced again at Vasili, and he could hardly keep from laughing out loud at her exaggeration of an adoring look. "So nothing would do but that he go and get me a jar. We were completely out, you see. In all that rain! And now look at his clothes here. He'll be lucky if his shoes aren't ruined, or at least shrunk two sizes too small. Well, it's his own fault. Any sensible man would have told me to roll over and go back to sleep. Tell me," she added, "what is your procedure now? Do you just warn him against doing such a thing again, or what? And is there anything else you want to see?"

Uncomfortable with a woman who spoke so freely of such things to someone who was not even a relative, the policeman looked beyond Vasili to his fellow officer. "Just look through the bedrooms," the officer said, "and let's get it done quickly."

Liana smiled graciously at him. "You can be glad," she said, "that it stopped raining by this morning. I should think your wife wouldn't like her husband having to go out in such weather any more than I wanted mine to. Would you like a glass of tea?"

"No, *Hanum*," he responded politely. "But thank you anyway."

IT WAS NOT UNTIL HE REACHED THE SHOP THAT VASILI HEARD THE news: The Smyrna city offices had been bombed the evening before. One official, working late, had been killed. Two others had been seriously injured. No perpetrators had been caught, but an Armenian separatist group was suspected. Vasili, standing at the shop door and looking out onto the busy street, listened to his father-in-law recount the news. After last night's storm, the sun shone brightly in a cloudless sky. A boy from a coffee shop, delivering morning coffee on a brass tray, leaped across a puddle in the narrow street without spilling a drop. And Vasili stared eastward toward the morning sun and thought of Ara.

Emmanuel moved closer to Vasili. "Whoever set that bomb was a fool," he said in a quiet voice. "He might have meant it for the best, but he has no idea what he may have started."

Vasili turned to him.

"And," Emmanuel added, "there is no telling who will take the brunt of it in the end."

CHAPTER 11

Vaia Melopoulos stood before the mirror, twisting her long hair into a coil at the back of her head. She stuck the pins in, one by one, the edge of each grazing her scalp, giving the satisfying assurance that it was doing its job, holding the coil in place, firm and controlled. She wore a dress of dove-gray wool, tight in the bodice and waist, full in the skirt, with a starched white lace jabot down the front of the bodice. She knew she looked smart, even though the dress was old. The jabot, at least, was new.

She watched her reflection as she fluffed up the lace, then leaned forward and turned from side to side. Small lines spread from the outer corner of each eye. She was forty-five years old, married twenty-nine of those years. She had one son, born in the first year of her marriage, a point of pride that she carried like a medal. She smiled even now, thinking of it. She had done her duty: a fine, tall, handsome son. She had proven herself in the first month of marriage by her almost immediate pregnancy. That was back in the days when the house that stood so still and quiet around her now was peopled with family and servants, when there was no question but that the young couple would live in the house with the bridegroom's parents, when she had allowed her swelling body to excuse her from waiting on her mother-in-law, when her father-in-law's pounding on the floor with his silver-headed cane had brought a servant girl running.

But those days had gone, drained away with the land that turned out to be mortgaged, root and branch; with the warehouse that lost more money each year; with the servants, who departed one by one, until all that was left was a thirteen-year-old village girl who had to be taught how to care for fine wood, how to wash clothes clean without beating them to death, how even to set a table or, for that matter, to iron a sheet.

Her mother-in-law had died first, of apoplexy, her whole side going numb to begin with, and finally, within only hours, her eyes bugging out as if by the force of her soul fighting to escape, her mouth twisting into horrid contortions, as Dimitri stood by, wringing his hands and wondering what to do, until, with a final release of breath, she collapsed in a faint from which she never recovered. Then the drinking came in earnest, her father-in-law never leaving his room, the frightened servant girl pushing meals at him through a half-opened door, the cane pounding through the night, the sound of falling chairs or his own body blundering against a wall or the bed or an armoire, his own hoarse voice talking to his demons or singing himself to sleep, until at last one day there was silence and she looked at Dimitri and he looked at her, and she knew that he would not go and there was no point in calling the girl, that it would be she who would have to walk into the stench of that malodorous room and make sure that the man was, at last, dead.

The silver-headed cane paid for his coffin, and four Bergama carpets paid off the last of the debts, and the warehouse was finally gone, and she had been left with a house half empty of its furnishings and a husband who went each day to a little shop where he sold the only thing he knew how to sell and a six-year-old son who had stared wide-eyed at his grandfather's body, as he had done two years before at his grandmother's, and who was her only hope.

The problem was that, when the time came, her son refused to consider medical school, even though she'd brought him up from childhood on her cherished plans. He went instead into his father's shop, and she watched in silent fury as she saw her husband drinking more, and her son following her husband to the shop, each of them mindlessly trampling on her dreams.

She spread her hands now on the dressing table; they were still as smooth and white as they were the day she'd married. *I've given them six months*, she was thinking, six months to go their own way, to get their idea of married life out of their systems. At the time the arrangements were made, she had swallowed her objections, holding her silence within, the flavor of it bitter against her tongue. She had promised herself to give them six months and she had held to that promise. But no more; the time was up. And not a moment too soon. She could guess that it would take a firm hand and a wily mind to bring them back to the house in time, before they could plead that it was too close to the birth.

They would come to where they had belonged in the first place, filling the house once again with people, bringing Liana's dowry furnishings to make this house once more what it should always have remained: a house rich with carpets on every floor and lamps lighted in every room, a mistress of the house and a family for her to oversee. But time was short now. When she'd given them six months, she'd had no idea that the baby would come so soon. Her hopes had never been that high, though she should have known. Her own child born in the first year of marriage—she'd given that to the precious Demirgis girl: a virile husband, a husband who could make a child on his first attempt.

And when their son was born he would grow up in this house and she would oversee his education, and this time she would not make the same mistakes. When the time came, this child would train to be a doctor.

But it would take care to accomplish all that. She had grown used to dealing with men, but this was different. She had learned that the Demirgis women, as soft and compliant as they might appear, could be a formidable force. She had not realized that on her first visit to Theodora's house. But now she remembered having seen the older daughter soothing a cranky baby with a bit of honey, and she smiled.

THEODORA LOOKED AROUND HER PARLOR AND BEAMED OVER THE rim of her coffee. Four daughters, two of them pregnant: Liana pregnant within the first month, perhaps even the first week, and Eleni expecting her third. God gave with a generous hand. It was rare these days for all four of them to gather at once—difficult for the pregnant ones to come out in the winter weather. But today was her name day. Since it was also Lent, there would be no big celebration, but this was more than enough—surrounded by her daughters and her grandchildren. She was used to quiet name-day celebrations: Hers almost always fell during Lent.

All of her grandchildren were here. Because it was Doroush's name day as well, there was a little pile of white-wrapped presents for the fifteen-month-old, to be opened later, when Emmanuel and the sons-in-law arrived. Despite Theodora's insistence that she wanted no gifts, a pile of presents for her had also appeared. Her eyes lingered on each precious face as she surveyed the room. Nine-year-old Naso fidgeted impatiently, eyeing the presents and eating sweets. Soula and Marina played quietly in a corner, the two four-year-olds mimicking their mothers' voices as they dressed their dolls, while two-year-old Constantine hovered at the edges of their play, absorbing every word in wide-eyed wonder, as if proximity alone made him part of the game.

Eleni, barely showing the child she'd been carrying for almost five months, held Doroush, who had fallen asleep in her arms. And Liana appeared as healthy as a child, her cheeks rosy, her eyes glowing.

The sound of the doorknocker surprised them all, everyone's eyes turning toward the parlor door, as if they could see through walls, as if they could envision who stood at the front door. It was too early yet for the men to have come, and who else could it be? Liana glanced at her mother and then down at the floor, absently smoothing a hand over her rounded belly. Beyond the chatter of the children's play, they all listened for the sounds: Despinise opening the door, muffled voices, then the maid's footsteps toward the parlor.

"*Kyria*," Despinise said, her face a mix of curiosity and doubt, "it's *Kyria* Melopoulos."

Liana started to rise, anxiety flooding her. Vasili? No, surely not. His father, then?

"No," Despinise said, nodding toward Theodora, "it's for you."

"Well, for heaven's sake," Theodora said, "invite her in."

Despinise gathered her apron skirt in her hands and wiped them, as if absolving herself of any misdeed. "I did, *Kyria*, but she says she only wants a word with you."

Theodora rose. "I can't imagine . . . What on earth?"

"Shall I come?" Liana asked, starting to rise.

"She asked only for *Kyria*," Despinise said, still worrying her apron.

"Oh, my," Theodora said, following the woman out of the room. "What in the world?"

Vaia Melopoulos stood in the entry hall, tall and erect. At that moment, Theodora realized that she and Vaia had not ever, in all these months, exchanged words between just the two of them. "Vaia, please, come in," Theodora said, beckoning with her hand as she walked forward. "It's just family here today, and you're . . . family. Come."

"No, I can't, really, Theodora," Vaia responded. "Though it is . . . kind of you to invite me. I have a number of errands . . . But I wanted to bring you a little something." She reached into a small fabric bag she carried on her arm and withdrew a tiny package, wrapped in white. "For your name day," she added.

"Why, Vaia, how kind," Theodora said, her mind suddenly racing: Had Vaia had a name day since the marriage? Had she been remiss in not giving Vaia something? And Dimitri? They had certainly missed his—Aghios Dimitrios's Day was late in October, already gone. "I . . . I hardly know what to say—so thoughtful of you." But they had never exchanged name-day gifts with their other sons-in-law's families. "Please, do come in."

Vaia tossed her head. "No, truly, Theodora, I mustn't. I only wanted to bring you a little something." She was already turning toward the door.

"But I couldn't let you stop in and then leave without even a cup of coffee." Theodora turned to the maid, who had remained standing nearby, as if waiting for instructions. "Coffee, Despinise. Medium, isn't it, Vaia?"

Vaia opened the door. "No, thank you, not today. Another time, perhaps." She stepped outside and closed the door firmly behind her.

Theodora stood for a moment, the gift in her hand, her mouth still half opened to say something in response.

"She didn't stay," Liana said from behind her, a statement, not a question.

"How strange," Theodora said, and she wondered how long Liana had been there, how much she had heard. And if she thought Theodora should have said something different to make Vaia stay.

Liana had moved to the door and opened it, looking out, watching as Vaia, head still held high, walked away, stepping around the puddles.

From behind them, in the parlor, came the high voice of a child—Marina, Theodora thought—"When I'm a mama, I will never say that!" And the raucous laughter from Theodora's other three daughters.

"I imagine she's lonely, out there in that big house," Theodora said. "No other children, what a pity."

"I can't understand why she wouldn't come in," Liana said, still watching as Vaia disappeared from sight.

"I suppose she didn't want to spoil it for us," Theodora said.

"Spoil it?"

"A mother and her daughters and grandchildren—she would feel like an outsider, wouldn't she?"

"Not even for a cup of coffee?"

"Liana, how a person feels is not always logical. Still, what a pity. And she didn't even wait for me to open her gift."

"Mama?" Christina appeared from the parlor. She looked around. "What happened to *Kyria* Melopoulos?"

"She left," Liana said.

"Left? Without even coming in to say hello? Why ever did she come, then?"

"She brought me a gift," Theodora said.

"Really? What is it?"

"I didn't open it."

"But you should have, if she was going to leave so soon."

"She didn't give me a chance. She gave it to me and left."

"Mama thinks she didn't want to intrude," Liana said.

Christina looked from one to the other. "How sad."

"Liana," Theodora said, looking down at the small packet in her hand, "do you go out there often?"

"Sundays," Liana said, then added, "sometimes."

"You must make a point to."

"She's not easy—"

"Never mind. You must make a point to. She's Vasili's mother, after all."

THEY WENT THE NEXT SUNDAY, RIDING OUT IN A RENTED CAR- riage, the cover pulled up because of the misty rain. Vasili seemed stiff and formal, as if he hardly knew how to act now in the house that had once been his home. But Vaia was, for once, all smiles. She greeted Liana with a kiss on the cheek and took Liana's damp coat and hung it in the hallway, near the stove. "You've never really seen the house, have you?" she asked.

It was true. In the few times Liana had been there, she had never seen more than the entry hall and the parlor and the din- ing room. Now Vaia took her through all the rooms, showing her the kitchen and the sitting room across from the parlor, and then leading her up the wide oak staircase to the bedrooms. Everywhere, Vaia pointed out the rugs, the pieces of furniture that had been in the family for generations, the photographs and paintings on the walls, the hand-embroidered towels that graced each bedroom commode. "It's beautiful," Liana said, examining more closely the handwork on a towel in Vasili's old room.

"I did it myself," Vaia said proudly. "For my dowry, of course. The silver threads," she added, pointing to the shimmer that threaded through the design, "do you know what they're called?"

"No."

"*Sim*," Vaia said. "Your father works with silver—so did I, once. It's almost out of fashion now, using *sim* in the design."

She's not so bad, Liana thought. "Mama loves the brooch you gave her," she said. "She put it on right away. Papa says it's very fine indeed."

Vaia allowed herself a little smile. "It was something I found that I thought she would like. Your mother sent me a kind letter of appreciation."

"It was very thoughtful of you."

Vaia nodded, accepting the compliment, and she led Liana back to the parlor, where the men still sat in desultory conversation.

If it were my house, Liana thought, *I would take down these heavy dark draperies and put up something light and cheery. Even in winter.*

"Soon, I suppose, you will not be able to travel out here," Vaia offered.

"Oh, that will be weeks away," Liana responded, laughing. *Especially in winter*, she thought. *I would want bright and cheery things in a house like this. And new furniture as well, something not so dark and cumbersome.* She was noticing, for the first time, the worn edges of the sofa. *I can't imagine what it would be like*, she told herself.

"Have you thought of names?" Dimitri asked, pouring a bit of something from a small flask into his tea.

"Dimitri," Vaia said, "it's not appropriate to talk of names yet."

"Not appropriate?" he asked.

"Unlucky," Vaia said tersely.

Liana looked at Vasili and he returned her gaze. "We haven't decided," he said diplomatically, and Liana smiled to herself.

"A child is a big responsibility," Vaia offered.

"Yes," Liana said.

Vaia cleared her throat, as if to say more, but Vasili stood up. "We must be going," he said. "It gets dark so early this time of year."

"It was good of you to come," Vaia said.

"It was," Dimitri echoed, struggling to rise from his chair.

He saw them to the door and watched as they walked through the gate and to the waiting carriage.

Without looking back, Liana imagined Vaia, still sitting at the window, watching as they left.

Vasili took her hand in his. "You were right," he said. "It *was* good of us to come."

"We should go more often," Liana said. "It must sometimes be lonely for her." She thought of her own mother, reveling in the presence of her daughters and grandchildren. She thought of what she had always dreamed of for herself: a house full of children, their shouts and laughter warming a home, defining a life full of love. Nothing at all like what Vaia seemed ever to have experienced. *We shall have to go again*, she thought, *until it is too close to the birth*. She made that thought a promise to herself, and to Vaia.

Vaia, sitting in her chair, watched the carriage disappear from sight, already reviewing the visit. It had gone well, she thought, better than she had expected.

CHAPTER 12

THE BABY CAME UNEXPECTEDLY EARLY AND HARD. THEY SENT for the neighborhood midwife and Liana's mother. And then the doctor, who looked at Liana, nodded sagely, and left.

The house was filled with steaming pots and scurrying feet and whispered orders. Liana clung to the bed and strained. The midwife hovered over her, alternately holding her wrist and massaging her distended belly. Theodora held cold compresses on her forehead, while Vasili paced the floor, measuring the time with his long strides.

When the baby finally came, his face was blue and the cord was wrapped around his neck. Theodora crossed herself and sent Despinise for the doctor. And the priest. The midwife finally slapped the baby's bottom, and he opened his eyes in surprise and let out a faint cry.

Liana held out her arms for him, but the midwife turned away. "You're too weak," she said. "And he is as well. You both need rest." And she took the infant out of the room.

The priest came and made the sign of the cross over the cradle and swung the censer above it and said a prayer, but only Theodora was there to see him. The doctor came again and looked at the baby and shook his head. The midwife had already gone on to another delivery. Kateri was back in the kitchen, boiling water to wash the soiled sheets, and Liana was still in bed, crying in Vasili's arms because she had not yet held her own child.

Vaia came as soon as she heard the news, leaning over the baby's cradle, frowning at his bluish skin, at the wispy hair, at the shallow, labored breathing, and, in fact, at the whole unanticipated turn of events. Unhealthy, she thought to herself, but she had the sense to say nothing and to greet Liana with a forced smile and a brush of her cheek. This had not at all gone the way she had imagined it would; but, then, it was what one might expect when a person allowed children to make such important decisions. Still, one had to be ready to size up a situation and play it to one's best advantage. Honey, she reminded herself, smooth the way with honey. "I understand it was difficult," she said.

Liana, lying in bed, looked pale and drained. "Maybe a little," she said.

"You must get your rest. I won't keep you. I just wanted to stop in and see the both of you. He's sleeping, by the way."

Liana nodded.

"I'll leave, then. You need your sleep as well." Vaia turned and walked from the room, stopping once more at the doorway to the baby's room, as if in hopes of seeing a healthier child this time. But he remained gray and still, lashless eyelids closed, swaddled to his pale cheeks in blankets. She took a long look and let out a deep breath. This was not what she had hoped for Vasili. Nor for herself. If they had been in Bournabat, things would have been different. She was mistaken to have thought she had the time to humor their foolish wishes. One never knew what unexpected turns of events might occur, but she had had enough experience to know that one must make the best of a bad situation.

Three days later, the baby died. He had never gained the

strength to suckle, and Liana had expressed by hand the milk that was overflowing in her breasts and she tried to feed it to him with a spoon, but most of that dribbled back out as soon as she put it into his mouth. And all she could do was look at him, heartsick.

After the baby's death, Vaia steeled herself and came once more to the house on Dionysus Street. Taking Vasili aside, she told him firmly that the dead child should not be named after any living person. "It's not right," she said. "It'll put a curse on the person whose name he carries into the grave." She looked away then, as if not wanting to meet his eyes.

"Liana and I will discuss a name," Vasili said.

Vaia said nothing more.

"Did you want to see Liana?" he asked finally. "I think she's sleeping right now," he added, hoping it was true.

"Never mind," Vaia said. "I wouldn't want to bother her." He nodded and led her back to the door and opened it for her, and she walked outside. Then, just as he was about to shut the door behind her, she turned. "Forgive me," she said. "Please."

He frowned. "For . . . ?"

She looked aside, at the doorstep, not meeting his gaze. "I made a terrible mistake. *We* made a terrible mistake—your father and I. We should never have encouraged this marriage. She's too thin; she'll never have healthy babies."

Vasili took in a deep breath and held it for a moment, then it burst forth. "No!" he said, surprising both himself and his mother with the vehemence in his voice. "This is not Liana's fault—don't make it out to be. Don't you dare say anything against her."

Vaia took a step closer, looking at him now. "I know," she whispered. "You think I'm just a bothersome old woman. But Vasili, I'm still your mother, and I love you and I only want the best for you."

"Liana is what I want," he said, his voice calmer, but it was still a sterner tone than he had ever before used with her. "Don't make me choose between you."

She forced a weak smile. "Of course," she said, reaching her hand to him. He took it in his own and gazed for a moment at the translucent skin and the thin blue veins before bending and holding it to his forehead in a gesture of respect. She *had* made a mistake, she realized. She had let her emotions overrule her mind. Never again, never again. *Honey.*

Then Vasili stepped back and closed the door.

In the next months she kept to her resolution, never speaking another word to him against Liana.

By custom, a woman stayed in seclusion, preferably in bed, for forty days after childbirth. Liana stayed ten, restless the whole time, her face pale and blotched with tears, her hair dull and straggly. She had risen just long enough to dress the tiny body in the white silk baptismal gown she'd sewn for him in the months preceding his birth and to place the body in the little wooden casket. She insisted on doing those things herself, despite the protestations of Vasili and her own mother. And she had stood at the window in her long white nightgown, a shawl thrown thoughtlessly over her shoulders, and watched the carriage bear the casket away. "Apostoli," she whispered as the carriage disappeared down the street. They had chosen the name according to Vaia's wishes. No family members or close friends carried the name, and it was a suitable one— Apostoli, now joining in death the apostles for whom he was named.

Vaia came back to the house a few times in the weeks after the baby's death, and Liana would walk on unsteady legs down to the parlor to sit with her.

"I've brought you a little something," Vaia said during one visit, placing a small wrapped packet on Liana's lap.

"How kind of you," Liana said. Her words came automatically, her voice dull with indifference. She had no need or desire for anything, save the one thing she had lost.

"It's something I've had for a long time. I thought you might like it," Vaia said, as if ignoring Liana's apathy.

Understanding what Vaia intended her to do, Liana unwrapped the paper slowly, and she saw among its folds a bracelet of silver rosebuds set into a slim silver band. Feeling Vaia's gaze upon her, she understood and looked for the mark. She found it, and suddenly she felt warmed, as if the sun had at last slipped from behind a bank of clouds. "It's my father's," she whispered, looking up at Vaia.

"So it is," Vaia acknowledged. "From years ago, when I was younger. Perhaps from before you were born."

Liana turned the bracelet over in her hands, letting it catch the light.

"Even then," Vaia added, "his work was impeccable."

"But do you really want to part with it?"

"Of course. You should have it."

"Thank you," Liana said. "Thank you so much." She rose then, moved forward, and planted a kiss on Vaia's dry cheek. "This is so kind of you."

"Vasili cares a great deal for you," Vaia said after a while.

"Yes."

"He respects you."

"Yes."

"That's good. A man should have respect for his wife."

Liana looked again at the bracelet, now encircling her arm. But the silver suddenly blurred, and all she could see was the small, pale, bluish body in its little casket and all she could feel was the throbbing of her breasts where the milk still came.

They sat in silence for a long time. Then Vaia spoke again. "Do you know what I was thinking? It would do you good to have a change of scene."

"Change of scene?"

"It's lovely in Bournabat at this time of year—really, it is. The flowers are just coming into bloom, the pines smell so good. You should come."

"Perhaps Vasili and I could come out on Sunday—"

Vaia's eyes narrowed. "Well," she said, "it's only been a few weeks. It's not suitable yet for you to be traveling back and forth. But"—she leaned closer to Liana—"if you were to come and stay for a while, that would be different."

Liana stared at her, hardly knowing what to say.

"After all," Vaia went on, "the country air is so much better for a person trying to recover. It would put the bloom back into your cheeks. Why don't you come for several days, a week or more?"

"Oh, I couldn't. How would Vasili—"

"Of course you could. Think about it." She gathered herself then and rose. "No, no, sit still. I can see myself out. But Liana, think about it."

VASILI STARED OUT THE SHOP WINDOW, WATCHING THE PEOPLE and the horses and donkeys and camels passing in the street. "What would you think of our going to Bournabat to stay for a while?" he asked finally.

"A while?" Emmanuel arched his eyebrows.

Vasili shrugged. "A few days, a week. Get Liana into the countryside, the fresh air."

"What does Liana think of it?" Emmanuel asked cautiously.

"She brought it up, though I think my mother gave her the idea. What's your opinion?"

Emmanuel cleared his throat. "I think it's your decision—yours and Liana's. Does it seem as if she wants to?"

"I can't tell for sure, but perhaps the change of scene, getting away from the house where . . ."

Emmanuel nodded.

"She still cries so much. Sometimes I don't know what to say to her."

"Vasili, women don't always need words."

The boy brought in the tea just then, and Emmanuel took a glass and saucer and handed it to Vasili and then took his own. He dropped two sugar cubes into it and stirred the tea gently with the tiny silver spoon. "I remember . . . nearly a year ago . . . meeting with you. Our conversation about where you would live."

"I remember it too. But Liana really seems to want to go."

"Why?"

Vasili shrugged and looked again toward the street. "I suppose it's what she says—that she could use a change of scene. That the fresh air would be good." He shrugged again. "I don't know."

Emmanuel gazed out at the street. That time, in the coffeehouse, when he and Vasili had met alone for the first time and schemed—yes, schemed—together, what a long time ago that seemed. And now they were on the edge of undoing it? And yet . . . one could hold too tightly to plans that had been made at another time . . . under other circumstances. "Then go, if that is what you and Liana want. And when the two of you decide to come back home, do that. If you go out there because it's what you want, then it's not your mother running your life. You don't have to always do the opposite of what she wants—if you truly did that, she'd be running your life just as much as if you bowed to her every wish."

"Sometimes it seems as if she might have mellowed in the last year," Vasili said.

"Perhaps she has," Emmanuel replied.

THEY WENT OUT THE LAST WEEK OF JULY, MOVING INTO THE ROOM that had once been Vasili's alone, with the dark oak bed and dresser and the heavy burgundy damask coverlet, and the matching draperies and the dull brown wallpaper. Awakening in that room the first morning, Liana turned to Vasili, who had already risen and was putting on his shirt, and she asked him to pull down the draperies. When she herself rose, she sent a message to her mother to bring out to Bournabat the white voile curtains from what had once been her own room in her parents' house.

She spent that first morning walking among roses and jasmine blooming in profusion in the garden, and under cherry trees where fruit was already ripening. In the afternoon her mother came with the voile, and the two of them went up to the bedroom to hang it. Vaia followed, standing wordlessly in the doorway as the two worked to make the curtains fit as best they could, and then she finally turned and walked away.

"She doesn't like it," Theodora murmured.

"It's only temporary," Liana responded.

"It's her house," Theodora pointed out.

"Yes." Liana fluffed out a curtain and stood back. Not a perfect fit, but good enough. "But it's not forever. And it does no harm. She doesn't have to look in here if she doesn't like it."

"Liana," Theodora warned.

Liana laughed suddenly. "I'll keep the door closed. How's that?"

Theodora stared at her daughter. It was the first time she had heard Liana laugh since the baby.

The weeks slid by, Vasili sometimes coming back for the noon meal and sometimes not, Dimitri never. A new fullness came into Liana's face, and her hair took on its old sheen and her step quickened. She took to pruning the roses, with Vaia's guidance, and the two of them would sit on the veranda in the late afternoons, drinking tea and chatting. Theodora sometimes joined them.

Vaia never mentioned the curtains. "I used to miss the city terribly, the bustle of it and all the shops," she said once as she and Liana sat on the veranda, the lowering sun dappling the garden under the trees. "But then I thought of all the dust, and how my skirts were always filthy, and how my shoes always had to be cleaned every time I returned home, even if it was only from visiting a neighbor. The dust and the mess from the horses and the donkeys and the camels," she added delicately.

"Yes," Liana said absently, watching a bee flit briskly from one flower to the next. She looked down at her own slippers and thought of the lines of shoes in her mother's entry hall when the whole family was there, everyone having changed to slippers as they always did when coming in from the street.

"And then, of course, when Vasili was born, I realized how much nicer it is for a child growing up in the country, where the sky is so blue, and the air so clear—not gray with coal smoke in the winter and brown with dust in the summer. And all the birds."

Liana gazed out over the garden to the trees beyond, imagining Vasili as a child, climbing trees, chasing butterflies with a net, staring at cloud shapes in the sky. He would have been a gangly boy then, all arms and legs, and she longed to hold his earnest childhood face in her hands and plant her kisses on him.

In the end, they stayed in Bournabat until the middle of September. Vaia had urged them to remain longer, but Liana had grown impatient with the days Vasili was unable to come home at midday, and she missed being able to see her family whenever she chose. So she took the voile down from the windows and put the damask back where it had been, and they returned to the city.

CHAPTER 13

LIANA WAS SURPRISED AT HOW CLOSED-IN SHE FELT ONCE THEY returned, and how she missed the sound of the wind in the tall pines, the deep blue sky, and the country smell of new-mown hay. And then there was the little room across the hall where the cradle had once held a tiny newborn and that now echoed in emptiness. Even though she kept the door closed, she could barely stand to walk past it. And whenever the family got together, there was Eleni's new baby, Eleftherios, to remind her, and even though no one said anything she could not help remembering little Apostoli, whom she had barely even held.

Vaia started coming to visit, bringing her handwork, and the two of them would sit together with long wordless intervals between occasional awkward conversation. Liana rarely knew what to say, but she thought it was kind of Vaia to come; and even Theodora, who was also present much of the time, thought that Vaia was at least trying to be sociable. On the days when Vaia was the only one who came, she would speak to Liana as a mother might to a daughter. "Wait," she would say. "Don't be in a hurry. You have years of marriage ahead of you, God willing." And when she said such things, it seemed as if Vaia might be the only one who understood.

Vasili hired a carriage one Sunday and they rode back out to Bournabat, and, walking under the trees, Liana asked Vasili to show her the places where he had played as a child. Chuckling, he took her to a little stream she had never noticed before. She dipped her hand into the cool water while he told her of catching toads, and of placing mantises in a glass jar and watching them fight to the death, each one eating the other until one finally succumbed. Then they walked back to the house, where Vaia and Dimitri sat waiting for them on the wide veranda in the cool shade of the sheltering pines.

And in the night, she dreamed of her Apostoli, who would have had a different name if he had lived, playing with Eleni's Eleftherios under the pines and at the little stream, catching toads and perhaps even finding mantises, though even now she shuddered at the thought.

While the weather was still fine they fell into the habit of riding out to Bournabat on Sundays. Vaia and Liana would sit on the veranda, watching the roses fade and the chrysanthemums bloom and listening to the birds. On the way home they'd hold hands in the carriage and Liana would lean her head on his shoulder, and one evening she pressed herself against him and he knew she was ready to try again.

The rains came early that winter, and once again the kerosene stoves were lit and shutters drawn against the weather, and the winter carpets were laid out and the *pekmez* vendor walked through the neighborhood and the houses smelled of cinnamon and honey and oranges. Vasili, walking home in the evening chill, was always cheered by the glow of the windows of his own home and by Liana waiting for him there with a smile and a kiss. But as the days and weeks passed, she didn't get pregnant, and Liana didn't know whether to be disappointed or relieved.

⥺

THE LETTER HAD TAKEN FOUR WEEKS TO ARRIVE. WRITTEN ON both sides of a page torn from a student's copy-book, it had been entrusted to an acquaintance headed for Malatya, who handed it to a relative going toward Kayseri, who gave it to a friend bound for Konya, who found a rug merchant about to take a shipment to Smyrna.

The rug merchant noted the directions on the envelope—*To be delivered only to Vasili Melopoulos, E. Demirgis & Son, Silversmiths, Eski Buyuk Pazar*—and smiled to himself. He had thought to do a kindness for his brother-in-law's cousin, but it was certainly possible that the favor might be returned. He'd been hoarding his profits for the day when he could afford to move his considerable family to Cairo. Surely a silversmith would reward a diligent messenger with some small token that would hasten that day.

Emmanuel was alone in the shop, Vasili having left to deliver an engraved cup and bowl set ordered as a christening gift. He looked up from his work when the stranger entered, noting the man's dusty clothes, and assumed he was bringing in cash he hoped to convert to jewelry. Provincials, even more than city folk, kept their wealth in jewelry—bracelets and earrings and necklaces, usually of gold but sometimes of silver. In the countryside, and even in some of the cities, jewelry was better than money. The face on the coins might change and with it their value, but an ounce of precious metal was always an ounce of precious metal. Two silver bracelets could buy a cow; half a dozen or more of them could purchase a husband.

"Do I have the honor of addressing Vasili Melopoulos?" the man asked.

"I'm sorry, *Effendim*, no," Emmanuel replied. "I'm his father-in-law. But since we're in business together, perhaps I can help you."

The man looked him over. The directions had been clear: He was to give the letter only to Vasili Melopoulos. "When will he return?" he asked.

Emmanuel shrugged. The delivery shouldn't take long, but it was late in the day; perhaps Vasili would go home afterward. "I can't promise he'll return today," Emmanuel said.

The rug merchant shuffled his feet. To deliver a letter was one thing. To have to come again and again was quite another.

"I'm his father-in-law," Emmanuel said again. "You can trust me to give it to him."

Sighing, the rug merchant pulled a tattered envelope from his pocket. "I have a letter here for him, sent from a friend. I don't know the name, but I do know that it's come a long way." He straightened his back, as if emphasizing the importance of his words. "I have no idea, of course, what the letter might say, but one must assume its importance from the distance it has traveled. I only tell you these things because I want to make clear that I have discharged my part responsibly." The man finished with a deep breath, the formality of his explanation completed, and waited in silence for Emmanuel's response.

Emmanuel took the letter and turned it over in his hand. Of course there was no return address. A letter delivered hand to hand was sent that way for a purpose. He could imagine who must have sent it.

Then the rug merchant began talking again. "In fact, perhaps I am wrong to give it to you. Perhaps it is my duty to stay and deliver it directly into the hand of this Vasili Melopoulos. Not that I wouldn't trust you, but, as I have already said, it must be an important letter, and perhaps—"

Emmanuel looked up at him and blinked twice. "I'm quite capable of giving it to my son-in-law."

"Nevertheless—"

Emmanuel understood. He opened a drawer and withdrew half a dozen coins. "Vasili will appreciate your diligence, I'm sure," he said, taking the man by the elbow and ushering him toward the door. "You must have traveled some distance. Please, take these tokens of appreciation, go to the baths, and wash off the dust of the road, and then have a good dinner." He gently shoved the man out into the street. The man hesitated a moment, perhaps wondering whether to hold out for something more substantial, but then he turned and left. Emmanuel watched until he was out of sight. In these times, given a choice, anyone would rather give away coins than jewelry.

When Vasili returned, Emmanuel gave him the letter. "This came while you were gone. Hand delivered."

Vasili took the letter, recognizing the handwriting. "From Ara," he said, opening the envelope. He scanned the letter quickly, then read it through more carefully.

> *My dear friend,*
>
> *I have come a long way since that last time we saw each other, and I've seen things I would never have dreamed of. There are so many people in this world, Vasili, and many of them are kind and hospitable, but too many others are not.*
>
> *Before I left, when you urged me to write, I thought I would be able to do so with relative ease, but I quickly learned that life is very different here, and one rarely has the opportunity to send a letter safely. For that reason, I have no idea when I will be able to write to you again.*

Please tell my family that I am safe and healthy and I am exactly where I want to be. But it is no doubt better for them not to be fully aware of where that is, because my mother will only worry and my father will think I have lost what little brains he thought I had. But Vasili, I cannot tell you how exhilarating it is to be in a place where Armenians are in the majority, where people talk openly about their political ideas, <u>and</u> where they are willing to fight for them. Yes, there have been battles in some places I have been, as I am sure you have heard. I have seen men and women killed for no reason except hatred of their religion. I have seen children wandering the streets, covered in their own mother's blood. I have been lucky to survive, but despite everything, I cannot deny the pride I feel in being part of this battle. We <u>will</u> win. We <u>will</u> have our own nation.

But Vasili, this Turkification that they talk about will touch Greeks as well. Even though Smyrna's population is mostly Greek, it may not be a safe haven for any of you. Take my words seriously. Vasili, listen to me. Things are changing.

Your friend,
A.

Vasili read the letter through again. The words were precisely the ones Ara would have used; the tone exactly Ara's. And yet he sensed that a very different man had written the letter than the one who had left his house in the night so many months before. Now and then Vasili had heard the rumors of uprisings and fighting in the east, but they had always seemed to be events happening in another place, with no connection at all to him. He refolded the letter and shoved it into his pocket, then he turned back toward Emmanuel, who seemed suddenly to be focusing all his attention on the lock of a display case.

"It was from Ara," Vasili said, though Emmanuel already knew that.

His father-in-law said nothing at first. Then, finally, he asked, "Was he in the fighting?"

"Yes."

Emmanuel let out a long breath. "No good will come of it," he said. "You know that, don't you?" Then he turned away toward the workshop at the back of the store.

CHAPTER 14

VASILI COULD NOT REMEMBER EVER HAVING CELEBRATED A name-day party for his mother—nor for his father, for that matter. But things were different in the Demirgis family, where nearly any excuse was used as a reason for a family gathering, name days especially. And now Liana had decided—and no amount of talking would convince her otherwise. He had looked askance at her when she had first mentioned it, and he'd argued that it would be too much trouble, and who would they invite anyway, and probably his mother wouldn't even want such a party. But Liana was determined, and in nearly two years of marriage, he had learned a thing or two about her determination.

Vaia had, at first, said an unequivocal *no*. They were sitting in the parlor of the Bournabat house, an early spring drizzle peppering the windows. But Liana had leaned forward and fixed a gentle gaze on her and asked, "When was the last party you had—just for you?" Vaia shrugged and turned away, not even responding. "It would be fun, wouldn't it?" Liana added.

Vasili winced at the word: *fun*. As if his mother had ever in her life done anything just for the fun of it.

"You could make up the guest list," Liana went on. "It could be here, and I would do everything. My mother would help. And Aspasia, of course. And I could bring Kateri. You wouldn't have to lift a finger."

Vaia frowned at that, and Liana realized that Vaia would, in fact, want to be in complete control.

But Vasili hadn't reckoned on Liana, whose voice took on a sudden seriousness. "You've been so kind to me. And to Vasili too, of course. You've done things for us; please let us do this one little thing for you. It wouldn't have to be a big party, if that's what you prefer, and you could make all the decisions and even order us around." She laughed a little. "But really, let Vasili and me do this one thing for you."

Vaia turned to her then and gazed at her as if suddenly trying to decide who this young woman was and what she should do with her.

"You could make all the decisions, if you want," Liana repeated. "We would do whatever you say."

Vaia's gaze shifted to the garden, to the trees beyond, and then she stiffened in her chair. A name-day party! What a waste of time and money and effort. And yet . . . she had not spent all these months trying to cultivate Liana just to throw it all away over a party. "Whom would you invite?" she asked at last, and Liana smothered a smile, knowing she had won.

"Whoever you like."

Later, when Liana had gone into the kitchen for tea, Vaia grumbled to Vasili, "I suppose she'll want her whole family there."

"She said whoever you want," he pointed out.

"I suppose we'll have to ask them."

"It wouldn't be so bad," Dimitri offered, his only words on the subject.

"Really, Mother, it's up to you," Vasili said.

And still later, when he and Liana were leaving and he gave

his mother a farewell hug, she whispered into his ear, "I suppose it would look bad if we didn't invite them."

"Do as you like," he murmured. And on the way home, he looked at Liana and saw her smiling. "You've figured out how to handle my mother, haven't you," he said with a grin, and he squeezed her tight as she laughed into his shoulder. And it seemed to be true, for in the end, Vaia had thrown up her hands and told Liana to do as she wished. It would not be her responsibility—if the whole thing turned into a disaster, it would be Liana's disaster, not hers. Though Vaia tried to grow used to the idea, the thought of someone else in charge of a party in her own home made her nearly ill with resentment.

Now Liana brimmed with excitement and plans: who would be invited (almost everyone she could think of), what the food would be and how it would be served (roast lamb and *itch pilav* and spring vegetables on long tables outside), and what sort of gifts Vaia would most appreciate. She smiled broadly as she made the preparations, head to head with one sister or another in whispered conversations, running off to her mother's in search of the perfect platter or an obscure recipe. The color was back in her cheeks and a new briskness in her step.

Vaia's name day dawned with perfectly blue skies and—finally—a warmth in the air that teased of the summer to come. Liana had spent the entire previous day at the Bournabat house, making preparations, and she and Vasili had stayed for the night. Vasili had at first been skeptical and then bemused at Liana's enthusiasm, but he'd been totally astonished at his mother's eventual willingness to let Liana engineer the whole event. He had never seen his mother so compliant, and even Dimitri had elbowed him in the ribs and chuckled over the way Liana had taken control.

Liana searched the house until she found, packed away in

an unused wardrobe, white linen tablecloths, and Vasili sent for the boy from the shop to help carry dusty tables from the barn and set them up on the lawn under the trees, something Vasili remembered seeing last when he was a small child and his grandparents had occupied the house and parties of friends came often.

Theodora came first thing in the morning and made herself busy bustling about. Sophie had come with her to help as well, as she often did these days, having no child of her own and Themo often gone on business. Liana had insisted that Vaia sit on the veranda and watch the proceedings, and had even tasked her with making sure everything was done to her satisfaction, but in fact Liana already had everything well under control. The lamb had been roasting most of the morning, overseen by Vasili and Dimitri, who had decided there was no point in opening his shop for only the morning and so had slept late.

"She's a determined one, that wife of yours," Dimitri said to Vasili. "And an organizer."

"She loves a party," Vasili responded, nodding his head, pleased at the pride he felt and the way Liana seemed to handle his mother. Sometimes, he often thought, Liana still took his breath away.

The others came in the late afternoon, when school was out, when offices and shops could be closed. There were more than thirty in all, mostly Liana's family, but also some old friends and business acquaintances of Dimitri's and Vaia's, and a few neighbors as well. Vaia stared in astonishment at the coming together of all of Liana's plans, at the children—eight of them, including two of the neighbors'—running through the yard, playing with Vasili's old croquet set, sporting dirty knees and dirtier hands. She said almost nothing, for there was nothing to be said. It had been clear from the start that Liana would not be dissuaded from this, and perhaps in the end there might be some advantage to it, and so she had girded herself with the determination that she would get through this day as best she could, though inwardly she gritted her teeth and simmered.

And at the end of the day, when the last of the lamb had been pulled from the bones, the last fingers licked, the last sweet popped into a mouth, when the last sleepy child had left and the clatter of the final carriage had faded, Liana gave her mother-in-law the gift she imagined Vaia longed for. "I wanted to tell you today, but not with all the others here," Liana said into the gathering dusk as she sat next to Vaia on the veranda. "I'm pregnant again."

Vaia sat in silence for a long moment, holding her breath, wondering if she was the first to know, hearing Vasili and Dimitri at the other end of the veranda, their voices soft in the evening air, and she imagined that surely Vasili knew. And with a surge of jealousy, she wondered if Theodora knew yet. "You must take care of yourself this time," she said finally.

THE NEXT MORNING VAIA ROSE EARLY, HAVING SLEPT POORLY. THE party had not been as bad as she had feared: Liana had done an acceptable job of it after all, but Vaia still held a lingering resentment at having turned her house over to a crowd of near strangers. And she had not really been happy that neighbors and friends had been invited, for, despite what she had said to Vasili, she would have preferred that only Liana's family had come. She hated having old friends see how tawdry her furnishings had become, and if a party were to be at her house, she wanted to know that it would be up to her standards in every possible way. If Liana and Vasili had made this their home from the start, then Liana's dowry furnishings would have come to this house, making it look almost new again, and Liana would be used by now to Vaia's ways. But that had not happened—not yet, anyway. Instead, Vaia had spent much of her own name day simmering, waiting for a catastrophe that, in the end, even she had to admit never happened.

And she had resented the noise and commotion of all the children. One child, especially if it were a boy, ought to be enough for anyone. But what could one expect from the Demirgis family—four daughters, and God only knew how many grandchildren they would finally end up with.

Liana had promised to come back first thing in the morning to finish the cleaning up, but Vaia could not—would not—wait. She would start early, and when Aspasia heard her already at work, she would rise, shamed that her mistress was up and working so early, starting all the cleaning and laundering that must now be done to put the place back the way it should be. In the last few days she had allowed others to wrest control from her, but today she could at last reclaim her own house. By the time Liana arrived, the floors had already been swept, the rugs shaken, and the laundry water was steaming on the stove, while Aspasia was busy rubbing borax into a grease-stained tablecloth. Vaia was in the dining room, standing on a chair, reaching with a feather duster to the farthest corners of the ceiling. "You shouldn't be doing that," Liana said, looking up at her.

"Well, you hardly can, in your condition," Vaia responded, her back still to Liana as she worked.

"But I said I would do the cleaning up, and now it looks as if you've done most of it already. And why are you dusting in here? Surely it didn't get so bad overnight."

"Aspasia always dusts on Tuesdays and Thursdays and Saturdays."

"Then let Aspasia do it."

"She's busy." Vaia's words were clipped, as if she were angry, though Liana could not imagine why she should be. *Wasn't it a wonderful party?* she wanted to say. She had imagined, all the way out from the city, sitting on the veranda with Vaia and talking over all the events of the day before. That's what she would have done if the party had been at her mother's or at one of her sisters'. Instead, she wandered into the kitchen and then outside, walking around the garden, picking up a plate that had been missed the evening before, finding a croquet ball hidden in shrubbery at the side of the house. She stood for a few moments, gazing over the lawn. It *had* been a wonderful party; and it was a wonderful place for a party—plenty of space for the croquet and whatever other games anyone wanted to play, room for tables spread under the trees and men standing around smoking and talking politics and children running and laughing—she could almost see and hear it all again now.

She took a deep breath. Vaia was tired. She was not used to so many people—and so many children. Everyone had a right to a cranky day now and then. There were a dozen reasons for Vaia's sharpness, but nothing could ruin this day for Liana. The sky was as blue as the sea and the birds sang lustily in the treetops and Liana was filled with a brightness and joy that could not be diminished. She had chosen to tell Vaia first, a true gift for her mother-in-law. Last evening she had told Vasili, and he had held her close and covered her in kisses. This afternoon she would tell her mother, and Theodora's face would brighten and she would break into a broad smile. When Emmanuel learned—when Theodora told him—his eyes would glisten and he would smile his special smile and nothing else in the world would matter. She turned back to the house and was walking up the broad front steps when she heard the crash.

Liana picked up her skirts and ran—up the steps, through the open door, glancing into the parlor on her left and the little sitting room on the right, running past the stairway and down the hall until she reached the dining room and saw Aspasia, aghast, long-handled wooden spoon still in her hand, staring over a crumpled pile in the corner.

"What happened?" Liana asked.

Aspasia stared at her, guilt written across her face, but she said nothing.

Liana knelt and gently cradled Vaia's face in her hands. "*Mitera*," she said softly, "*Mitera-mou*, can you hear me?" She bent closer and heard the shallow breathing. "Tell me," she said into her mother-in-law's ear, "what happened?" But there was no response. "Get a cold compress," she said to Aspasia without even turning around, and she heard the woman's footsteps hurrying away. "And the smelling salts," she called.

She laid the back of her hand against Vaia's cheek and decided it didn't feel feverish. She bent closer again to make sure she really did still hear breathing, and when Aspasia returned, she laid the cloth on Vaia's forehead and opened the bottle Aspasia had handed her. "Get the doctor," she said without looking up. "Hurry." And then she added, "But first . . ." But Aspasia had already run off.

By the time Aspasia returned with the doctor, Liana had straightened Vaia's skirt and was sitting on the floor, cradling Vaia's head in her lap. Vaia's eyes were open, but she was dazed and disoriented, and she seemed unable to speak.

"What happened?" the doctor asked, standing above the two women. "She fell?"

"She was standing on the chair," Liana said, motioning to the chair that was still overturned from Vaia's fall.

"She was dusting," Aspasia said, though no one seemed to be paying her any attention.

The doctor bent down then. "Madame?" he said. Then, louder, "Madame?"

Vaia's eyes blinked and she seemed to be trying to focus them. Finally they turned toward the doctor, but she said nothing.

"Madame?" he asked again. She stared at him wordlessly. He felt her forehead and her cheek, he held her limp hand. "Can she sit up?" he asked.

"I haven't tried. I was afraid—"

The doctor placed his arms around Vaia's shoulders and attempted to lift her to a sitting position, but she was limp as a rag and she collapsed as soon as he removed his hands. "Has she been stressed lately?" he asked finally. "Has she been over-excited?"

"We had a party," Liana said softly.

He stared at her.

"It was her name day," she added in her own defense. "Yesterday."

"And today she was standing on chairs?"

Liana looked at Aspasia, and Aspasia looked back, refusing to be brought into it. Liana gave a little shrug. "She was dusting," she said at last.

"Dusting." The doctor spit the word out. And then repeated it. "Dusting?"

Aspasia backed out of the room.

"Was it . . . ?" Liana started to ask.

The doctor took a deep breath and looked forcefully at her, as if forbidding her to say the word. And indeed, she was terrified to even think it.

He leaned closer to her and whispered, "I have always wondered if the ill can hear us, even when they seem most unlikely to." Then, louder, he added brusquely, "Are you and the girl the only ones in the house?"

"And my mother-in-law," Liana said, nodding down at Vaia, whose eyes had closed and whose mouth seemed now to have migrated over to the left side of her face.

"And your father-in-law? Your husband?"

"In the city. At their shops."

The doctor rose. "Send the girl for them. And you? Can you help me carry her to a sofa?"

VASILI ARRIVED FIRST, THOUGH ASPASIA HAD GONE IMMEDIATELY to Dimitri's shop before continuing on to Vasili's. Theodora came an hour later, to find that Vaia had somehow been taken up to her room. Liana and Vasili stood on each side of the bed, but Dimitri hovered in the doorway, as if frightened that Vaia's condition might be contagious.

"Shouldn't she be in the hospital?" Theodora asked.

"The doctor says there's nothing they can do for her there," Liana responded. "She might as well be at home."

"But who will care for her? You can't expect Aspasia—"

"We could hire a woman," Vasili responded.

"She would hate that," Liana said. "Just as much as she would hate being in the hospital." *Vaia would think it dirty*, she thought, and it would be. Vaia would indeed hate it.

"But what else can be done?" Theodora pressed. "She must have care."

"Liana can take care of her," Dimitri said from the doorway, his voice husky and dry.

"No," Vasili said.

"I could," Liana said softly.

"No," Vasili said, "not now. Not in her condition."

Theodora turned quickly to Liana. "Liana . . . ?"

Liana nodded, but "Yes" was all she said.

Theodora rushed to Liana and enfolded her in her arms, tears already coming to both their eyes. "I was going to tell you today," Liana whispered apologetically.

Emmanuel Demirgis smiled broadly. "Well, that is wonderful—"

But Dimitri, Vasili's father, interrupted, changing the subject back to what it had been. "Pregnant isn't disabled," he said.

"I could do it," Liana said determinedly.

"But—" Vasili started, but Liana interrupted him.

"I can. I should." *Has she been stressed lately?* the doctor had asked. *Has she been overexcited?*

"No," Vasili said. "We will hire someone."

"No!" Liana insisted sharply. "I will do it." She then turned back to Vaia, whose eyes were still closed, her breathing shallow, her face pale and immobile. It would not be so bad to stay here for a while. The roses in the garden were coming into bloom, new leaves on the trees fluttered pale green in the breeze, and the country air was warm and sweet and full of birdsong. It might almost be pleasant.

Vasili said, "Liana—" but then he could think of nothing to convince her. He looked imploringly at Theodora, but Theodora simply sighed. It was not her place to argue against it. "Only for a week or two," Vasili finally said. "If it's necessary after that, we find someone to come in for her."

Liana nodded, saying nothing, and Dimitri turned away and wandered downstairs, satisfied that a decision had been made.

They moved once again into Vasili's old room, Vasili telling himself it was only for a week and Liana thinking that it really wouldn't be so bad. During the day, Liana sat with Vaia, sewing garments for the new baby and watching Vaia's face for any sign of consciousness. On the third day, Vaia opened her eyes and gazed around in wonder and dismay, as if she had just discovered a new world and wasn't so sure she liked it. Then she spoke, but the words were guttural and garbled, though Liana thought she understood what her mother-in-law was attempting to say, and she replied in reassuring tones, trying not to notice that Vaia's mouth was still askew and her left eye was pulled down at the corner.

Liana sent for the doctor, and he listened to Vaia's heart and noted her breathing and asked her a few questions, even though he didn't understand any of the answers. Then he took Liana out of the room. "Now that she's conscious," he said, "she needs to be where there's activity, where she will hear people talking, not shut away up here. You need to have your husband put a bed downstairs, where she can be part of things."

"Of course," Liana said, wondering what Vaia would think of such a thing: a bed in the parlor.

When Vasili came, he sat down on the bed and held his mother's hand in his. "I'm so glad you came back to us," he whispered to her. "We were all so worried."

She stared at him wordlessly.

"The doctor thinks you should be downstairs, where you can be part of things. What do you think?"

She gripped his hand tightly, and a stream of nonsense came out of her mouth.

He looked at Liana, standing at the foot of the bed.

"Of course it's not ideal," Liana said gently, "but perhaps it's for the best right now. It won't be forever, just until you get a little better."

Vaia's gaze shifted to Liana, and when her words came they were still unintelligible, but at least they sounded less agitated.

They sent for a couple of porters to move Vasili's old bed to the parlor, as the doctor had suggested, instead of Vaia's, which was heavier and harder to carry downstairs. Vaia had grumbled incoherently, but Liana smiled at her and reassured her. Upstairs, Liana and Vasili moved into his mother's bedroom at the front of the house. That night, in the bed that had been Vaia's for as long as Vasili could remember, he held Liana tightly and whispered, "She's better already. I was afraid—"

"I know," she said against his chest. "We all were." She

closed her eyes, breathing in his scent. There were worse things. There could be much worse things.

Liana still spent her days at Vaia's side, gently coaxing her into language, praising each attempt, cheering each recogniz- able word or phrase, and ignoring Vaia's flashes of anger and frustration and, even, resentment.

It could be worse, Liana often told herself, though it was sometimes hard to think what might be worse.

And they stayed on in Bournabat, for it seemed as if, for the time being, at least, they had no choice.

CHAPTER 15

DIMITRI MELOPOULOS, THE SECOND SON OF VASILI AND LIANA and the first to survive past his first few days, was born on the eighth day of November in the same room and the same bed in which his father had been born.

The pregnancy had been easy, and, despite Vasili's protestations and those of her own mother, Liana had insisted on staying at the Bournabat house. Even her father had pulled her aside at the end of the summer, four months after Vaia's accident, and spoken to her in a gentle voice. "You mustn't feel guilty, Liana," he'd said. "It wasn't your fault. Let Vasili hire a woman."

If I hadn't insisted, she'd thought to herself. But she had never told the others what the doctor had asked her, and she knew, despite what anyone else might say, that it was indeed her fault. And she knew as well that Vaia would not put up with a strange woman caring for her and running her house. It was bad enough, Vaia too frequently made clear, that she was dependent on Liana and Vasili.

Vaia could talk now, though sometimes her words came slowly as she searched her mind for the ones she wanted. Her left hand was nearly useless, and she had no control at all over her left leg. Bedridden, she remained in the parlor, furious in her dependency.

This time Liana's baby was healthy. Vasili had told her to choose the name, but she had insisted they follow tradition and name the first son after his paternal grandfather. "We could name him after your father," he had offered. "After all, he has no sons of his own to give him a namesake."

She giggled wickedly, leaning against him as he sat beside her on the bed. This delivery had been so much easier than the first, and now the new baby lay cradled in her arms. "Perhaps we should," she said. "It would bring your mother right up out of her sickbed if we did such a thing."

He grinned and nodded, looking at the round, red face of the infant in her arms. "Emmanuel," he said.

But she raised her head slowly and *tsked* in a negative response. "The next one will be Emmanuel, as he should be. This is Dimitri."

The baby opened his eyes briefly at the sound of her voice, then closed them again.

"You see," she said, "he likes his name. Dimitri."

This time the baby's eyes remained closed.

SOPHIE STAYED ON, INSISTING THAT LIANA STAY IN BED THE USUAL forty days, though Liana often refused, rising on her own when she heard baby sounds. One day Themo came, having returned from some trip or another, and was looking for Sophie. Without asking, he lifted the baby from his cradle, chucking him under the chin. "Liana, you did yourself proud, this handsome boy," he said.

Liana flushed, remembering the crush she once had on Themo when he and Sophie were first married.

With a smile, Themo put baby Dimitri into Liana's arms and he gazed for a long time at the little one, and at Liana holding him now, before he brushed a hand gently down Liana's arm as he said, "Take care of this little fellow." Then he took Sophie by the elbow and led her from the room.

ONCE LIANA WAS OUT OF BED, THEY KEPT THE BABY'S BASKET in the parlor with Vaia during the day. The baby was a welcome diversion for her, and she kept an eye on him there, patting the blankets that bundled him if he cried and calling Liana to come and see what was the problem or to walk with him if Vaia thought he needed a change of scene. It was a harmless enough occupation, Liana thought, something to keep Vaia distracted so that she wasn't constantly demanding to know if Aspasia had scrubbed the floors yet, or why the windows hadn't been washed in the last week, or what had happened to her favorite embroidered pillow slips, or why dinner was late. If Liana had to share baby Dimitri with her mother-in-law, it was little enough pleasure to give to a woman who had been housebound for so long and who still had to remain in bed all day, except when her son was around to carry her to a chair.

The gold damask draperies in the parlor/bedroom remained closed much of the time at Vaia's insistence, and the windows in the house were kept shut as well, because Vaia preferred it. And the baby had to be picked up as soon as he began to cry because his squalling sometimes started Vaia's headaches. But even so, Liana found herself settling back into the routine of her mother-in-law's house. In the morning she would sit with Vaia and do her handwork, nursing the baby or changing his diaper whenever Vaia thought it should be done. In the afternoon, Vaia napped and Liana was allowed to take the baby elsewhere so that Vaia's sleep would not be disturbed. She'd carry him upstairs and play with him, or nap with him, or bathe him, marveling at how chubby his legs were growing, or how his eyes followed her as she moved around the room. When Vaia awoke, she would ring the bell on the bedside table, and Liana would return and place the baby in his basket, where he usually fell asleep again, and Liana would be excused to go about her own affairs for an hour or so. In the evenings, she and Vasili usually sat with Vaia, who insisted Vasili tell her all the news from the city: what new shops were opening, what he'd heard of the new cinema (though none of them had ever seen a moving picture), the automobiles that were starting to be seen on the streets. The political news and the rumors from the outlying areas farther east he kept to himself. There was enough to worry about closer to home.

Finally Vaia would grow fretful and Liana would call for Aspasia and the two of them would gently remove Vaia's bed jacket, then brush her hair and wash her hands and face for the night.

When the baby was newborn, Theodora had come to help, but she managed to stay less than three days before Vaia demanded that Theodora get out of her house. The two women disagreed on how often Liana should nurse the baby, and how often the baby should be bathed, and when Liana should be allowed out of bed, and what was the proper way to wash linens or cook rice, and how often floors should be scrubbed, or silver polished, or babies' diapers checked.

Theodora still came, but only twice a week, for two hours in the afternoon, while Vaia slept. She and Liana huddled together in the little sitting room, discussing the baby's progress and gossiping. Occasionally Theodora would ask an oblique question that related to whether or not Vaia still decided when the baby should be fed and changed, but Liana laughed off her concerns. A baby was little enough entertainment for a woman who was bedridden, she would tell her mother. And little Dimitri seemed to thrive on all the attention.

CHAPTER 16

A COLD, DAMP JANUARY WIND BLEW ACROSS SMYRNA BAY, SHOV-
ing the waves ahead of it, dashing them against the break-
waters. Boats rocked in the gray, roiled waters. Soon most of
the shipping would cease, the waters of the Aegean too wild in
winter for all but the largest of vessels. Since before the time
of Odysseus, sailors had been wary of winter in the Eastern
Mediterranean.

In winter, Smyrniots retreated to brightly lit parlors smelling of oranges and dried rose petals. Women—at least in their
own homes—dressed like tropical birds, wearing bright colors
against the damp and chill outside, and they even more often
entertained each other with coffees. Men retired to the common rooms of their sporting clubs to gamble and to read the
European newspapers and speculate over the fighting in the
Balkans. And some of the men of Smyrna spent their evening
hours at places like Fahrie's.

Dimitri closed his tobacco shop early. He'd been closing
early more and more in recent months, and why not? Few
enough customers came; it hardly mattered if the shop was
open or closed, and certainly a man could be excused for taking pleasure now and again. And there was little enough pleasure these days.

The Abyssinian eunuch who served as doorman at Fahrie's swung the door open for him, and Dimitri was immediately enveloped in the familiar sights and smells and warmth. The polished brass and mahogany of the furniture and the bar reflected the glow of the lamps. He caught one girl wink at another across the room, and laughter floated around the room like a haze of smoke.

Then a girl took his hat and his coat, and he smiled at her. The girls at Fahrie's knew him and always greeted him, even though these days he only sat at a table and sipped *mastika*. They hung on him and pulled up chairs beside him and laughed with him, parting their perfectly painted lips and showing their young teeth and their rosy, round tongues. And they leaned close, their smooth, eager cheeks begging to be touched, until he was overwhelmed by their powdery scent and the musky civet of their perfumes.

He didn't bother ordering brandies for them because he knew what it was they really wanted, and he was fortunate enough to be able to provide it: high-quality tobacco, the finest in Smyrna—the finest in the world, in fact—saved for his few remaining old customers and for the girls at Fahrie's, who lounged at his table in their lace undergarments beneath silky peignoirs and their colored silk stockings and pointed slippers.

He didn't go to the upstairs rooms anymore—he hadn't done so for years. And he didn't go to the back rooms either, where Tiffany lamps overhung baize-covered tables and the men of Smyrna could indulge in their favorite pastime. In those rooms could be found tables for cards—baccarat and escambile—and also for dominoes, backgammon, and dice. It was said a man of Smyrna would gamble against tomorrow's sunrise, if the odds were good enough, and at Fahrie's a man could always find good enough odds. But Dimitri Melopoulos wasn't a gambler. One addiction was enough for any man.

He sat at a table in a corner of the room, sharing cigarettes with two of the girls and vaguely listening to the ragtime pianist, candy-striped sleeves rolled up to the elbows. Someone brought him another drink and he smiled his thanks. Dimitri loosened his collar and sat back in his chair. The girls were talking among themselves, their low voices punctuated by silvery laughter. He didn't care; they were company, and that was enough. He closed his eyes and his head nodded forward.

When he opened his eyes again, another girl had joined the table. She was smoking from the store of tobacco in the tin box he'd placed on the table. She smiled at him, and he managed a smile in return. Then he lifted his brandy and was surprised to discover the glass was empty. He put it down, and one of the girls took it away to be refilled. He gazed after her, watching the soft curve of her leg above her stocking.

She set the empty glass on the bar and turned for a word with a man standing beside her. He nodded his head, as if agreeing with her, and she touched his arm in a soft, caressing way. She took the refilled glass and then paused for one more word with the young man before moving away from the bar. He half turned to watch her leave, and for a moment Dimitri thought he recognized him. But then Dimitri's head became muzzy and the young man turned away, and the moment passed.

The girl brought his glass and bent to kiss Dimitri's cheek, then with pale fingers she dipped into the tin box and sprinkled tobacco along a cigarette paper. She rolled the paper and licked its edge with a pink tongue darting from crimson lips, and then she smiled conspiratorially at him and strolled back to the bar. He watched her leave, watched her touch the young man again on the arm, watched the young man throw back the rest of his drink and follow her to the stairs. He was still watching as the two of them mounted the carpeted steps, the young man's hand already around her waist. And as they turned at the top of the landing so that Dimitri could see them in profile, the young man's hand was moving across the girl's breast. She leaned into him and whispered in his ear and he laughed and turned away, and Dimitri saw him full on and recognized him at last: The-mistocles Panayotis, Vasili's wife's brother-in-law Themo.

It went without saying that one never mentioned what or whom one had seen at Fahrie's, but it occurred to Dimitri just then that if he and Themo happened to be leaving the place at the same time, perhaps Themo would think to offer him a ride to Bournabat in his new automobile. It would be far out of Themo's way, of course, but perhaps he would take pity on his sister-in-law's husband's father, and that would mean that Dimitri could ride home in relative comfort, compared to the chill of an open carriage. Automobiles were undepend-able, noisy, expensive, and garish, but on a night such as this, it would be quite convenient to have an automobile to take one all the way home to Bournabat.

And so Dimitri settled back into his chair and smiled at the girls and sipped his drink. Now and then he nodded off, and perhaps it was during one of those times that Themo had walked down the steps and gathered his coat and left, but Di-mitri didn't see him again that evening. Eventually the drink was no longer able to hold its focus for him, and he wandered to the door, and someone put his coat and hat on him and the door-man called a carriage and gave the driver directions, and Dimitri settled back in the shelter of the carriage and, well fueled with alcohol, barely noticed the wind and the damp chill after all.

But the driver was a new one, unfamiliar with Bournabat, and he managed to get the street wrong, convenient street signs not being a consistent feature in the outlying areas, and he mis-takenly let Dimitri off one street away from the correct ad-dress. Dimitri, too hazy to realize, paid the driver and cheerily waved him on his way, then turned to the unfamiliar gate and couldn't figure out how to open it. And after trying unsuccessfully for a time, he sat down on the ground to think it over, wishing he had another drink, and then he nodded off, and in the night the temperature got down close to freezing—an unusual event for so early in the season.

In the morning, the maid of the household, coming out to sweep the walk, tried to open the gate. That was when she discovered a man's body wedging it shut, and it wasn't until she called the master of the house to come help her move the dead man that anyone realized that Dimitri Melopoulos, who lived only a street away, had died in the night, propped against a gate he couldn't open in front of a house for which he had no key.

THE CHURCH WAS FILLED WITH MOURNERS: THE MELOPOULOS family still had wide ties in the Greek community of Smyrna. Themo offered to take Vaia in his new automobile, and after vigorous refusals on her part to ever ride in such a noisy, dirty vehicle, Vasili managed to talk her into it. The two men carried Vaia out in their arms and placed her in the front seat, having decided that the front was easier for an invalid to manage. Then Liana climbed into the back with Sophie, and Vasili waved them off. He would take a carriage—and, no doubt, arrive before they did.

Vaia was uncharacteristically silent during the ride, and Liana and Sophie, in deference to the occasion, were quiet as well. But Liana had noticed that Sophie's cheeks seemed to hold an unusual glow, and she wondered if it was the cold or if Sophie was . . . possibly . . . but she hesitated to ask, just in case it wasn't true. Sophie would share the good news soon enough. If it was true. And Themo was a rock. One would think Dimitri had been a beloved uncle, the way he hovered over Vaia, tucking in the blanket that covered her feet, driving slowly so as to avoid the worst of the bumps in the road, talking to her in low, confident tones.

Liana sat behind Vaia, looking at the back of Vaia's head, at the precise knot of hair and the proud, stiff neck. *She is ours now*, she thought. In all the months since Vaia's accident, Dimitri had seemed to become a mere presence in the house, as if Vaia's diminution of power had affected him as well. But it had still been his house, his wife, his—nominally at least—responsibility. Now all that had changed.

And the little house in Smyrna, tucked away on a street only minutes from her own parents' home, locked and silent for all those months, would stay locked now maybe forever because there was no way Vaia could or would ever be moved there.

And then Liana knew what should be done. The only thing was: How would she tell Vasili?

CHAPTER 17

"IT'S MUCH WORSE THAN I THOUGHT," VASILI SAID. IT HAD BEEN A quiet morning in the shop. Outside, a fierce wind blew the rain against the windows. Few people ventured out in such weather unless it was necessary. "He was running his shop mostly on good will built up years ago. He owed everybody. A boy even came around yesterday with a bill from Fahrie's—close to thirty pounds for *mastika*! No doubt it was the drink they gave him that killed him in the end."

"The house was all he owned?" Emmanuel asked.

Vasili shook his head. "He'd even borrowed on that! Everything I've saved for us to enlarge this place and hire more assistants will instead go to pay off his debts. I haven't the heart to tell Liana. Of course, there's no point in mentioning it to Mother."

"We'll work it out somehow," Emmanuel said.

"It's just not fair to Liana. She's been so patient all this time. She's an angel with Mother." He let out a long breath and turned away. "Well, there's nothing to be done. We can't afford to keep two houses. Mother will hate it—she'll make life hell for Liana if we have to share that house. Even more so now."

Emmanuel Demirgis stared at his son-in-law's back. It had become harder and harder for the shop to support Vasili's growing family responsibilities—his mother's care and now a second child on the way. They'd agreed months ago that the best solution was to expand the shop, take in another assistant or two, and they'd set aside a percentage of the shop's revenues for that purpose. Now Vasili's father's debts would devour those savings. Vasili was right: It wasn't fair to Liana. Nor to any of the rest of them. Emmanuel gazed absently out the shop window. But that was the way of life, wasn't it? God sent His rain on the just and the unjust. You did your best with what came your way. "Perhaps there are ways we could cut back . . ."

"How? *How?*" Vasili demanded, and Emmanuel suddenly realized how frightened his son-in-law was.

"A family is a terrible responsibility, Vasili," he said. "But in the end, one always finds a way."

But Vasili, for the life of him, could not imagine a way.

"DIMITRI SAID 'YAYA' TODAY. CLEAR AS A BELL: YAYA." LIANA WAS sitting on the divan, knitting something for the expected baby. She'd begun to show lately, and it pleased him, seeing the rounding of her stomach. It was late, and little Dimitri had been asleep for hours and even Vaia had been put to bed. This was the only time of day they had for each other.

"Really? What did my mother say to that?"

Liana sighed and took a closer look at the stitches she'd just knit, as if trying to decide if she'd made a mistake. "I don't think she heard. I tried to get him to repeat it, but he just babbled, and she turned impatient."

Vasili chuckled. "Of all the names he could say, that hers should be the first—"

She chuckled. "I thought so too. Too bad she didn't appreciate it. But still, one can't control . . . well, I suppose I should say that—"

"Liana—" Vasili interrupted her, and his voice was suddenly so serious that she laid down her knitting. "Liana, I've been putting together all the bills I've gotten from Father's affairs. He owed nearly everyone in Smyrna."

She stared at him, saying nothing.

"It goes without saying I'll have to use the money we've been saving to enlarge the shop."

She shook her head. "Never mind. We can start saving again. It's not that important."

"But even that won't be enough, I'm afraid."

"I'll let Aspasia go. I can keep the house by myself."

"She doesn't cost that much, Liana. And besides, with another baby, you're going to need her more than ever. No, you can't let her go. But I think we should move."

She stared at him. "Move?"

He looked about the room. "Sell this house—what's left of this house. He'd borrowed on it too. Move into the house on Dionysus Street."

He'd expected to see an almost pleased expression on her face. At last she'd be back in the house she loved so much, near her parents and her sisters. For a long moment she said nothing, but when she finally spoke, her response surprised him.

"No, Vasili. We can't do that."

"We haven't a choice, Liana. Mother will get used to it."

"No. Listen, I've been thinking about these things since your father died, even though I didn't know then about his debts. No, our home is here now, and it's where your mother is most comfortable."

"We can't afford to stay."

"We could if we sold the house on Dionysus Street. It would bring a good price. We could use the money to pay off his debts, and we could stay right here."

"Sell the house? Your dowry house? We couldn't do that."

"Why not?"

"It's your house, Liana. It's the promise I made you—that you'd never have to leave your family, that you would always live close to them."

She laughed lightly. "We haven't lived close to them for months, Vasili."

He reached for her hand. "It hasn't worked out at all the way we—"

"No," she interrupted him. "I know you meant that promise when you made it. But that was a long time ago; everything has changed since then. Soon there'll be two children. And maybe more, God willing. And your mother. The house on Dionysus Street is too small."

"We'll enlarge it."

"We'll stay here, Vasili. Please, it's what I want."

"You only say that because you know Mother would fight against moving."

She rose and walked to the window, where she pulled the curtain back. It was dark, and the rain drove against the window. "I used to dream of living by the sea, of watching the sea in good weather and bad, the way the sea is never the same, every day different." She turned and faced him, letting the curtain fall back over the window. "This is the house you grew up in, Vasili. It's filled with you, every room of it. It's a big house, a house longing for children and a garden waiting for children's games. The house on Dionysus Street was a promise, Vasili—I understand that, and I love you for it. But that was never what this house has become. Our son was born here, as you were, and this is the house he knows as home, as it will be for this next child and the one after. This is really our home now, isn't it?"

CHAPTER 18

Vasili stayed home from work to help pack up all their belongings from the house on Dionysus Street, although he wondered why he had bothered. Liana insisted on overseeing all of the packing and helping in any other way that she could. He was amazed at her renewed energy and her enthusiasm. "It's an adventure!" she would say. "Here, look at this little tea set! Papa bought it for me once when I had the mumps and I had to stay in bed for a week. How I hated that!" Or: "Be sure to pack every book. A house isn't a home without books." And her eyes would glow with memories. It was only then that she paused to remember what she would miss: the quick, easy trips to her parents' home, and her sisters'; the milkman who came every other day with his donkey bearing two large milk cans, from which he would pour milk for her into a big crockery bowl. He always had a remark about the weather: *So much rain I almost drowned in a puddle. The wind is from the south, missus—watch out for a* melteme. *It's so hot you could cook an egg on the flat of your hand!* There was a milkman who came to the house in Bournabat, of course, but he was not so clever, nor so engaging. On the other hand, the shoeshine man in Bournabat had an astonishing kit, with all kinds of bottles topped with polished brass lids and cloths and leathers and even a rabbit fur with which to shine women's delicate shoes.

The whole moving process took almost a week, and it was more exhausting than Liana had assumed it would be, but with the house on Dionysus Street finally sold and all of its furnishings moved to Bournabat, Liana and Vasili felt themselves truly settled in at last. From the parlor, Vaia ordered the placement of every stick of furniture, every platter and vase and spoon. With a mental picture of the entire house, she mandated where every last possession should be kept. She offered a couple of particularly shabby chairs to Aspasia, but for the most part she insisted on keeping everything, determining that one divan or table be nudged over to make room for another, filling Vasili's old room with their marriage bed from the Dionysus house, storing extra dressers and chairs in Dimitri's old room. Liana nodded and agreed with all she demanded, then arranged the furniture in the upstairs rooms to please herself. It was not really a tug of war between them, because Liana simply ignored most of Vaia's orders. Aspasia looked on silently, taking no side. Vasili too listened to his mother's demands and smiled and assured her that Liana was taking perfectly good care of the house—there was no need at all to fret.

But fret she did.

"He doesn't sleep with you, does he?" Vaia asked once, her froggy voice coming from the bed.

Liana had thought Vaia was sleeping, and she turned to her mother-in-law in surprise. "Of course he does. Why would he not?" She could not understand what had prompted her mother-in-law to ask such a question. But of course, she realized, how would Vaia know for sure who slept where when she never even left the parlor?

Vaia *tsked*. "There are plenty of bedrooms upstairs," she

added, her voice rising. "And plenty of beds. Even with this one here, where no bed ever belonged."

Liana looked away, saying nothing. But wondering. Her parents had always shared a bed—and still did.

"I never slept with Dimitri after Vasili was born," Vaia said. "One child is enough if it's a son."

"But we—"

"Peasants do it all the time, of course. Like animals."

Liana didn't respond.

"But a respectable woman only sleeps with her husband if she's ready to have his child. It's the only reason to. You know, Liana, a man won't respect a woman if he thinks she likes it. Whores do that."

Liana turned to her, astonished she'd used the word but not knowing what to say in response.

Vaia lay with her eyes closed, worn out from the conversation. Liana picked up her sewing, and finally Vaia's voice came again from the bed. "And of course, I understand your mother . . . Four girls. Well, of course she had to keep trying for a son, poor woman."

"My father was perfectly happy with daughters."

"Yes, dear, of course, he would say that. But still . . . once a woman has done her duty . . . well, there are plenty of places for a man to find pleasure."

Liana kept her eyes fastened on the fabric in her hands, a little white gown. She'd decided to embroider it in trailing leaves and tiny yellow roses.

"Well, what's done is done," Vaia said at last. "But really, Vasili ought to be sleeping elsewhere now. And you . . ." Her voice lowered, as if she suddenly feared Aspasia might be lurking close enough to hear. "Pregnant again. And so soon. It's unseemly. I'll speak to him."

"Please. I'd rather you didn't."

Vaia turned in the bed and opened her eyes, staring at Liana. "Child, do you want him to lose all respect for you, rooting about like an animal?"

Liana felt her face flush and her hands grow cold. "I . . . I'll . . . speak to him," she said at last. Yet she wondered what she could say to him, and how she could sleep at night alone in the big bed, with no one to hold her. And besides, what would he think if she asked him to sleep somewhere else? And why should she, anyway? But although the idea needled at her mind, it took nearly a week before she had the courage.

"Do you love me, Vasili?" she asked one night as they readied themselves for bed.

He held her close. "You know I do."

"Do you want any more babies?"

He chuckled and placed his hands on her belly. "It's a little late now to ask that, don't you think?"

"But after this one?"

"We'll have as many babies as you want," he said, pulling her closer.

"But how many babies do *you* want?" she asked him.

"Lianoush." He kissed her forehead. "We used to talk about having dozens, remember? A garden full of children."

She nodded and smiled against his chest.

And then he went on. "But back then, when—when I saw you there in the bed, back then, the first time . . . you were so pale, and it was so difficult, and you were in such pain . . . when it went on and on and on for so long . . . I swore to God then that I couldn't make you . . . I had no right to make you go through that again. Not ever again—unless you yourself wanted it. Thank God little Dimitri came so much more easily. And this one, I hope, will too. But in the end, Liana, it has to be your choice."

She leaned back, barely seeing the outlines of his face in the darkness. "But you, Vasili, what do *you* want?"

"I want what makes you happy."

She sighed impatiently, and he pulled her close again. "A man wants his wife to be happy. If two children are enough, then so be it, and the two of them will fill our hearts. And if it's to be a garden full of children, then . . ."

"Then . . . what?"

He chuckled into her ear. "Then so much the better. As long as it's what you want."

She smiled into the darkness.

He kissed her neck. "Lianoushjum," he said.

A man won't respect a woman if he thinks she likes it, Vaia had said. Liana could not imagine what kind of life that would be, but it was not the life she wanted.

CHAPTER 19

VASILI SAT BENT OVER THE PAPERWORK ON HIS DESK, HIS FORE-head cradled in the palm of one hand.

"Is it still that bad?" Emmanuel asked him.

It took a moment for Vasili to realize that his father-in-law was asking about the accounts. He kept staring blindly at the papers in front of him, the figures swarming in his head. *Would there never be an end to the debts*, he wondered.

Suddenly the shop door burst open, bringing in the street sounds of the market and a stranger, small and hawk-nosed, his clothes covered in dust. The man looked about himself, his eyes squinting as if he had difficulty seeing. "Vasili Melopoulos?" he asked, looking from one man to the other.

"Yes?" Vasili said, expecting another outstanding bill to be presented.

"You are Vasili Melopoulos?"

"I said I was."

A smile cracked the man's lined face. "Please to excuse that I made certain to whom I speak. I was asked to be certain before I gave the letter." He took a step toward Vasili and held a battered and dirt-smudged envelope toward him. "I was asked to deliver this to your hand, none other."

Vasili looked at both sides of the envelope but saw no writing; then he opened it cautiously and looked at the signature: the simple letter *A*. He looked again at the man, still standing in front of him, and saw now the road weariness in his eyes. "Come in, sit down," he said. "Let me send for tea."

IT WAS LATER THAN USUAL WHEN VASILI RETURNED HOME, AND HE walked through a summer evening redolent of roses and oleander and jasmine. Liana was sewing in the glow of a lamp in the parlor/bedroom, listening to Vaia's fretful voice complaining that the quilt on her knees must not have been washed and rinsed properly because it didn't feel as soft as it should.

He bent and kissed Liana first, on the cheek, breathing in the sweet scent of her hair. Then he kissed his mother's forehead, and Vaia asked him why he was so late, as she always did, not really expecting an answer but just wanting to register her disapproval.

He shrugged an answer, starting from the room, loosening his tie and unbuttoning his collar as he went.

"Did Aspasia clean the lamp chimneys today?" Vaia was asking.

"I'm sure she did, dear," Liana responded. "But if not, we'll take care of it first thing in the morning." She'd begun calling Vaia "dear" in the last few weeks, Vasili had noticed.

"Work done today is work not needed tomorrow," Vaia said.

"Is little Dimitri in bed already?" Vasili asked from the doorway.

"Yes," Liana answered guiltily. "It seemed you were late, and I wasn't sure—"

"Never mind," he interrupted. "But is dinner ready?"

"Of course," Liana said, jumping to her feet. "We can eat right away."

Later, while Aspasia washed the dishes, Vasili read aloud and the women listened, Vaia silent most of the time and Liana sewing again. At the end of a chapter, he laid the book down in his lap and gazed at the two women, thinking again of Ara and wondering, if he had been able to send a letter to Ara, how much he would tell him.

As if his pause were a signal, Liana brought a bowl of cool rosewater and washed Vaia's face and hands and arms. She removed the pins from Vaia's hair and brushed it one hundred strokes, plus ten more, in case Vaia had lost count. Then she helped Vaia out of her bed jacket and wrapped her in a quilt, and Vasili carried his mother the few steps from her chair to the bed and laid her on the smooth sheets while Liana pulled up the covers. They each kissed her good night, then Vasili turned down the lamp and followed Liana out of the parlor and up the broad staircase.

"I got a letter from Ara today," he said as he opened the door for her.

She tilted her head in surprise and curiosity. "Where is he now?"

"Zeytoun—in the mountains. You knew about the fighting there? The killing and routing of the Armenians?"

Her hand went to her mouth. "Oh Vasili—is he all right?"

"He seems so, but he's concerned about us. He seems to think it could happen to us here too."

"How could it? This is *Smyrna*, after all. It's not at all the same. This is not some . . . some God-forsaken little town in the middle of nowhere."

"He thinks it could."

She stared at him for a long moment. "No," she said. "Surely not."

"Your father worries about it too."

"Oh Papa, he worries about everything."

"Still . . ." he said.

"Let's not think about those things," she whispered, pressing her body against his and running her hands down the length of his back.

He took her face in his hands and kissed her, and he felt himself stiffening. With one hand he held her close and with the other he unfastened her hair so that it hung down, the way he liked it. Then he began undoing the myriad of buttons at the back of her shirtwaist. She startled as his hands touched the bare skin of her back.

"Your hands are cold! How can they be cold on such a warm night?"

He moved his hands to the curve of her neck. "Then warm them for me."

She giggled and began unfastening his shirt, but he stopped her by taking her hands in his. "We can't," he said.

"Why not?"

"What about the baby?"

"Oh Vasili, it's weeks before it comes."

In response, he finished unbuttoning her shirtwaist and drew it from her. In the pale lamplight he nuzzled her neck, and she giggled softly. She unfastened the buttons of his pants and he unbuttoned her skirt, drawing her toward the bed as he did so.

"Not on the bed," she whispered. "It creaks so, your mother is bound to hear it."

"Let her hear," he murmured into her skin.

Let her hear indeed, she thought.

In the night, she dreamed of Ara and of people dying, but when morning came, she didn't tell Vasili.

Our most basic instinct is not for survival but for family.

—Paul Pearsall

CHAPTER 20

LIANA STEPPED OFF THE VERANDA INTO THE GARDEN AND TURNED to the two girls who trailed after her. "Soula, Marina, serve *Papou* and *Yaya* first, then the others." Her ten-year-old nieces walked carefully along the path, eyes fastened on the trays they carried. On each tray, ice *clinked* softly in half a dozen lemonade glasses.

Liana stopped beside the chair at the edge of the garden. "Lemonade, dear?" she asked.

With her good hand, Vaia reached for a glass, but her eyes were on the two girls. "You should not let them do that. One of them is bound to trip and drop a tray," she said. "Maybe both. And then where will you be? Heaven knows how many glasses broken."

"They're being very careful," Liana said.

"You'll be picking up broken glass for the rest of the summer. And heaven only knows how much new glasses will cost."

"They like to help."

"Mama! *Mama!*" Dimitri called.

Liana turned toward the field that bordered the garden to see little Dimitri jumping up and down, pointing excitedly into the air. "Look at my kite! Look how high!"

She balanced her tray on one hand and shaded her eyes with the other. Vasili was helping Dimitri manage the yellow kite as it swayed in a high, gentle breeze. "I see," Liana called back. "It's wonderful!"

"The baby needs her diaper changed," Vaia said.

Liana turned her attention back to Vaia, and to the thirteen-month-old playing contentedly on a blanket at Vaia's feet. "I'll check her in just a minute."

She moved away, but not fast enough to avoid hearing Vaia's grumbling comment: "It's too bitter; you should have used riper lemons."

Liana made her way toward Eleni and Sophie, who sat on a blanket at the edge of the field. Sophie held Eleni's youngest—three-year-old Evangelos—on her lap. "'Leni, the girls are such a help."

"They love it, you know. You treat them like grown-ups."

"They almost are! In not so many years they'll be as old as you were when you married Aleko."

Eleni took a long drink. "Don't remind me! I can't imagine where the time has gone. Liana, such good lemonade!"

Liana turned to Sophie. "I hope Themo manages to come."

Sophie hugged the squirming Evangelos and blew softly into his hair. "I do too. I'm sure he'd hate missing it. You always have such lovely picnics."

Liana looked away toward the field where the other adults were helping the children with their kites and wished she hadn't said anything about Themo. She hadn't planned to; it had just popped out. There was so much one couldn't say to Sophie these days. Nothing about the children—in case it made her feel bad. Although she always asked. Asked, and then sat in silence when one told her, as if she were imagining what her own children would be doing, if only she had had any children.

And now Themo as well, who used to treat Sophie with the utmost care and respect—and now almost never paid her any attention and rarely came to family parties anymore. It was as if, for him, Sophie had become a piece of rare china that he kept on a shelf and admired now and then when he thought about it, but something for which he could no longer think of any actual use. No, she should have bit her tongue, she should never have mentioned Themo's name.

She walked across the field and offered the tray to Vasili, who took two glasses, handing one to Dimitri. "Perfect day for it," Vasili said.

Liana sipped from the last glass. *No*, she thought, *it's not bitter at all*.

"Have you told your mother?" he asked.

"Not yet. I was waiting to get her alone."

"In this crowd?" He laughed. "Not likely." He leaned over and kissed her nose, and the kite in his left hand, ignored for just a moment, made a sudden swooping circle, lost wind, and settled to the ground.

"Papa!" a disappointed Dimitri called.

"Pay attention to what you're doing," Liana teased. She turned around and gazed toward her parents, who were standing with Christina, watching Spiro help their two boys, Naso and Constantine, manage their kites. As one would expect of the oldest, Naso had gotten his kite to fly the highest. Now the string drifted perilously close to the highest branches of a pine tree.

If Themo would only come, she thought, *it would be perfect, with everyone here. Naso, for once, was distracted enough that he wasn't teasing the younger ones, while the day was warm but not as hot as it could be for late June. Even Vaia was managing to not complain too much.*

Vaia, who had made no secret of her distaste for Liana's last pregnancy, seemed to hold Liana at fault when the child turned out to be a girl. Even when they'd named the infant after her, she disapproved. Vaia had more than once made her opinion perfectly clear: As soon as a woman gave birth to a son, her duty to her husband—and his place in her bed—was finished. Now how was she going to tell Vaia this news? But thinking of babies reminded her of the diaper that might or might not really need changing, and she turned back toward the house for a clean one.

Rounding the corner of the house, she saw Themo just leaving his automobile, and her initial reaction was relief. He had come, at least. "Themo!" she called, waving a hand. But then she saw his face, his mouth set in a firm line, his eyes tense, and she thought: *Oh God, what is it?* Because every day her prayer was for Sophie's marriage. Not that Sophie ever said anything, but some things didn't need saying. If ever a man had distanced himself from his wife and all who cared for her in the last few years, it was Themo.

"Liana," he said, coming close.

She thought it was just a greeting, but he paused, and she knew there was more.

"It's begun," he said.

"What?" *What? What's begun?*

"It'll happen now for sure—war. There's been an assassination in Serbia, just the excuse the Austrians have been looking for."

She tried to think what that would mean. "But they've already been fighting in the Balkans."

"Not like this. This time they'll pull us all in."

"Us?"

"The Ottoman Empire, Greece. The Russians, the Germans, the British and the French. Everyone."

"War," she whispered, trying to think what it would mean.
He was looking at her, his eyes searching her face.

"Oh God," she said. Men going off to fight. Dying. She
thought of Vasili—surely he would not have to go.

Suddenly Themo moved closer and cradled her face in his
hands. His eyes were still on hers, and for a moment she had the
wild thought that he might be going to kiss her. Themo. Sophie's
husband. Instead, he said, "Who knows how it will all end?"

She pulled away from him, and he too backed off and
turned toward the garden. She followed him with her eyes as he
strode toward the rest of the men, completely ignoring Sophie,
who had seen him and was already rising to greet him.

Blinking in astonishment at what she had thought he was
about to do, Liana watched him go, watched him speak first
to Spiro, and then watched Vasili and her own father move
closer. *War?* But surely that wouldn't affect her family, here
in Smyrna, far away enough, she thought, from Europe. And
then she saw the slump of Vasili's shoulders as he received the
news, and that subtle gesture terrified her more than anything
Themo could have said or done.

FROM THE BEGINNING, VASILI AND EMMANUEL HAD WORKED OUT
an arrangement that suited them both. Vasili, the titular owner
of the shop, greeted customers, settled them into chairs if the
negotiations were apt to be long ones, sent the boy running for
coffee or for glasses of tea, smiled politely at complaints, and
complimented customers on their good taste. From the start,
Emmanuel had been immensely pleased to be relieved of these
chores: *I'm too old to be polite to people who have nothing better to
do than complain*, he'd said.

On the other hand, Vasili had spent most of his life trying
to please his mother. He could smile and listen to a woman who

insisted a necklace was too expensive or too long or too short or too much like everything else in the shop or too different from what everyone else was wearing, and he would nod agreement with everything she said, and in the end, not wanting to disappoint the nice young man, she would reach for her purse and count out the money. Meanwhile, Emmanuel sat at his workbench in the back of the shop, surrounded now by three or four assistants, and made the delicate filigree work that attracted customers from all over the city.

The Demirgis shop was something of an anomaly, the lone Greek-owned shop sitting along a row of Armenian goldsmiths in the old district known as Eski Buyuk Pazar. Emmanuel Demirgis had come from a family of ironworkers, makers of ornate fences and fancy grilles and elaborate candelabrum for churches and the fine houses along Smyrna's seafront Kordon. But Emmanuel, from childhood, had been enthralled with the delicate tracery of filigree work. While his father and uncles labored in the heat of their shop, cutting the iron bars and heating them over the fire until they could be bent into the twisted rods and curlicues of an iron fence, Emmanuel, as a child, had found scraps of paper on which to draw intricate designs of leaves and flowers, of interlocking hearts and fragile rosettes. His father, having seen the designs his child made, had recognized the artistry and apprenticed him to a silversmith.

When no one was in the shop, Vasili would sometimes look over Emmanuel's shoulder, watching him coat the ends of the silver strands with wax and ease them through the holes of a steel drawing plate, each hole smaller than the last, each time coaxing the silver strand into an ever-finer thread, sensing by touch and by the vibrancy of the wire when it needed annealing to prevent breakage. For the finest of wire, Emmanuel kept copper disks with bored pieces of diamond in the center through which to pull the gossamer thread. And sometimes he passed twisted lengths of silver through flat rollers, creating a smooth tape with ridged edges. With a variety of threads—fine ones, flatter ones, broader ones, plain and twisted ones—he could create the fine filigree work for which he was known.

"I'd never be able to do anything even close to that," Vasili would say with a sigh.

And Emmanuel would nod. "The fingers need training when they're young."

Vasili watched now as Emmanuel's forceps deftly shaped two twisted threads into a tiny, perfect heart. Then, taking two identical heart shapes, he soldered them together into an overlapping pattern to form a larger heart. He worked with the precision of a craftsman, the full powers of his concentration apparent in the task at hand. Then, unexpectedly, he laid the material aside, straightened, and turned to Vasili.

"So. What have you heard?"

Taken by surprise, Vasili was confused and almost asked, "About what?" before realizing what: *the war.* Bournabat had become—for him, and for Liana even more so—a retreat from the vicissitudes of politics, including the impending war. "Nothing," he said. "What about you? What do you think?"

"The Empire—what's left of it—will join the Central Powers, almost certainly."

"For what? The Empire's already bankrupt from the Balkan Wars. What could we contribute? And we've lost so much already—half the Balkans, Libya already gone to the Italians, Thessaloniki lost. And even before, Tunisia, Egypt. The Ottoman Empire is no longer an empire at all."

"Still," Emmanuel said, "the Germans want us."

"Everyone wants us," Vasili responded cynically.

"Everyone wants the Mosul oil fields," Emmanuel corrected.

He stood and moved closer to Vasili. "War does things to people, ugly things. And now I've seen the beginning of it here," he whispered. "On a wall near the Konak this morning there was a poster showing a Greek bayoneting a Turkish baby. It was crudely done, but that's how these things begin."

"No one believes such nonsense. When did you ever see a Greek bayoneting any kind of a baby?"

"What does that have to do with it?" Emmanuel asked. "If people see enough pictures of such things, they begin to believe them. That's how these things start: people making enemies of those who live among them. Us against them, them against us. Things start to fall apart. No, it will get much worse before it gets better, believe me. You should take Liana and the children and go."

"*Go?* Where would we go?"

"America?"

"How could we do that? Liana's pregnant."

"When the baby is born, then."

"You saw a poster? That's not so bad—one poster is not the end of everything."

"How many posters, then, Vasili? Two? Five? Twenty? When will it be time, when will you know? Maybe when it's too late?"

"We can't just up and go, leaving everything behind. We have only just moved to Bournabat, and now you tell us to go to America? Liana would never do that and leave the rest of you here. And for what? For one poster in the Konak?" Then he narrowed his eyes. "Have you mentioned this to Spiro, to Aleko?"

Emmanuel lifted his chin, a gesture meaning *No*.

"And anyway," Vasili said, "this talk of leaving is crazy. You know Liana won't leave without you. And I—what kind of job could I get over there? What do I do here? Run the shop? It's nothing; it's you who pulls the people in." Then he stepped back, as if he suddenly were too close to Emmanuel. When he spoke again, his voice was distant and ragged. "Besides, if we left, what would happen to my mother?"

CHAPTER 21

EMMANUEL, THE THIRD SURVIVING CHILD OF VASILI AND LIANA Demirgis, was born on the last day of February, 1915. He was a large, chubby, healthy "ten-month baby" as the midwife called him. His parents cooed over him; his four-year-old brother, Dimitri, laughed at the seemingly random movements of his arms and legs; and his two-year-old sister, named by custom after her paternal grandmother but called Vaioush, tried to climb into the cradle with him.

Downstairs in the parlor, his grandmother Vaia, into whose house he was born, simmered. She was still bedridden, almost five years after what her son and his wife continued to call her "accident," managing with help the few steps between her bed and a chair. Occasionally, for a change of scene, when the weather was warm enough and there was no wind, Vasili would carry her to a chair on the veranda. Vaia still deeply resented the loss of control her immobility had forced upon her. There were parts of the house she hadn't seen in years—heaven only knew what condition they were in by now. Vasili was, after all this time and all those babies, still so besotted with his wife that he wouldn't notice if the house were falling down around him.

And the new maid was worse than a disaster as far as Vaia was concerned. Aspasia had left in the fall, going to America as a bride for some man who'd come back to Smyrna long enough to find himself a wife. Aspasia had proudly brought him to the house, showing him off as if he were some fat prize, but Vaia had observed the ill-fitting suit and the grime under his fingernails and the too-long hair and the untrimmed mustache and she had nodded to herself. Aspasia had taken the nods for approval, but they had only been Vaia's way of confirming to herself what she had suspected from the first: a village girl from a family of no importance at all, twenty-five years old now if she was a day—she'd come to Vaia fifteen years ago from a family who claimed she was twelve, but Vaia had suspected at the time that the girl was only ten—what kind of husband could such a girl hope to get? There was no one to guarantee she was even a virgin. A husband in America was probably the best she could hope for.

And then Liana had hired a new one—a Turk, no less, a woman with three half-grown children and a man she claimed was her husband but who was rarely in evidence. And as if that weren't bad enough, the older of the Turk's children were twins, two girls as different looking as possible—one dark and slight, the other robust and red haired. Clearly there had been two fathers, and that, one could only assume, was without doubt only the beginning of a story that was too tawdry to tell.

Oh yes, the Turk made a big show of working, polishing the floors every morning without having to be told, but you could be sure there was dust in the corners where no one else would bother to look, and the silver was only shined when the occasion demanded instead of every week, and the *imam bayildi* had too little olive oil.

And now the new baby had upset the routine completely.

Its mother's mother had practically moved into the house, and its mother's sister—whose husband seemed to have gone off and left her—actually *had* moved in, occupying Vasili's old room, of all inappropriate places. And when Vasili came home in the evening he went upstairs first to see his wife before coming in to greet his own mother, who had devoted her whole life to making him happy, and for what? So that her house could be taken over by a bunch of women who paid her absolutely no attention at all.

And they didn't even bring the baby down to lie in a basket next to her bed, as they had done with Dimitri and his younger sister when they were infants. Such a simple and obvious pleasure they had denied her.

LIANA FELT THE MILK SURGE INTO HER BREASTS AND KNEW IT WAS time. And yet . . . In the rocking chair by the window, Sophie held little Emmanuel next to her breast, and the baby, lost in a dream, made soft suckling sounds in his sleep. Sophie's gaze was fixed on the infant's face, as if no matter how much she looked at him she couldn't quite get enough.

Around them, the house was quiet. Little Vaioush was deep into a morning nap, while Dimitri was off for the day with Theodora, who'd come bright and early to take her grandson for a day's excursion into the city. A lark sang in the tree outside the bedroom window, and in some other part of the house Hamdiye's broom swept rhythmically. Downstairs in the parlor, Vaia no doubt fretted impatiently, but here . . . *Let her wait,* Liana thought.

Sophie's hair was caught in a glint of sunlight, and her round, pale cheek rested on the baby's head, as if she were a Madonna in a painting. Liana was so used to aching for Sophie that she barely knew how else to feel anymore. Empty arms, except to hold other women's babies. And now an empty house as well, Themo gone to America more than six months, and never a word.

He'd closed the carpet warehouse and left in October, with promises to send for Sophie when he had a good job and a place for her to live, and Sophie had built up her courage for the long trip, certain she'd be seasick, certain she'd be terrified in a boat—no matter how large it might be—sailing through the Mediterranean and then out onto the vast Atlantic. Certain that America would overwhelm her, that she would never learn the language, that she would be kidnapped by red Indians.

Less than two weeks after Themo left, Turkey had joined the Central Powers and declared war on the Allies, and Sophie had begun—even then, with Themo almost certainly still at sea—watching for the postman. Because if he didn't send for her soon, and if the war grew too fierce, it would be even more difficult for her to leave. And if America ever entered the war, it would become impossible; and besides, eventually the war would isolate them and the mail would stop altogether.

But time had passed, and Sophie had kept her house tidy in case she was called upon to leave in a hurry, and she sewed gold coins into the lining of her coat against the chance that a thief would attempt to rob her on the streets of some American city, and she thought about cutting her hair so as not to tempt an Indian to take her scalp, but a letter from Themo never came, not even one saying that he'd arrived safely and had found a job.

When Liana's new baby was born, Sophie had moved into the house in Bournabat to help, but she smiled less and her eyes had dulled, and Liana knew she had almost despaired of ever hearing from Themo. Liana kept telling her all the reasons that could have delayed a letter—the war, and Themo's exhaustion after such a long trip, and the need to get acquainted in America first—but all of it sounded hollow, even to Liana's ears. The fact was that Themo had slipped farther and farther away even when he'd lived in the same house as Sophie; now that he was half a world away, what was there to hold him to her?

Liana felt a trickle of milk slide down her breast, but she thought: *No, let them enjoy this time.* She snuggled deeper into the quilts and tried to think of something to distract her, something to keep the milk from coming. She thought of the things that Vasili had told her lately: German soldiers were almost everywhere in the city now, and most of the foreign ships in the harbor these days were German. She was glad to be living in Bournabat, away from signs of war, and she turned her mind to other things—to five-year-old Dimitri, who would be starting school soon. And to little Vaioush, who was probably right now in her room playing with her dolls, dressing them up, pretending to mother them. She smiled at that image in her mind—and yet worried. Vasili seemed to laugh away her concerns about the war, but she felt, somehow, that he was more worried than he let on.

"What will happen to us if the war comes here, to our country?" she had asked him once.

He'd laughed and smoothed her hair and kissed her. "Surely that won't happen," he had said. "The Germans have the best army in Europe, and Smyrna is the gem of the Mediterranean. Who would want to destroy it? And General von Sanders is based right in Smyrna. We couldn't be safer."

And indeed, Smyrna did seem safe. In reality, if it hadn't been for the British naval attack on an Ottoman minelayer in Smyrna harbor, it would almost have been possible to forget that the country was at war. Tobacco, cotton, and figs still grew in the fields beyond the city, though it was true that the tobacco and figs were sometimes now left to rot for lack of access to overseas markets, and the cotton was mostly requisitioned by the government, or by the Germans, for the use of the military. But the fishermen still sailed out of the harbor, albeit more cautiously now that it was known that French mines had been laid there. But still, a regiment of the German army was stationed right in Smyrna, to protect it no doubt, though they seemed to spend most of their time marching back and forth along the Kordon.

WHEN VASILI ARRIVED AT THE SHOP EACH MORNING, MORE OFTEN than not he would find Emmanuel grumbling over the latest news. After a horrendous, nearly year-long struggle, General Kemal had finally wrested victory over the Allies after their attack on Gallipoli. But that was the beginning and almost the end of the good news for the Ottoman Empire. As the war had ground on, year after year, the news seemed mostly bad. The Russians took Erzurum, the empire's major eastern Black Sea port, while the British took Baghdad and then Jerusalem. By the time the war ended, the Ottoman army had also lost Damascus and Beirut, and an allied fleet was occupying Constantinople. In November of 1918, what was left of the Ottoman Empire surrendered unconditionally. It seemed as if the war was finally over, and even though it was a shameful ending, everyone could at last breathe a sigh of relief, especially the residents of Smyrna and its surroundings, for in all the four years of war, Smyrna had never come under attack.

During all this time, Dimitri—with the other children in the neighborhood, or with his cousins, Eleni's sons, Eleftherios, whom they all called Taki, and Evangelos—played at war, fashioning guns from whatever came to hand: a stick, a broken branch, a piece of metal found in the trash, even a carrot stolen from the kitchen. They ran across the lawns, shouting and making gunshot sounds as best they could imagine them, or snuck silently through the trees in attempted ambush. In their games, the German army had always been victorious. But after the Turkish victory at bloody Gallipoli, Taki began to insist on playing the victorious General Kemal.

In the end, when the German army left, its naval ships having slunk away, and General Kemal accepted surrender terms, the cousins could not imagine what kind of military force could have defeated such a formidable army. Dimitri listened to the men of the family talking about the armistice and what depredations the Allies were about to inflict on the empire, and the boys at school laughed now at the Germans, whom they had so recently admired. And when the men talked of tens of thousands or hundreds of thousands dead, the numbers seemed to be too great to comprehend.

LIANA HEARD IT IN THE NIGHT: DIMITRI COUGHING. SHE ROSE and threw on a shawl, then slid her feet into the slippers at the side of the bed and made her way into the children's bedroom. She could only just make out their forms in the faint light of a half moon through the window shutters. On her left was Vaioush, a snuggled lump under the quilt; on her right, Dimitri was still coughing. She sat down on the side of the bed and put her hand on his forehead and was astonished at how hot it felt.

"*Mama*," he said in a gravelly voice, "it's so cold tonight."

"I'll bring you some lemon tea," she whispered. "Does your stomach hurt?"

He lifted his chin: *No.*

"Try to go back to sleep. I'll bring you another quilt."

In the dark, she opened the chest at the end of the bed, pulled out a quilt, and wrapped it tightly around him. Then she lit a lantern in the hall and tiptoed down the stairs with it.

In the kitchen, she lit a match to the stove and set about making tea. *Feverish, cold, a cough, but no stomachache.* Something he'd picked up at school, perhaps, probably only a twenty-four-hour thing; he could be better by morning.

By the time she got back upstairs he seemed to be sleeping, and no longer coughing, but now he seemed to have a slight difficulty breathing. She stood for a few moments, the tea glass in her hand, and then she told herself to let him sleep. It would be the best thing for him, so she turned and went back to bed.

In the morning, Vaioush was up early, complaining that Dimitri's coughing had kept her awake, but Dimitri himself was sleeping, his bedclothes, including the quilt Liana had added, twisted around him. Liana stood in the doorway, watching him sleep, noting that his dry cough seemed to have returned, as had his ragged breathing. *Let him sleep,* she thought; *he shouldn't go to school anyway.*

But Vaioush complained that he got to stay home from school, and she didn't, even though she was the one (she insisted) who had hardly gotten any sleep, while he had slept the night through. Liana didn't argue with her, but gave her a square of *lokum* as a treat (a bribe, she admitted to herself) to eat on her way to school.

By late morning Dimitri was awake and seemed a little better, and he even asked for a piece of bread with rose-hip jam, but when she brought it, he'd already fallen back asleep. She sat with him for a time, watching him struggle for breath, debating with herself if she should send for the doctor. But when Vasili came home for the midday meal, she was taken aback by his news: Emmanuel had come into the shop in the morning saying that Eleni's Taki had taken seriously ill the previous day with chills and a headache, and aches all over his body.

"Taki too?" Liana asked, alarmed now. "What is it?" She looked in fear across the table at little Manoush.

"Influenza, no doubt," Vasili answered.

Liana's hand went to her mouth in alarm. "Can it really be? Dimitri has influenza too, do you think?"

Vasili nodded his head. "Probably," he said. "They were playing together on Sunday."

Suddenly she ran from the table, already hearing Dimitri's coughs as she mounted the stairs. She felt his forehead—still hot—and she noticed now his shivering under the two quilts and the rattled breathing. She called to Vasili, and when he came she told him, frightened, to send for the doctor.

When Doctor Andreoglou came and looked at the sleeping Dimitri from the doorway, listening to him cough, he asked, "Is he feverish?"

Liana nodded. "And he doesn't seem to want to eat anything."

"He must drink warm drinks. Lots of them. Honey and tea is good. Warm broth is good."

"Is it . . ."

"Does he hurt anywhere?" he interrupted.

"Yes, he says especially his back."

The doctor nodded. "Influenza, yes," he said.

"What can we do?"

"Let him sleep. Keep him warm and dry, and well hydrated. There is nothing else for him."

She looked him straight in the eye. "There must be something."

"There is no medicine," he said briskly, and he pursed his lips in emphasis. "Prayer," he added, then he turned and left.

Four days later, word came that Taki had died in the night, and Liana, panicked, flew up the stairs to find Dimitri asleep, with rattled breathing. But breathing. And then she burst into silent tears for Taki, only a little older than Dimitri, the two boys the best of friends, and playmates whenever the family got together, and now Taki gone so suddenly. She crossed herself three times, and for the next few days she hovered over Dimitri, plying him with lemon tea and chicken broth, wiping his sweating forehead and murmuring softly to him. She couldn't imagine it. She missed Taki's funeral, but she knew Eleni would understand. She sent her sister notes and letters of compassion and sympathy; and at last, almost a week after Taki's passing, Dimitri awoke and squinted at her as if he could barely see her and asked for an orange.

They did not tell Dimitri for a long time about Taki's death—even Vaioush managed not to reveal it—and when they finally did, Dimitri took a sudden deep breath and stomped up the stairs, as if he would beat to death their words, and he did not come back down until the next day.

The whole Demirgis family grieved over Taki. Liana visited Eleni often and held her closely as the two of them cried over the loss of a child; at home, Liana held her own children closer, their lives ever more precious to her, and her own mind refused to accept that any mother should have to lose a child in that way—or, indeed, in any way. But she had long known that nothing at all could be done to salve the heart of a mother who had lost a child.

CHAPTER 22

VASILI HAD LEFT WORK EARLY TO GO HOME. EMMANUEL UN-
derstood: on this day, of all days. When Vasili arrived, the
children were in the garden laughing and teasing; he could
hear Dimitri's shouts and Vaioush's squeals and little Emmanuel's husky voice, but he didn't join them as he might have
done on another day.

He peered in at his mother and was relieved to see that she
was dozing in her chair. From the kitchen came the sounds of
Hamdiye working on dinner. He climbed the stairs and found
Liana in the nursery, sitting on the floor in the waning light of
early evening. From here the children's sounds were fainter,
and she didn't seem to hear them. On her lap lay a small pile
of baby clothes.

"Liana."

She turned and saw him standing in the doorway, then
frowned. "Is it so late already?" She made to rise, but Vasili
motioned to her. "No, stay where you are," he said.

"Dinner's almost ready, I'm sure."

"It'll wait." He came closer and bent to kiss her.

"Did you have a good day?" she asked.

"It was all right." He crouched beside her and took a little
infant cap from her lap.

"He would have been ten years old today," she said.

He nodded. "I know."

"We haven't any babies anymore." Little Emmanuel—Manoush—would be four soon.

"We have three beautiful children."

She took the cap from his hands and with her fingers smoothed the pale satin ribbon ties. "He was a beautiful baby too, in his own way."

"Yes, he was."

"I was with Eleni today," she said.

"How is she?"

Liana took a long breath. "A lost child," she said finally, "makes a hole in your heart that never fills." Her mind suddenly went to Sophie and her heart turned over in her breast. *And a lost husband*, she wondered, *what does that do to a person?*

Vasili hugged her and kissed her on the neck, then he rose and walked to the window. He couldn't see the garden from here, but he heard Manoush's excited shouts. He couldn't imagine what his life would have been without the children.

"I got a letter from Ara today," he said finally.

"Ara?" she repeated, as if she almost didn't remember the name. "How is he?" Then: "He survived it, then? Where is he?"

Vasili pulled the letter from his coat pocket and handed it to her. She withdrew the flimsy pages from the envelope, and they crinkled in her hands.

10 March 1919

Dear Vasili,

Do not be surprised at the return address on the envelope. I am indeed living in another world, and I have been through hell to get here.

*When last you heard from me, I had just come to
Zeytoun. I stayed there some time, and while I was
there I became a husband—married to a lovely girl
by the name of Siranoush. When Zeytoun became
threatened by the Turks, Siranoush was expecting our
first child, and I decided to take her to some place I felt
would be safer.*

*I can only tell you that was the most horrendous
mistake of my life. While I was gone for a few days
on business, Siranoush and our baby, Vartan, were
killed—in our own home! Horribly, brutally. Their
bodies left in our house to molder, not even buried.
Even now I cannot bear to think of it. And our village
was completely destroyed. Those who survived were put
onto that long road toward Aleppo that you have no
doubt heard about—a small part of the multitudes who
were thrown out of their homes in similar ways all over
the country. And killed, or forced into that long march
through the Syrian desert without food or water, and left
to die where they fell.*

*When I returned to our home, there was nothing
left—nothing, except dead bodies and the trails of those
who were forced into the desert. I cannot tell you the
horrors I myself saw along that road—the dead and
dying. The murdered and mutilated. Those starving
and dying of thirst in the desert. Most of them old men
and women and children—the younger men having
almost always been killed in their own towns. Only a
few, like me, were lucky—no, surely unlucky—enough
to be absent from home when the renegades came, or
for some other reason managed to survive. Hundreds
of thousands died. Perhaps millions.*

*When I finally reached Aleppo—relative safety—
I lived like a peasant, taking whatever work I could
find and sleeping in doorways. I saved every piastre,
and when I finally had accumulated enough—it took me
more than three years—I booked passage for America. It
was the only way I could think to put all of that horror
behind me.*

*I have found, here in California, many
Armenians like me who escaped the terror. We share an
awfulness—a vast hole—in our past that can never be
forgotten, but we have more or less put our lives back
together, one way or another. I still think of Siranoush
and Vartan—I will never forget them.*

*I haven't heard of such depredations in Smyrna,
and so I hope you have escaped them, but I have not
forgotten what I wrote to you—that you too should
think of leaving. That is still true, and for all I know,
perhaps you have taken my advice; if so, you have been
wiser than I, who waited too long. I only wish I had
taken my family out of our wretched country before it
was too late.*

*I pray that I may someday hear from you and know
that you are safe.*

Ara

Liana folded the pages slowly. "How awful," she said.
She'd heard stories—even close to Smyrna there were towns
that were rumored to have been destroyed, villagers killed or
made homeless—but none of it had seemed real. *So much death,*
she thought. So much war and death. These things were not
supposed to happen. That was some other life, some other peo-
ples' lives, not hers, not here, not in Smyrna. Now, holding

Ara's letter in her hand, it suddenly seemed as if it really could have happened—and did happen. Over and over again, one way or another. But surely it would end.

Vasili bent to her and held her close, and she ran her hand along the side of his face. "What terrible things he must have seen. I can't even imagine."

"Don't think of it, Liana. Don't even think of it. The wars are over; things will be better now." He slipped his arms around her and pressed her against him, and she clung to him, smelling his closeness and hearing the sounds of the children's laughter outside, blessedly innocent of all such horrors.

CHAPTER 23

C AN YOU KEEP A SECRET?" HIS *PAPOU* ASKED HIM.
Dimitri nodded and leaned closer.

"It's for your mother," his *papou* whispered. "Even your father doesn't know."

Dimitri leaned back on the high stool, trying to catch a glimpse of his father through the gap between the curtains. Vasili was in the front of the store, where the cases displayed engraved silver trays, filigree baskets, bracelets set with elegant jewels, and delicate earrings.

Dimitri especially liked a silver basket there, made of open filigree work, with an intricate pattern of leaves and flowers, and a base that looked like a wreath of acanthus leaves. He liked to imagine it on the dining-room table at home, filled with figs and cherries.

Now he could see his father's back as he spoke to a customer. All the ladies liked Dimitri's father, it seemed, and whenever Dimitri visited the shop, the ladies would sometimes run their fingers fondly through Dimitri's hair and ask if he wanted to run the store, like his father, when he grew up. Sometimes he would lie and say he did, and then they would smile and pinch his cheeks. "Isn't he sweet?" they would say. "Such a healthy boy! Lips like *koftes*!"

But what he really thought he wanted to be was a silversmith, like his *papou*. And now he looked from the filigree hearts to his grandfather. "For her name day?" he asked.

His grandfather raised his chin slightly, *No*. "For no occasion at all. Just because I love her. I'm making one for each of my daughters. All different. Your mother's has hearts."

Dimitri nodded. He had already counted eight pairs of hearts in graduating sizes, the smallest smaller than his fingernail, the largest twice that size. He pointed at the one his grandfather was completing. "Is that the middle one?" he asked. He knew there would be an odd number; his grandfather had told him long ago that odd numbers were more beautiful in art than even numbers.

"Ummm," his grandfather said, concentrating now on the task at hand. Like all the other hearts, this biggest one was formed from a delicately ridged strand of silver, shaped into matching patterns of branches and swirls that composed the two halves of the heart.

"I think she'll like it," Dimitri said.

His grandfather had already drawn the outline of each heart onto a thin piece of sheet metal, and now he delicately nudged a piece of the heart design into place, letting the gum solution hold it there. He stared for a long moment at the heart before finally turning back to the boy. "Do you want to go see the Greeks land?"

Dimitri's eyes widened. "*Could* I?"

In the last few days, the boys at school had been gossiping about the Greek landing—when it would be and what the Greek army would do when they came ashore. "They'll kill every Turk in sight," one of the boys had announced.

"No they won't," another had said. "The Turks will already have run."

"They carry guns as tall as you."

"They eat raw meat and drink blood for breakfast."

"They shoot bullets so fast their guns get too hot to hold."

"My papa says they can march thirty miles in one day."

"*My* papa says they can march *fifty*!"

All the boys had nodded sagely, each with the same thought: *And then at last the priests can finish the holy* litourghia *in Constantinople.* They all knew the story of how the Turks had taken Constantinople on Easter Sunday nearly five hundred years before, and the priests, in the midst of Easter services, had snatched up the Communion cup and the jewel-encrusted Bible and rushed them into a little side room and locked the door, which had never been opened since, and would not be until the day the Greeks retook Constantinople.

His grandfather interrupted Dimitri's thoughts, saying, "I'll take you to see them land if your papa says it's all right."

Dimitri slid down from the stool and dashed through the curtain. At the front of the shop, his father was talking to a tall Turk with a great mustache. On the counter between them was a filigreed fruit basket. *The* fruit basket. The one with the base that looked like a ring of acanthus leaves and the basket itself an openwork design of leaves and flowers. *Not that one!* Dimitri thought, but he said nothing. He knew better than to interrupt adults, especially at the shop.

The Turk looked down and smiled at Dimitri.

A tea boy walked into the store carrying a brass tray with two tea glasses in silver holders, two glasses of cold water, and a small bowl filled with sugar cubes and another bowl of cherry preserves and two tiny silver spoons. Vasili motioned the Turk to a chair and took a chair for himself, and the tea boy placed the glasses and the bowls and spoons on the table between them. Then he turned and hurried out of the store.

"It looks to be a fine summer," the Turk said, gazing out the window.

"Ah, yes, it's warm already," Vasili responded.

"Your family is healthy?"

"Fine. All fine."

"This is your boy?" The man nodded toward Dimitri, who shuffled from one foot to the other, impatient for the Turk to get his business over and leave.

Vasili put an arm around Dimitri and pulled him closer. "My oldest."

"*Mashallah!*" the Turk said. "You have others, then?"

"One other son."

"*Mashallah!*"

"And a daughter."

"Ahhh."

"And you?"

"No sons. Unfortunately." And then he motioned with his hand. "Come here, boy."

Vasili's hand released Dimitri's shoulder and pressed against his back, pushing him forward, and Dimitri took a step closer to the Turk.

The Turk rummaged in his pocket and brought out a single bead, the size of a small marble. On each of its four sides was a ring of yellow, which enclosed a thin ring of white, which enclosed a center of the deepest blue. Dimitri turned it over in his hands. He had seen countless blue beads against the evil eye before—all the boys at school had them, for luck. He knew Turkish mothers pinned them to their babies' clothes to ward against evil, and carriage drivers and *bah-chevans* pinned them to their horses' harnesses. But this was not a mere painted bead; this was made of something more like glass, and the colors seemed to go all the way through it and out the other side, pulling him with them into their depths.

"What do you say?" Vasili prompted.

"Thank you," Dimitri whispered.

The Turk ruffled his hair. "*Mashallah!*" he said again. Then, almost as if he had suddenly forgotten all about the boy, he turned to Vasili. "My wife—" Then he interrupted himself. "The basket is worth, I believe, ten pounds."

"I'm sorry. I was asking twenty."

The Turk lifted his chin. "For such a piece? But it's rather small, don't you think?"

"But fine workmanship."

"Humph."

Vasili gazed at the bowl. "I could let you have it for eighteen," he said at last.

The Turk took a sip of tea. "You know how things are these days." He reached over and took the silver basket in his hands again and turned it over once. Then he made a disparaging face. "Not up to his usual standards," he said. "Eleven."

Vasili took the basket gently from the Turk's hands and placed it back on the table between them. "No one in Smyrna does the work better than my father-in-law. No one."

"Twelve," the Turk said. "Last offer."

Vasili slowly lifted his head and *tsked*. "I've already gone the lowest I can go, my friend. And only for you. At that price we would have to take a loss."

The Turk rose then. "I had thought of taking something from the Demirgis shop before we leave. But my wife actually was asking for gold."

"You're leaving?" Vasili asked, rising as well.

"For Istanbul," the Turk said, using the Turkish name for Constantinople on purpose.

"A farewell gift from me then," Vasili said. "Seventeen."

The Turk shrugged and started toward the door. As he reached it, he turned. "Twelve and a half."

Vasili glanced at the basket, then at the Turk, and back at the basket. Then he sighed. "You would rob me blind. Sixteen."

With his hand on the doorknob, the Turk smiled. "Split the difference. Thirteen."

Vasili stiffened. "I have a wife and children to feed. And my in-laws eat from the store as well. Fifteen."

The Turk opened the door and stepped across the threshold.

Vasili said nothing.

Finally the Turk, still in the doorway, sighed. "You drive a hard bargain." Then he pulled out a handful of coins and began counting them.

Vasili patted Dimitri on the shoulder and said, "Run to the corner and tell them to send more tea." Then he turned to the pile of old newspapers he kept on hand to wrap the basket.

Dimitri took one last look at the silver basket. He had imagined giving it to his mother, and the astonishment and joy on her face when she unwrapped it. He had imagined her wide smile and her arms coming around him and holding him close in the pure pleasure of the moment, and being wrapped in the jasmine smell of her. He could not imagine what this Turk's wife was like or what she would think of the basket—if she would like it, if she would know whose hands had created it, if she would set it on her table with pride and put cherries and figs in it, or if she would pack it away in some cupboard or chest and never use it or even look at it.

Then he left the shop, running to the corner to get the boy, as his father had said, holding back the tears, promising himself that when he was grown, and a rich man, he would pay his grandfather to make the most beautiful silver basket in the world.

By the time Dimitri returned, the two men were sitting again at the small table, smoking and chatting like the oldest of friends, with the basket, now carefully wrapped in newspapers and tied with string, on the table between them.

CHAPTER 24

THERE WAS NO SCHOOL, THOUGH IT WOULDN'T HAVE MATTERED. Dimitri's grandfather had promised to take him if his father said yes, and his father *had* said yes, and a promise was a promise, school or no school.

He had spent the night at his grandparents' home, sleeping in the bed that had been his mother's, with the white quilt and the tiny yellow roses on the wallpaper and the pale blue ceiling, a room that made a person feel as if he were in a garden. "We'll have to get up early," his grandfather had warned. "You know soldiers: They get right to business first thing."

He was awake and dressed before dawn, and his Theodora *Yaya* and his Emmanuel *Papou*, hearing him, rose and fixed tea, and he and his *papou* sat at the little white table in the kitchen and ate bread with great gobs of jam and drank tea. His *papou* was dressed in his best suit, and he himself wore his nicest shirt and his best navy-blue short pants. "This is a historic occasion," his *papou* said, and he knew that meant he should try to pay attention to everything that happened so that he could remember it and tell his own children in the years to come. "Smyrna is, after all this time, coming back to its home," his *papou* added, and Dimitri nodded seriously.

Dimitri had always loved walking in the city with his *papou*. Often Emmanuel took him down to the quays, which were always busy and where there was so much to see. They would watch the *hamals* bending under their heavy burdens as they trudged, like human ants, in long lines up the gangplanks. Hamdiye's husband, whom he had never seen, was a *hamal*. He sometimes tried to guess if one of the scores of men bearing large crates and bundles on their backs might be husband to Hamdiye, father to Husseyin, who was only two years older than Dimitri and who had been apprenticed to a box maker since he was seven.

Dimitri was always captivated by the plethora of ships in Smyrna's harbor, ships that traveled all over the world, some still sail-driven and others, more modern, powered by coal-burning engines, and even some with oil. And everywhere there were scores of lighters, flat-bottomed vessels like barges, each driven only by a single long-handled paddle powered by a boatsman standing at the back of the craft. These were the vessels that serviced the very largest of the boats anchored farther out in the bay. Today, though, the city was different. The streets were decorated as if for a holiday. Blue and white bunting hung from all the buildings along the seafront, and from rooftops and balconies blue and white Greek flags fluttered in a gentle breeze. In the distance he could hear firecrackers. Even so early, crowds of people jammed the streets, smiling and laughing. All the schools had let out, and most of the businesses had closed for the day.

"Look sharp, now. Don't get lost," Emmanuel said.

Dimitri reached for his grandfather's hand. He was noticing something strange. There were crowds of Greeks, and there were Armenians and Jews too. But almost no Turks were on the street, and it seemed odd to him: no *hamals* on the streets, carrying loads stacked high on their backs; no *bahchevans* with carts piled with vegetables and fruit; no policemen; no carriage drivers; no officials of the city. He put his left hand into his pocket and felt the blue bead the Turk had given him. He had taken to keeping it in his pocket—for luck. Now he rolled it between his fingers, feeling the ridges of color on each side, feeling its smooth, glassy surface.

He could hear the brassy sounds of a military band playing up ahead, and now, to his right, through the early morning mist of the bay, he saw a ship approaching. No, two ships. Three. He stopped in amazement. Six ships, and more still coming.

His grandfather pointed to the lead ship. "It's a destroyer. British."

Dimitri felt a surge of disappointment. "I thought they were going to be Greek."

"They will be. That is just the lead ship. The others are all Greek."

Dimitri counted again. Ten ships in all, and one of them was huge. "Even the big one?"

"The battleship. Yes."

Dimitri grinned with pride. The German army, as proud and as disciplined as they appeared, had been defeated, and the Greek army had been on the winning side. If they had beaten the Germans, they must indeed be wonderful, he thought, the best army in the world—braver than Turks, just as all the older boys at school said. And now, because Greece had been on the winning side, the Allies had given Greece what it had dreamed of for almost five hundred years: Smyrna.

His grandfather pulled him along now, pushing through the crowds. He saw a woman with so much white powder on her face she'd have looked like a ghost if it weren't for the bright red of her lips. He saw a man with a boy sitting on his shoulders, and the boy was waving a Greek flag. He saw now a lone Turk wearing a fez scurry along the side of a building and disappear into an alley, and it occurred to him that perhaps a Turk might have reason to be afraid.

The lead boats were pulling right up to the quay. His grandfather found a place along the seawall where Dimitri could stand on a donkey cart and see above the crowds. Now the boats were docking, and now the gangplanks were being lowered, and now the Greek troops were disembarking. Dimitri craned his neck for a better look, then turned to his grandfather in confusion. "They look like girls!" he said. In fact, the men disembarking looked like the pictures of ballet dancers in one of his mother's books: white tights and short, full, white skirts.

Emmanuel nodded. "*Evzones*. The best of the best of Greek soldiers."

"Why do they dress like that?"

"It's their custom. But don't let the fancy dress uniforms fool you: They're the best and the fiercest of fighters."

From somewhere on the other side of the bay a siren began to wail, the sound coming at him in waves as the tone rose nearly to a scream. All over the city, church bells were pealing, first one and then another claiming his attention. Aghios Dimitri's at first, and then Aghios Giorgios's. Then the mellow tones of the cathedral, Aghia Photini's, joined by the excited bells of the Armenian cathedral—Saint Stepanos's—and, finally, the Italian Saint Polycarp's. The chimes of the church bells were met with the thunder of cannon salutes from the warships in the harbor. Cheers rose from the crowd as the first Greek soldiers stepped onto the quay, and then a military band drowned out the cheers with a rousing march. All around him the sounds bounced against the buildings at the seafront and echoed back, rolling across the bay, from one side to the other. It seemed as if the whole earth was celebrating.

But from the Muslim quarter came only silence.

Up ahead now, Dimitri saw the tall, gold-embroidered miter of the metropolitan, Archbishop Chrysostomos, his white beard flowing over his bejeweled robes. Surrounded by a retinue of priests carrying holy icons and great candles, Chrysostomos met the troops as they walked up the quay, his arms upraised, blessing them. The Greek general paused before the metropolitan and bent to kiss his ring, and the crowd cheered. The metropolitan and the commander in chief each gave a little speech, too far away for Dimitri to hear. Then, together, they reviewed the troops as they marched smartly by. In the meantime, a troop of dancers had forced the crowd back to form an open space, and they began a Greek dance for the benefit of the officials and the debarking army.

When the troops were finally able to reach the Kordon, they turned smartly to the right and headed directly toward the Konak, the government buildings. In a holiday mood, the crowd followed along, cheering wildly, shoving each other in the rush to follow, and now excitedly shooting guns into the air. From a balcony, someone ripped a Turkish flag to shreds and threw the pieces of it like confetti to the crowd below.

Losing sight of the soldiers, Dimitri jumped down from the cart and pulled his grandfather along. "Let's go!" he shouted.

"Time to go back home," Emmanuel said.

"No!" Dimitri urged. "I want to see!"

"It's foolishness," Emmanuel said, holding his ground. "It's starting to get out of hand."

"You *promised*!"

Emmanuel gazed at him for a long moment.

"Let's *go*!" Dimitri repeated, pulling his grandfather along.

Emmanuel finally succumbed, allowing himself to be dragged along after the soldiers. It seemed everyone was laughing and cheering, and Dimitri, caught up in the excitement, was running now, and jumping into the air, shouting along with the crowd, *"Zito! Zito!* Bravo! Bravo!"

And then the shots came. In the confusion of sounds, it was hard to tell from which direction the first ones had come, but then there were more, and it became clear that they were coming from ahead, and then others from behind as well, and then from a rooftop to the left. Excited shouts turned to screams; the crowd panicked and turned, people running now in all directions. Emmanuel grabbed Dimitri and ran with him, back the way they had come. A horse, frightened by the shots, bolted through the crowd, scattering people in its wake. Someone running beside Dimitri was shot and fell, bloody, against him, knocking him to the ground. Dimitri screamed in fright, and Emmanuel shoved the limp body aside and lifted Dimitri to his feet and dragged him forward, disregarding the boy's skinned knees, protecting him against the onrushing crowd. From behind, from the sides, the stampeding crowd beat at the two of them, shoving him this way and that, but Emmanuel kept going, holding the terrified Dimitri in front of him, catching him up each time the boy stumbled, until, finally, Emmanuel saw a break in the crowd and he veered left, pulling Dimitri with him, dragging him to safety on the far side of a pile of sacks of figs waiting on the quayside for shipment.

CHAPTER 25

LIANA LAUGHED. TWELVE-YEAR-OLD DORA, ONE OF ELENI'S daughters, had just knocked Liana's croquet ball halfway across the garden. The girl looked up at Liana proudly, daringly, and Liana laughed again and hugged her. "Doroush, must you have hit it so hard?"

"It's the game, *theia*," she said.

"So it is. But still, how will I ever win?"

"*I'm* going to win."

Nearly all the children were playing, from the fifteen-year-olds down to the youngest, Liana's Manoush, who was only four and a half. Of all the cousins, only Naso wasn't in the game. Barely nineteen, Naso stood with the men, drinking *raki*, smoking cigars, and talking politics.

"It was stupid," Emmanuel was saying. "Stupid to fire guns in the first place."

Spiro dismissed his father-in-law's statement with a wave of his hand. "Since when do we Greeks do anything intelligent? Besides, have you ever heard of a Greek celebration that didn't include firing off a gun or two?"

Naso nodded in agreement with his father. "Besides," he said, "it was Turks who fired first."

"Did you see it?" Emmanuel challenged. "Were you there?"

"I heard it from someone who was," Naso retorted.

"And anyway," Emmanuel said, dismissing Naso's argument. "All that nationalism, that Greek dancing and everything, and all the Turkish signs replaced quick as a wink with Greek ones—it's just plain stupid to rub their noses in it."

"They've been rubbing our noses in it," Spiro said. "All these years we've been second-class citizens. Five centuries of it. Why shouldn't we celebrate when the tables are finally turned?"

"Because it's not seemly."

Spiro chuckled. "Celebrations are rarely seemly. Especially Greek celebrations."

"They're just a bunch of peasants over there," Emmanuel said. "The world thinks of Greece, and immediately they think of Aristotle. Every Greek is another Aristotle. Or Demosthenes. *That* Greece is dead—the Greece of Socrates and Plato. Even the patriots: Ypsilanti, Kolokotronis. They're all dead."

Aleko turned to him in surprise. "I thought you were happy to see the Greeks come."

"I was. In theory. It's the reality that makes me nervous. Do you think the Turks are just going to sit back and take such insults? Do you think they're going to sit by while their nation is cut into pieces?"

"Pieces?" Aleko said. "It's just Smyrna, after all."

"*Just* Smyrna?" Emmanuel snorted. "The gem of the nation. And do they mean to take only to the city limits? Not the outlying areas? Not here? Not Manisa, or Sardis or Bergama? How far will they go?"

"Smyrna was never Turkish. It's always been Greek," Spiro said. "In the Bible, it's Greek. For thousands of years it's been Greek."

"Smyrna is the gateway to the sea," Emmanuel pointed out. "For all of Anatolia. *We* may think it's Greek, but—"

"Well, it is," Naso interrupted.

Emmanuel frowned at him. Just because Naso was old enough to smoke with the men didn't mean it was appropriate for him to interrupt his grandfather. "*We* may think it's Greek," Emmanuel repeated, "but there are plenty of Turks here, and for them Smyrna is the door to the world. Not Constantinople, Smyrna. And the Turks are desperate to be admired by the world."

"They've acted pretty damned stupid, if that's what they want," Aleko said.

Emmanuel shrugged. "Still, it's only prudent—"

Spiro clapped him on the back. "Prudent! Since when was a Greek ever prudent?" Then he leaned closer. "Emmanuel, Naso has some news." He glanced at his son, and Naso smiled proudly.

Twenty feet away from the men, Theodora sat with three of her daughters on a blanket, gossiping and watching the croquet. Vaia sat in her chair, farther away.

It was the name-day party for Eleni and for Christina's Constantine, and the party was, as almost all the family parties had been for years, at Liana and Vasili's house. And for good reason: It was the biggest house, and it had the biggest garden. Besides, having the parties there always solved the problem of what to do with Vaia, because there Vaia was at home, and if she grew tired, she could always be taken inside and put to bed. And in the last few years, Vaia grew tired more and more easily and complained less and less.

"It's not a good sign," Liana had worried to her mother.

"I think it's a very good thing," Theodora had said. "She's much easier for you to live with now."

Liana had sighed. "Easier, yes. No doubt. But it's not her, not the way she's always been. She's turning in on herself."

"Giving up?"

"I don't know, but it worries me."

Now Theodora watched from a distance as Vaia's eyelids fell heavily and her head lowered. She thought of the irony of it, remembering that evening, years ago, when the marriage agreements had been made. It was true that Liana had helped with that meal, though by no means had she cooked any of it herself, regardless of how Theodora had made it sound. All mothers of eligible daughters did the same. And then, when they had finished, when they were settled in the parlor and Emmanuel had unveiled his surprise, she had been shocked, and Vaia too. He had offered the business to Vasili, but only, it seemed, if Vasili and Liana would live in the city, close to her parents. And Vaia had had to weigh that—one could almost see her mind sorting it out—before she finally agreed.

But Theodora had, from the start, guessed that Vaia would renege on the deal at the first opportunity. And, to be honest, Theodora had been suspicious of Vaia's fall, and of the illness that seemed to have overwhelmed her. Theodora had imagined someone—herself, perhaps—coming upon an unaware Vaia and discovering it had only been a sham, that Vaia was as fit as anyone. But that revelation had never happened. Vaia had, for nearly ten years, remained an invalid: cranky, querulous, demanding—but an invalid nevertheless. She had indeed, in the end, gotten Liana and Vasili into her home, for all the good it did her. More than once, Theodora had gazed at Vaia and remembered the old adage: *Be careful what you pray for . . .*

I should have been kinder to her, Theodora thought now. *I should have visited her more when she was first bedridden.* And then, excusing herself: *But there was always so much to do. Always another new grandchild. Ten of them—no, nine, now that Eleni's Taki was gone. Millions around the world had died in that epidemic, but numbers were only numbers; it was those one knew and loved whose loss one truly felt.*

A cheer went up from the croquet game, and Theodora glanced over to see Doroush jumping up and down in victory, for once beating her older cousins. All the children were crowding around Doroush; and then, directed by Liana, they lifted the girl onto their shoulders and carried her precariously in and out among the croquet wickets, laughing and chanting out her name: "Do-roush! Do-roush! Do-roush!"

Halfway around the course Liana left them and, still laughing uncontrollably, collapsed onto the blanket with her mother and sisters. Vaia, hearing the commotion, opened her eyes. The children made one more round before dropping Doroush unceremoniously to the ground. As if that were a signal, Emmanuel motioned to the others with his hand, and they joined him as he walked toward the women. Curious, the children followed.

"I'm not a man given to speech-making," Emmanuel said, by way of introduction.

"Speech! Speech!" Spiro shouted, laughing good-naturedly.

Christina frowned at her husband.

"But this is definitely a special day," Emmanuel continued. "First of all, we honor our own Eleni and Constantine." He reached into his pocket, pulled out a gold coin, and handed it to Constantine. "And, of course, we always honor our dear mother and grandmother and my dear wife." From the same pocket he withdrew a small packet wrapped in tissue. Theodora, taken by surprise, rose, and Emmanuel kissed her cheek and placed the packet into her hands. "With all my love," he whispered.

Intrigued, Theodora unwrapped the tissue, and her face broke into an astonished smile as she discovered a silver filigree necklace of alternating designs: four roses, four stars, four tulip shapes, and four hearts. And the center segment, the largest and most intricate, was composed of intertwined palm fronds. "Mano," she whispered, "it's beautiful."

"And that's not all," he said in his speech-making voice. From another pocket he withdrew four more tissue-wrapped packets and, noting the tiny designations he'd marked on each packet, he handed one to each of his daughters.

"Oh Papa," Eleni said. She held up a necklace of seventeen star segments.

"Papa," Liana murmured. "It's beautiful." Her necklace of hearts lay in the palm of her hand, and her eyes suddenly clouded. She reached over to her father and hugged him tight.

Christina and Sophie moved forward to embrace their father, and he gave each one a quick hug, then he raised his hands to address the family again. "Before we get too carried away with tears and thank-yous," Emmanuel said, still in his speech-giving voice, "Naso has something to tell us." He stepped back then and left Naso, suddenly, as the center of attention.

Naso cleared his throat.

Christina moved closer to Liana and took her hand.

Naso cleared his throat again. "I'm going to join the Greek army," he said finally.

The men moved in close, clapping him on the back, giving him their encouragement and congratulations. But Liana turned to Christina. "Did you know?" she murmured.

Christina nodded, unable to speak, tears running down her cheeks.

Liana enfolded Christina in her arms. "Why didn't you tell us?" she whispered.

For a moment, all she heard was Christina struggling for breath. Then: "I hoped he'd change his mind."

"Of course," Liana said, running her hand up and down Christina's back. "And we'll all miss him."

"The army," Christina whispered. "What if the Turks start fighting back?"

Liana held her at arm's length. "Don't worry. All the Allied nations are behind the Greeks," she said. "They won't let them fail."

Dimitri stared wide-eyed at his cousin. Naso, the oldest of the cousins, always teased the younger ones, sometimes shamelessly, but he was never actually mean. Still, you had to put those things aside when you were a soldier. You had to kill people if you were sent into battle. For a moment, he thought of the noise of the gunfire, the screams of terror, and the man—blood running down the side of his face—who had fallen right over on top of him, and the frightened horses, and his own terror. And he squeezed his eyes tight to keep the memory of it away.

CHAPTER 26

EMMANUEL DEMIRGIS THREW DOWN THE NEWSPAPER. VASILI looked up from the other side of the shop, where he'd been working on the store's accounts, and raised his eyebrows. Emmanuel rose and strode restlessly to the shop window to stare out into the late March rain. Outside, men hurried by, heads bowed against the wet. There had been no one in the shop all morning. In the back room, the assistants were still bent over their work, but Emmanuel had taken half an hour for a cup of Turkish coffee and a look at the newspaper. Now Vasili waited; he knew the signs.

When Emmanuel turned back, his face was dark with fury. "So! I thought it would happen, and now it's as clear as can be. They're going to abandon us, no doubt about it."

Vasili set down his pen, making note of where he had stopped. "What?"

Emmanuel stormed back and forth between the display cases.

"*What?*" Vasili asked again.

"The Italians have signed a deal with the Kemalists. First it was the French, last fall. Same thing: currying favor with the Kemalists. So certain"—his voice was bitter—"so certain that in the end the Greek army will lose to the Turks. And even before that. Yes—when the British withdrew from the southeast, that's when it began. That's when the Turks started treating the Anatolian Greeks the same way they treated the Armenians, the very same: throwing them out of their villages, sending them off to God knows where . . . killing them. Knowing they could get away with it. Knowing no other nation would raise a finger."

"But Smyrna is—"

"Vasili," Emmanuel interrupted, "listen to me. In the end, Smyrna may not be any different. Why should it be? And anyway," he said, raising his hands in a gesture of helplessness, "what difference would it make if it were? The Greek army was never content to just take Smyrna. This was never just about Smyrna. No, they had to take the outlying areas, of course. Of course, because what good is Smyrna without the outlying areas? And then, of course, Constantinople, despite the agreement, because, after all, Aghia Sofia is the center of our Greek faith, is it not? And the *litourghia* has to be finished, doesn't it? Because the icons must no longer be cold in exile. And then, of course, they must claim the whole Aegean coast, because, after all, it was settled by Greeks long before the Turks arrived, was it not? And then, of course, of course . . . on and on. That is how politicians think!"

Vasili stared at him in astonishment. It was not like Emmanuel to speak so cynically.

"Now, in Constantinople, do you know what it is they have begun to argue about? Well, I'll tell you: Is Smyrna worth the fight? That's what they argue about in their coffeehouses. In case the Kemalists start fighting back—*really* fighting back— should those Greeks up there just hand over Smyrna to the Kemalists, in order to maintain the peace, keep themselves and their precious icons safe? That's what they spend their afternoons discussing."

"No, I don't believe that," Vasili said. "Why should they think such things? The Greek army is winning everywhere."

"Don't believe it if you like. But I'll bet it's true. Mustafa Kemal has not yet begun to fight, that's what they believe in Constantinople. He was a hero at Gallipoli, don't forget. Responsible for the Allied defeat there. No, not the German generals, Kemal himself."

"Why should the Kemalists want Smyrna? It was never Turkish."

"Because, Vasili"—he spoke as to a child—"because it's the commercial port, the doorway to Europe. Because they need it to export the products of the interior. Why would they want such a valuable asset in enemy hands?"

"We're not their enemies. We've lived with them for centuries."

"Among them, Vasili, not with them. There's a difference."

Vasili shook his head. "You never talked this way before."

"We never acted so stupidly before—nor were we ever in a position where we could change the outcome. And the handwriting on the wall was never so clear before. Do you know what the glorious Greek troops have been doing in the villages? Killing everyone in sight, that's what. No better than the Turks, it turns out. My own grandson out there—Naso—can you imagine him doing such things? Naso and boys like him, killing people just because they're Turks. And killing their animals and destroying their crops and burning down the villages as well. Stupid, stupid. Forgetting the inhumanity of it—although one would hope Christians would know better than to act as badly as Turks— forgetting that, it's just plain stupid. Do they think the tables will never turn back? Do they think they aren't giving the Turks the rope that will eventually hang us all? You know the saying, Vasili: You don't sell rope to the hangman."

Vasili tapped his pen on the desk. It was littered with papers. On a slow day, he did the store's accounts. "That's just it, Emmanuel. Why would the French and the Italians side with the Kemalists—make separate treaties with them? Why would they undercut their fellow Europeans—their fellow Christians—to curry favor with the Turks?"

Emmanuel strode closer and leaned over the desk. "You know why, Vasili."

Vasili stared at him and shook his head in confusion.

"What do you know about naval power?" Emmanuel asked. "In the war, what were the ships that were the most successful, the most powerful at sea, eh? What do they run on, Vasili?"

Vasili blinked. "Oil, of course. But Europe isn't at war anymore."

"*Commercial ships*, Vasili. They won't be running on coal anymore either. No, it's commerce, and it's oil. And all those new automobiles. All of it runs on oil." Emmanuel leaned closer. "And where are the world's biggest oil fields, eh?"

Vasili knew that, at least. "Mosul."

And now Emmanuel's face was inches away. "And who holds Mosul?"

Vasili blinked back at him. "They would sell us for oil?"

"They would sell their own mothers for oil. In the days to come, whoever owns the oil will own the world."

Vasili shoved his chair back and let out a long breath. "Then what can we do?" He was astonished at the look that passed over Emmanuel's face, a look of great sadness.

Emmanuel straightened, though his whole body seemed to have shriveled. "We've talked about this before. Take your family and get out of here."

Vasili half laughed. "You're joking."

"It's not a thing to joke about."

"Will you go?"

"If all my daughters went, I would go too."

Vasili rose. "That's the thing, isn't it. Liana won't go and leave the rest of you here." He looked down at his hands. "You know, Ara has urged me to leave, to get out, go to America, to California, where he is. I've even talked to Liana about it, in fact, but she won't go and leave you here. You're all too important to her."

"You have to make her leave."

"You should talk to Spiro and Aleko. If we all decided to go—"

Emmanuel shook his head. "I've been going over and over all this in my mind. Aleko, nice as he is, is not perceptive enough. And Spiro and Christina—even if I could convince them of the wisdom of it—wouldn't go, not as long as Naso is out there somewhere. And who could blame them? Would you go, Vasili, if you had a son in the army here? But *you* could go, you and Liana and the children."

Vasili shook his head. "She won't go without her family. I already know that. And she'll say the baby is too small. And my mother—what would we do with her?"

VASILI LEFT WORK EARLY. SOMETIME AROUND NOON THE WIND had come up, rushing down the bay from the west, blowing the rain clouds ahead of it. Now the sun was out again, glittering off the waves of the bay, and the sky was clear. Only the damp crevices between cobblestones remained to remind one of the morning's rain. The air smelled fresh, like spring; everything seemed new, bright with promise.

On the horse tram ride home, he noticed that the windows

had been washed. It seemed to him that the whole city looked cleaner now that the Greeks had taken over. He noticed a *bah-chevan*, late on his rounds because of the rain, lettuces green and crisp, tomatoes in a rounded pile, leeks laid end to end—white against green and green against white. A nut vendor on a corner poured pistachios into a newspaper cone, folded over the top, and handed it to a portly man dressed in black. A stray dog, gaunt behind its ribs, trotted along a wall, tail lowered warily. A shepherd in a long felt cloak herded a dozen sheep, their wool splashed with magenta dye.

When he got out at the Bournabat stop, he could smell the pines, the aroma that had always meant Bournabat to him, its tall pines sheltering the houses. On the street he nodded to the shoeshine man, his portable wooden stand trimmed in brass, the brass-capped bottles of polish lining its ends.

He paused in the street outside his own house, the square stone house that—except for their first months of marriage—had always been his home. Growing up, he had thought of the house as cold and dark. Now its broad front veranda seemed to hold out its arms in welcome. He had lived in this house with Liana for more than ten years. Ten years, and long ago it had slipped out of Vaia's hands, out of her control. It had become Liana's house, filled with sunshine and the laughter of children.

She had pulled down the dark, heavy, damask draperies and put white lace in their place. When Vaia had clucked over that and complained that the sun would ruin the carpets, Liana had smiled indulgently and rolled up the carpets for the summer. She'd had the dining-room chairs recovered in pale green and hired men to paint and paper the sitting room in white and yellow. The front parlor, where Vaia spent her days and nights, was left in brown and dusty rose.

Now he saw Liana in the garden at the front of the house,

bending over a rose bush, examining its tiny buds. She hadn't seen him, hadn't expected him so early, and he watched as she moved from one bush to another. In the back, he supposed, his daughter was playing with her dolls under the grape arbor. Two sheep grazed in the field at the side of the house, keeping the grass there short for games of croquet and tag and hide-and-seek and for flying kites.

Liana, sensing him, looked up, shading her eyes, and then waved to him as he walked closer. She would be thirty years old this year; in August they would celebrate thirteen years of marriage. Four surviving children. Her smile held him as he walked toward her.

"You're home early," she said as he approached. "There's nothing wrong, is there?"

He bent and kissed her. "Not a thing. Your papa sends his love." Emmanuel always sent his love. "Where are the children?"

She brushed her hair from her face. "Dimitri is studying, of course." Of course. Dimitri was a diligent, if not brilliant, student. "Vaia is with her dolls. Somewhere. Sophie took the younger ones for a walk after Giorgi's nap." Sophie was with them again. Since Themo had disappeared into America, she had made it her custom to stay wherever she could be of use, like a maiden aunt. Liana, having the youngest child of the family, was experiencing the pleasure of Sophie's company again. Vasili had to chuckle indulgently at the sisters, who often sat with their heads together, gossiping or giggling or planning the next family gathering. "Your mother is, I think, still napping," Liana added. The birth of each new child seemed to arouse Vaia, who still insisted on having the bassinet beside her all day long, even though she fretted if the baby cried and complained of too many children in the house and grumbled that four children was at least twice as many as any decent woman would have. Then, once the babies were old enough to leave the bassinet, she fell back into her drowsy existence, sleeping the days away and lying awake at night, fretting and grumbling to herself.

Vasili put a hand to Liana's waist. "What's for dinner?"

"Fish. *Barbunya*. Hamdiye found some beauties."

"We have some time before, don't we?"

She studied his face. "Something is wrong, isn't it? Is it Papa?"

He kissed her again. "No, it's not your papa, not your mama. Well, maybe in a way your papa: He says we should think about going to America." Maybe if he couched it in those terms it would seem more reasonable.

"Who is 'we'?"

"Us. You and I and the children."

"Whatever for?"

"He thinks it's not safe here."

"Oh Vasili, Papa is such an old worrier. He's worried all my life. What's ever happened to us?"

"It's not what's already happened; it's what could happen."

"What? What? Aren't the Greeks winning every battle?"

"And if they start to lose?"

"It's foolish to borrow trouble like that. We've never worried about the future, and everything has always worked out fine." She took his face in her hands. "Hasn't it?"

"Liana, your father thinks it's important." He wished he hadn't sprung it on her this way. It was foolish not to have built up to it.

"Are he and Mama going?"

"Maybe." Maybe she would take it more seriously if she thought they were.

"When they decide to go, and my sisters, then of course I'd go too. Besides, what about your mother? What about Sophie?"

"Sophie can come if she likes. My mother—well, I guess she wouldn't have a choice."

"She couldn't stand such a trip. Vasili, it's *weeks* on the boat! And can you imagine Giorgi? He's such a climber—we'd be having heart attacks all the time for fear he'd fall overboard. And *America* . . ." She looked about her, at the profusion of roses, at the jasmine climbing up the side of the veranda, at the masses of bougainvillea growing nearly to the roof . . . "I can't imagine leaving here." When she turned back to him, there was a frown on her face. "And where would we live? What kind of work would you find?"

"Ara thinks we should come to California. He says he can get work for me."

"Ara." She shook her head. "You know Ara, how he is. God knows what kind of work he's doing. Do you know?"

He said nothing. In fact, Ara had written and told him, but he hadn't understood. Something about motion pictures.

"So," she said. "And you know why Ara had to leave. But for us it's different."

"The reason Ara left is the same reason we should think about it."

She let out a long breath. "When Papa and Mama go, that's when I'll go."

He said no more about it, walking beside her up the veranda steps. He was almost relieved she had refused to think of going. How could he support a family in America? And where could they find a house as inviting and comfortable as this one had become?

THE EVENING ROUTINE HELD A PLEASANT FAMILIARITY. VASILI FED his mother in the parlor early, while Liana gave Giorgi his supper and put him to bed. Then Liana, Vasili, and Sophie ate dinner with the older children, reviewing their day, hearing about Dimitri's and Vaioush's classes, admonishing Manoush to sit up straight and to use his fork properly. They had often urged Vaia to eat with them, and once Vasili had even brought home a wheelchair in which she could come to the table. But Vaia had refused to sit in the contraption, which, she was sure, would collapse or, perhaps, hurt her back. And she insisted the children's chatter gave her headaches.

After lingering over dinner, telling stories with the children, they would hustle them off to bed. If Vaia was still awake, Vasili and Liana would sit with her, reading to her or sharing the day's news (at least, whatever of the day's news would not upset her).

Eventually Sophie would rise, excuse herself, and go to bed, while Liana and Vasili would linger a little longer. Finally, they would turn down the lights and climb the stairs to their room. *Their* room. For the first thirty years of Vasili's life it had been his mother's room: wine-colored draperies always drawn, deep blue and wine Kirghiz carpets on the floor, deep blue quilts on the bed. Now, like the rest of the house, it was Liana's room: ivory lace at the windows, pale rose and ivory covers, rose and moss-green carpets on the floor.

Tall, his father had said all those years ago. *Very black hair—pretty hair. Nice eyes, good complexion, a sweet girl, they say. Perhaps—a little thin.* Lying in bed beside her, he remembered those words. He loved the smell of her, the feel of her. Her breasts, warm and milky when she was nursing, soft and cool when she wasn't. The ridge of her collarbones, her long, slim arms, her hands, soft as butterflies against his skin, her stomach gently rounded now after five pregnancies, the warm, damp place between her legs. He reached for her now, his hand finding its way under her nightgown, caressing her soft belly, feeling the dampness between her breasts, feeling the nipples grown taut beneath his fingers.

She turned toward him and said his name, soft as a sigh, and her hand was between his legs. He felt it cupping him and stroking him, and he held himself back, wanting this to last. She rolled over onto him, her mouth on his, her tongue teasing his, and her fingers were unbuttoning his pajamas, and now her mouth was on his chest, kissing him. He lifted his head and smelled the jasmine of her hair, and then his hands were on her back, and his mouth found her breasts, sweet and cool, and he felt her against him, the whole length of her, and she pulled him into her, closing around him, like a warm mouth, like a dark, warm, gentle sea, holding him in warmth and safety, holding him forever in a warm and safe embrace.

Afterward, he thought again of what his mother had said to him once: *No decent woman likes it, Vasili; you can't expect that. Respect your wife and she will make you proud.* It was the extent of her advice on the subject, and he wondered if that had been what her own mother had said to her, if that was indeed how she had lived her own life: alone in this bedroom. Decent. Respected. And he held tight to Liana in love.

CHAPTER 27

EASTER CAME EARLY THAT YEAR, AND, AS USUAL, THE PREPARA-tions began long before. On Red Thursday—the Thursday before Easter—came the dyeing of the eggs. The children, covered with Vasili's old shirts, knelt on dining-room chairs and leaned over the table as Liana stirred the red dye into the bowl. Sophie carefully placed upon the table nine hard-boiled eggs—one for each member of the family, and an additional one for the Virgin Mary. As the only daughter, Vaioush would have the privilege of dyeing the first egg, the one for the Virgin Mary. Then it would be popped into the top of the loaf of Easter bread, to be saved and eaten early Easter morning when the family returned from church.

The boys watched longingly as Vaioush slowly dipped her egg into the dye. "She always gets to do the first one," Manoush complained, though in fact he didn't actually remember any other Easters.

Vaioush, a born actress, took the complaint as her cue to move even more slowly. Dimitri shuffled impatiently but said nothing.

"Maybe next year we'll do it differently," Liana suggested, though in fact she couldn't imagine doing it any other way. "Maybe next year someone else will get a chance to be first."

"Me!" Manoush shouted, waving his hand.

Vaioush glanced sideways at him, then turned her attention back to the egg. Using a spoon, she slowly revolved the egg in the bowl of dye.

Giorgi toddled from one chair to another, hanging on with one hand while he sucked the thumb of the other. When he reached Vaioush's chair, he leaned forward and grabbed her leg, trying to hoist himself onto the chair.

"Mama!" Vaioush protested.

Sophie stepped forward and lifted Giorgi away, chucking him under his chin and taking him to the other side of the room, where she distracted him with a crust of bread.

"I was thinking maybe of Dimitri—he's the oldest," Liana said. She bent over Dimitri and gave him a hug from behind. Sometimes she wondered if he was her favorite. Though she knew better than to have favorites, sometimes she felt that she loved him both for himself and for the lost Apostoli. Manoush would have wriggled out of such a hug, but Dimitri pulled her arms tighter around him.

"Mama, she takes so long!" Manoush complained.

"I think that's enough, Vaioush," Liana said. "Let's give someone else a chance now."

The girl lifted the egg and looked it over appraisingly. "It's not red enough yet," she announced, then plunged the egg back into the dye.

"I think it is," Liana said gently. She moved from Dimitri to her daughter, and Vaioush reluctantly took the egg from the dye and laid it on a piece of newspaper on the table.

She is not a bad girl, Liana told herself, *just headstrong*. She would need watching. The time would come when the issues would be a great deal more important than who colored an egg or how long they took to do so. "It's beautiful, Vaioush," she said. "Just the right shade of red, don't you think?"

The girl beamed at her, a wide smile below blue-black eyes.

She'll be a beauty, Liana thought, *and the world is changing so fast.* Automobiles were not uncommon on the streets now, and—with the Turks no longer in even nominal control—women were seen more and more, with less and less to cover them. Even some Turkish women wore Western dress these days. To keep a girl a virgin until her wedding day would be, she was certain, much more difficult than when she was young. She sighed at the sudden remembrance of her own naiveté and wondered if it was even possible to expect such innocence of a child in the 1920s. By the time Vaioush was old enough to marry, it would be the 1930s, or nearly so, and God only knew what life would be like then. She hugged her daughter and kissed her hair. "Dora *Yaya* is coming this afternoon to help us cook," she whispered.

"Can I help?" Vaioush asked.

"Certainly."

"Can I?" Dimitri asked.

"If you like."

Six-year-old Manoush screwed up his face. Dyeing eggs was one thing; helping the women cook was something entirely different.

As usual, on Easter Sunday, the tables fairly groaned under the weight of the food: stuffed grape leaves and *tzadziki*, eggplant dip and fish roe puree, spinach pies and cheese pies. Huge loaves of crusty bread, *pilav* cooked with pine nuts and currants, small new artichokes in lemon butter, *imam bayildi*—eggplants slit lengthwise and cooked with onions and tomatoes in olive oil. There were dried bean salad and beetroot salad and lettuce with carrots and young spring onions, and four kinds of olives. There was Theodora's special recipe of *baklava* and Christina's *galactaboureko*, and sesame cookies and walnut cake.

The men stood by the fire pit, drinking *raki* and overseeing the turning of the spit. The children took turns at the handle, watching the lamb grow brown and crispy as its fat sizzled and popped and ran down into the fire.

"We called him Frisky," Manoush said, looking up at his Uncle Aleko.

Aleko nodded. "That's a good name."

"We always call them Frisky. Papa says that's the best name for a lamb."

Emmanuel ruffled his namesake's hair. "So it is," he said.

"*Papou*, when do *I* get a turn?" Manoush asked. Constantine, Christina's fourteen-year-old, had been turning the spit for the last five minutes.

"You had a turn already."

"Another one."

"Oh, I imagine you'll have all the turns you'll want," Emmanuel said. "How about a game of ball?"

"I wanted to play badminton, but the girls won't let me."

"You'll have a turn," Emmanuel said. "Where's your brother?"

Manoush pointed to where Dimitri and his cousin Evangelos, only a year younger, were kicking a ball back and forth. His grandfather grabbed Manoush's hand and ran with him to the boys at the edge of the field.

"Here! Kick it to me!" he shouted.

Evangelos, in the process of trying to dribble past Dimitri, half turned and kicked with all his might. The ball sailed six feet wide of Emmanuel, who, nevertheless, made a diving save, just barely managing to stop the ball with his foot, but losing his balance in the process. He fell, sprawling, to the ground.

"*Papou!*" Manoush said, standing over him. "Are you hurt?"

"My dignity only. Help me up." He held out his hand and let his grandson pull him to his feet. "But, my goodness," he said, breathing heavily, "you boys are too much for me." He handed Manoush the ball and turned back toward the roasting lamb.

On the other side of the garden, Spiro poured more *raki* into his brother-in-law's glass. "Has he talked with you?" he asked.

Aleko frowned. "About . . . ?"

"About leaving."

"No," Aleko said.

"He has to me," Vasili said.

Spiro nodded. "That goes without saying. What did he say about it?"

"Just that he thinks we should leave. It's not the first time he's talked of it. He mentioned it years ago, before Turkey joined the Germans in the war."

"And?" Spiro asked.

"I don't know. Liana doesn't want to."

Aleko laughed. "Don't tell me a woman runs your family!"

"Well," Spiro said, "there's no way we can go."

"Would you go if it weren't for Naso?" Vasili asked.

"What difference does it make? It *is* for Naso. How can we leave here with him God knows where?"

"Do you ever hear from him?"

"Not in almost a year."

"They say the king is going to take charge of the fighting."

"God help us then. Despite his history, Constantine is no general," Spiro responded.

"The troops love him. They'll fight to the death for him," Aleko said.

"God help us," Spiro repeated. Then he turned to Vasili. "Maybe in the end the wisest course would be to leave. Go to America? What do you think, Vasili? The land of opportunity? Is that for you?"

Vasili shrugged. "My friend Ara's there. He says he's making money hand over fist—in California. Can you imagine?"

Spiro nodded. "Maybe you should go. Leave all this craziness behind."

Liana, walking up to the men with a platter of *mezes* in her hands, heard this last exchange, and Vasili, catching sight of her, saw the look of consternation that passed across her face.

THE SHOP WAS CLOSED FOR WHITE MONDAY, THE DAY AFTER EASter. After the big party of the day before, the family relaxed, cleaning up the rest of the residue from the family gathering, munching on leftovers. Vasili took all the children out—even little Giorgi—and they flew kites in a high blue sky, while Liana and Sophie sat on the veranda in the sun, did needlework, and relived the party of the day before. In the parlor, Vaia sat alone in the semidarkness, the curtains closed against the sun, alternately dozing and fretting that she had grown too hot.

The day was indeed warm. In the afternoon the children begged to be taken to the beach, but Vasili laughed and reminded them of the old saying: *It's warm enough to swim only when you see melon rinds floating in the sea.*

"And when will that be?" Manoush demanded.

"Oh, June, July," Vasili said.

"How long is that?" his brother persisted.

"*Months*," Dimitri said impatiently. He loved swimming, the water cool and smooth as silk against his skin.

"We could just go put our feet in," Vaioush suggested.

"*Please*, Papa," Manoush begged.

"All the way to the seaside, just to put your feet in?" Vasili asked. "It's not worth it."

"Yes, it is," Dimitri insisted.

"Please?" Vaioush urged.

Vasili laughed and scooped up Vaioush, lifting her high into the air, knowing she loved such treatment. "Please?" she asked again when he had set her down.

Vasili looked at her and then back toward the house, where Liana and Sophie sat in the sunshine. *Well,* he thought, *it is quite warm for only April. And it* was *almost the end of April.* "We'll ask your mother," he said finally.

THE NEXT DAY VASILI WAS LATER THAN USUAL FOR WORK. THE whole family, as it turned out, had gone to Bayrakli, where the beach was long and empty at that time of year. He and Liana walked on the sand, leaving Sophie behind to watch the children, with strict instructions that they only go into the water as high as their knees. The two of them strolled arm in arm along the shore, mesmerized by the rhythm of the rolling wavelets, glancing now and then down the long throat of Smyrna Bay. *We could go to Greece, maybe to one of the islands just off the coast here—to Chios, for example,* Vasili thought a time or two, but he didn't suggest it. He had seen the look of alarm on Liana's face. Even a Greek island would be too far. Until he married Liana, he had longed for family, and now he was wrapped in it as tightly as she. If they left here, what would they take with them that would anchor them? How would the children grow, with no sense of who they were or whose they were or where they belonged? It would be like falling off the edge of the earth. No, there was no point in even discussing it. A man like Ara, a man who had lost everything—such a man could make a home in a new place. But not a person who had to give up so much to leave. He couldn't even imagine what America must be like, filled with people who had left their homes. Filled with people who had let go of their anchors.

A pair of gulls wheeled overhead, and Liana watched them.

"I wonder what it's like to be so free," she said, as if she knew what he'd been thinking.

He didn't respond.

From the distance came the sounds of the children laughing. Liana looked back toward them. "Dimitri's up to his waist in the water, and Manoush is with him, up to his chest, it looks like."

"Did you think they wouldn't be?"

Liana laughed and put her arm around his waist. "They'll probably have colds for a week."

"Pneumonia, no doubt. And Mother will tell you all the things you should have done to prevent it."

"Beginning with not taking them to the beach in the first place."

"Such terrible parents!" He kissed her forehead, then they turned and started back. "It's time to think about Dimitri's school," he added.

"Vasili, he's still only a child. He shouldn't be riding all the way into the city for school."

"I did."

"We always said when he was twelve."

"He's almost twelve, Liana."

"He's ten. He has time yet."

"He'll be eleven in November."

"That's months from now. Let him be a child. He has plenty of time to be an adult."

Vasili let out a long breath. "You spoil him."

She laughed. "We both do, then."

He laughed too. "Such terrible parents." Ahead of them, the children romped in the water. "I'm glad we brought them," he said. "It's been a lovely day."

As the sun dipped below the sea, they ate their picnic on

the beach, then took horse carriages back to Smyrna, where they stopped for syrup-soaked *loukomathes* from a street vendor before taking the horse tram back to Bournabat. A long day. A lovely, long day. Nowhere else in the world could they have had such a beautiful day.

When they returned, they found that Hamdiye had already fed Vaia and put her to bed. Liana wrapped a big chunk of left-over lamb in oiled paper and filled bowls with *pilav* and sweets and pressed them on Hamdiye to take home to her family.

And the next morning, with the older children still on holiday from school, Vasili left late for work.

And that was why, when he entered the shop at nine-forty, he was astonished to see the assistants milling in a corner. They looked uneasily at him until one of them finally stepped forward and led him to the back of the shop, where Emmanuel was slumped over his workbench, just the way he had fallen: alone in the shop he had founded, without anyone to hear his cry—if there was a cry; with no one to send for a doctor or to loosen his tie and make his last breaths easier; with not one of his loved ones to hold his hand or comfort him as he slipped from life.

CHAPTER 28

LIANA WORE BLACK FOR A YEAR. IN THE FIRST FEW WEEKS, VAIA asked almost every day, "Who died?" But after a while the questions came less often, either because Vaia grew incurious, or because she had become so used to seeing Liana in black that she no longer bothered to ask why. But she did manage to point out at least once a day that it was inappropriate to wear jewelry when one was in mourning. Liana ignored the comments; since the day she'd put on the black, she wore the necklace of filigreed hearts that her father had given her. It made her feel closer to him.

And for the first time in years, she wished she lived in the city, near her mother and her sisters and all her childhood memories, close to Vasili's work—so he could come home for dinner every noon. With Emmanuel gone, the full burden of running the shop fell on Vasili's shoulders, and it was all he could do to keep up with the work.

The church had been full. Everyone in Smyrna, it seemed, had known Emmanuel Demirgis, and half the city came to his funeral. Near the back stood a stolid corps of somber-faced Armenians. Vasili was reminded of how Emmanuel used to joke about being the one Greek silversmith on a street full of

Armenian goldsmiths. Vasili had always thought the Armenians clannish, but, one by one, the goldsmiths had stopped by
the store to offer their condolences, and the wives had brought
platters of sweets and pans of *dolmas* and jars of fruit preserves.

After the first shock of the death had worn off and the shop
was reopened for business, Vasili wondered if, in Emmanuel's
absence, any customers would come, but it seemed as if business doubled. Everyone, it appeared, wanted to buy one last
piece of Emmanuel's work before it was gone. And once they
came, they took a look at the assistants' work as well, and sometimes they decided that those things were almost as good and
not nearly so costly.

Sophie moved in with her mother. She fretted about leaving
Liana, but Liana insisted she go. Manoush would start school
in the fall, and then she would have only Giorgi at home.

"I'll be back when the new one comes," Sophie promised,
but Liana laughed her off. That was months away yet—and
so far, only her mother and Sophie and Vasili knew she was
pregnant.

In the weeks immediately following Emmanuel's death, Liana visited her mother almost every day, but when full summer
descended, she talked her mother into closing the house for a
time and moving out to Bournabat, where it was cooler under
the pines.

Vaia grumbled about so many people in the house until
she noticed that Theodora spent most mornings with her in
the parlor, sewing or reading aloud, not even seeming to be
insulted if Vaia fell asleep in the midst of a particularly interesting passage. After a time, she complained only when the
cousins came to visit, shouting in the garden outside the window and running through the house on what she was sure were
dirty feet. Theodora took over much of Vaia's care, bringing

her breakfast in the morning and dabbing rosewater on her hands and face when the days grew long and overly warm, and helping her settle into bed for the night.

"Your daughter has too many children," Vaia said to her one evening, interrupting Theodora's reading. The words seemed to come from thin air, nothing in the book or in previous conversation seeming to have prompted them.

"Do you think so?" Theodora asked mildly.

"There are too many children in this house most days."

"Do they bother you?" Theodora asked.

"Yes."

Theodora raised her eyebrows but said nothing.

"And they probably have destroyed the floors and the furniture by now."

Theodora looked about her, as if assessing the damage.

"Not in here," Vaia said impatiently. "In the rest of the house, where I can't see."

"Would you like a wheelchair, so you can see what the rest of the house looks like?"

"I'm sure I'd rather not know."

Theodora patted her hand. "That's all right, dear. The rest of the house looks perfectly fine, take my word for it."

"Humph."

Theodora found her place in the book and began to read again—and almost immediately interrupted herself. "I've always thought . . ." She paused so long that Vaia finally turned to look at her. "I've always thought children and grandchildren were a blessing as one grew older."

But Vaia stared at her, saying nothing, not giving an inch.

The summer passed as in a dream—a haze of coming and going, packing up for days at the beach, cousins taking turns staying overnight at each other's houses. Liana's Dimitri and

Eleni's Evangelos were ten and nine, and Eleni's Dora and Christina's Constantine were both fourteen, and Eleni's Marina and Christina's Soula were both seventeen—young ladies already, pretty and giggly and whispering about boys. Only Vaioush and Manoush had no one their own ages to play with. But Vaioush seemed almost to prefer being by herself, not having to share her dolls with anyone; and Manoush spent most of his time tagging after his older brother. And of course Giorgi, the youngest of them all and built like a little bull, toddled around and made himself at home with whomever he could find.

In July, when King Constantine's army began the new campaign that was designed to end the fighting, everyone thought of Naso—the one cousin who was missing—still somewhere far away, and they crossed themselves and prayed for his safe return. And in August everyone was so busy with getting the children ready for school that they hardly noticed when Greece's former allies in the Great War decided among themselves that Greece and Turkey were involved in a private war in which the other nations should remain strictly neutral. If Emmanuel were still alive, he might have read between the lines and known that neutrality in this case meant that European ships could supply war matériel to the Turks with impunity, while at the same time almost certainly preventing the Greeks from applying any kind of retaliatory blockade. But Vasili, working long hours at the shop, trying to keep up with everything by himself, barely had time to read the headlines.

WINTER IN SMYRNA, AS USUAL, WAS FILLED WITH RAIN AND WIND. *Bahchevans,* bundled thickly against the cold and rain, rode gloomily on their wagons, their winter vegetables—carrots and onions, potatoes and beets—dripping with rainwater.

Milkmen's donkeys stood downcast, their backs to the wind, as their owners poured sweet, raw milk from giant milk cans. *Pekmez* vendors strode through the evening darkness, calling their ware: the thick, dark syrup that cooks used as a sweetener and mothers added to winter drinks for their children. In every house the wood stoves and the coal-oil stoves burned brightly, fighting off the damp winter chill while clothes dried on racks nearby.

Baby Dora was born on a January evening during the worst storm of the year, when the wind howled over the top of the house and rattled the gate in front, and the shutters, closed over the windows, clattered against each other. She was almost small enough to hold in one hand, and her eyes, from the first moments after birth, were wide and curious.

Sophie moved in the next day, and the baby became hers in a way none of the other children had been. Little Baby Dora, with her round, pink face, her rosebud mouth, her wide eyes, and her small, pointed chin, was the picture of a porcelain doll, just as Sophie had been as a child.

Alone for the first time since Emmanuel's death eight months before, Theodora came almost every day, making the ride out from the city on the horse tram by midmorning, staying until nearly dinnertime. Sometimes her daughters insisted she stay the night, and she frequently did, helping Sophie manage the children and oversee the housework, urging Liana to stay in bed.

"Don't you think Liana's too pale?" she whispered to Sophie, and Sophie nodded her agreement.

"She doesn't seem to have the energy she had after the others," Sophie added.

"Well"—Theodora shook her head—"five children."

"And *six* pregnancies," Sophie whispered.

Theodora crossed herself three times. "God grant that's enough for her."

Sophie tucked in her chin as if she herself had been accused of some wrongdoing. "They're all good children."

"Thank God." Theodora crossed herself again. "All my grandchildren are." Then she clasped her hands in front of her breast. "Christina got a letter from Naso. The first she's heard from him since I don't know when."

"Where is he?"

"Oh, heavens, out there somewhere. Some little town no one ever heard of. Cold, not enough clothes to keep warm, barely enough food to stay alive, I imagine."

"What does Christina say?"

"What can she say? There's nothing to say. A boy joins the army when everything looks fine, when you imagine the victories will come easily and soon, and then it drags on like this." She took a deep breath. "Well, I certainly can't understand it at all. If Emmanuel were alive he'd have made sense of it, I suppose. Christina says that Spiro thinks they've stretched the army lines too far. He's surprised the Turks haven't taken advantage of it. I say, praise God they haven't."

"Sophie *Hanum*."

Both women turned at Hamdiye's voice. She was the third in the triumvirate that kept the household running, and she stood now in her coat, with a scarf covering nearly all of her head.

"Hamdiye! I'm so sorry. I completely forgot!" Then Sophie turned back to Theodora. "I promised she could go home early. It's Husseyin's circumcision tomorrow." To Hamdiye she added, "Wait just a moment, I have something," and she hurried off.

"His circumcision is so soon?" Theodora asked. "Isn't he only about ten?"

"Thirteen," Hamdiye said proudly.

"Oh, my goodness. How time goes." Theodora clasped Hamdiye's work-roughened hands in her own smooth ones. "You'll have a big party? All the neighbors and relatives? You must give him our best wishes."

Hamdiye leaned forward. "*Hanum*," she murmured. "Will you stay this evening and tomorrow? Your daughter needs you here."

Theodora frowned briefly. "Certainly," she said, nodding. "Certainly I'll stay. I think that's a very good idea."

Sophie returned to the room and placed some coins into Hamdiye's hand. "For Husseyin," she said. "From the whole family."

"*Mashallah!*" Hamdiye responded. "And Husseyin thanks you." She stuffed the money into her coat pocket and started for the door, but then she turned. "Don't let the baby keep Liana *Hanum* awake. She needs her sleep."

Sophie placed her arm across Hamdiye's broad back. "We'll do our best. Now, don't worry. Have a wonderful party. Use some of the money to buy those sweetcakes that Husseyin likes so much."

ONCE AGAIN THERE WAS A BASSINET BESIDE VAIA'S BED IN THE PARlor, and even though Liana still spent the evenings in her own bed upstairs, Theodora stayed in the parlor with Vaia. "You should tell your daughter to stop having children," Vaia said crankily. They were alone in the parlor; Vasili was upstairs, helping Sophie put the children to bed. "Five is too many," Vaia added. "It's even more than you had. And at least you had an excuse."

Theodora laughed with embarrassment. "Since when does a grown woman pay attention to her mother?"

"Who else would tell her?"

"It's your son, after all. He has something to do with it." Then, rising to the argument: "He's the one who should be spoken to. Surely you don't think she asks him for it."

Vaia shook her head. "They should sleep in separate rooms. I've said that from the start. That would solve it right there. Imagine, five children. God knows when they'll stop if no one does anything about it."

Theodora said nothing. She missed Emmanuel the most at night, the bed beside her so empty.

Vaia closed her eyes. "I'll have to speak to him, I suppose," she said with a sigh.

Theodora gazed at her. All these years an invalid. What would it be like? She leaned closer to the bed and patted Vaia's arm. "We're both very fortunate to have Liana and Vasili. They couldn't be kinder to us." *All my daughters and their husbands,* she thought to herself.

Except, of course, for Themo, who in the end had proved to be worse than worthless, leaving poor Sophie alone to fend for herself, no man to care for her or to make her a home. She ached for Sophie. At the time, Themo had appeared such a good match, well settled in business with his Uncle Constantine. But after his uncle died, Themo seemed to have lost direction, drifting farther and farther away, until he finally landed on America's shore, and God knew what had become of him there.

One did the best one could. A person chose a husband for a daughter with care, but—as Emmanuel used to say—no one can see into the future. She herself had been skeptical about Vasili because of his mother, and yet look how things had turned out: Vasili the best of husbands, and even Vaia had become bearable in her infirmity. Bearable, if not agreeable. But agreeable would probably have been too much to hope for.

She gazed at Vaia, lying still as death on her pillow, her eyes closed. *Whatever I may have thought of her—may think of her still,* she told herself, *she's Vasili's mother. And whatever she may say, she and I are fortunate beyond words.*

Vaia remained immobile, her eyes closed, saying nothing at all.

CHAPTER 29

SUMMER CAME EARLY, THE CHILDREN TRUDGING HOME EACH AFternoon sweaty in their woolen school uniforms. Liana would sit in a wicker rocking chair on the veranda waiting for them, greeting them with hugs and kisses. It annoyed her that she hadn't recovered from the birth of the last baby as quickly as she had with all the others. "Well," Vasili had teased, "after all, you're an old woman now, aren't you? Over thirty." But even as recently as last year she'd been running and playing with the children. Now it seemed she hadn't the energy for more than an occasional game of croquet.

It was a good thing her older three were all in school, with only Giorgi and the baby to look after. Hamdiye helped, of course, but most of the time she was too busy cooking or cleaning. Since Baby Dora's birth, they'd hired Hamdiye's daughter Kafiye—the slimmer, darker of the twins—to help with the household chores. Vaia was no trouble, lying in bed most days, saying little and demanding less. She too seemed to have lost what little energy she'd had. It was as if an exotic germ had entered the house and infected Liana and Vaia and left the others untouched. And Vaia no longer showed much interest in the house or the people in it. She didn't even care whether Baby

Dora's basket was beside her anymore, and she no longer re-marked on the damage she was sure the older children were in-flicting on her house; and if she noticed that it was now Kafiye who polished the floors and beat the rugs, she didn't comment.

Liana had invited her mother to spend the summer in Bournabat again, but Theodora had declined. The marriage arrangements for Christina's Soula were being made, and Theodora had promised to help with the betrothal party, so it seemed much more sensible to stay in town. The wedding itself would be celebrated in August.

Liana rocked back in the rattan rocker, her eyes closed, lis-tening to the faint call of a distant dove. Fourteen years ago the arrangements for her own wedding were underway, an August wedding as well, and in the same church—Aghios Giorgios. She thought back to the heat and the closeness of the church and the way she had almost fainted. And Vasili had stood close, letting her lean against him. *Vasili.*

Last Sunday in church an announcement had been read from the metropolitan, Archbishop Chrysostomos, urging the conscription of all males between the ages of seventeen and fifty. Liana had looked anxiously at Vasili, who was forty-one. Surely they wouldn't expect a man to go to war if he had a wife and five children—and a mother—depending on him. And then she had thought of Christina's Constantine, fifteen years old now. Surely they wouldn't lower the age to fifteen, would they? Christina had already given one son; it wouldn't be fair to ask her to give another. And what about Spiro, what about Aleko? No; no reasonable person could expect fathers of young children to go. And thank God Dimitri was not old enough.

She longed for the days when things seemed so simple. The Greeks went to church and the Turks went to the mosque, and each of them went to their own schools. There was no talk of wars, and no one's son joined the army and went off to God knew where with months going by between one letter and the next. You wanted your children to grow up, to live happy, adult lives. And yet . . . and yet you also wanted to hold them close, to save them from all the pain and loss the world might hold for them.

Vasili was urging that they send Dimitri to the Evangeliki School in the fall, but she was holding back. It was true that they had agreed Dimitri would go when he turned twelve, but that had been when he was small, when twelve years seemed a faintly distant future. Now he was eleven; his twelfth birthday would be in November. She'd asked Vasili for one more year. She wanted that one additional year for Dimitri at the local school, walking home with his younger sister and brothers, before he had to ride the horse tram each day for school in the city. Was it wrong, she wanted to ask Vasili, for a mother to want to hold her child close?

She rocked slowly in the chair, hoping for just a little more childhood for Dimitri.

In the distance now she could hear children's voices on their way home from school. This was what she'd always wanted, wasn't it? Her own home full of children, a garden of roses and jasmine and children. *I would never make you leave your family.* Vasili had promised her that, on the bench beside the wall in Sophie's garden. He had meant, then, that they would live in the city, near her parents, and at the time she had thought it an important promise, a gift to her. But neither of them had foreseen that the time would come when the promise couldn't be kept—nor that, instead of closing her out, moving to Bournabat had widened the circle, bringing the whole family again and again to this house that had become her own.

She watched the children coming toward her, Dimitri

running ahead, his hair plastered to his head with sweat; Vaioush walking determinedly with a small frown on her face, as if she were trying to remember the words of a song; Manoush lagging behind, drawing a stick across the wrought-iron posts of the neighbors' fences. Giorgi came running from the garden at the sight of his brothers and sister, the ball he'd been kicking suddenly forgotten. Upstairs in the nursery, Baby Dora slept.

What I wish for you, she said in her mind to the soon-to-be-married Soula, *is all the love and warmth and happiness I have known. And I wish for you as well,* she thought, *a garden of children for you to love.*

Dimitri burst through the gate and ran up the steps. "Mama! It's so hot! Can we go to the beach tomorrow?" His face was red from the exertion and the heat. He bent over her to plant a kiss on her cheek, and she breathed in the smell of him—soap and sweaty hair and damp wool.

"Have you seen melon rinds in the sea yet?"

"Oh Mama! You always say that. And anyway, how could we? We're *miles* from there."

She wrapped an arm around him and held him close to her chair. "Sunday," she promised. "Sunday your papa will take you."

ON SUNDAY FLAGS FLEW FROM EVERY WATERFRONT BUILDING along the Smyrna quay. Bunting-bedecked portraits of the king and the Greek cabinet hung from balconies. Smartly dressed bands paraded in the streets, and precisely at three o'clock in the afternoon a motor launch pulled up to the quay and General Giorgios Hadjianestis stepped ashore in a neatly pressed uniform and polished boots. And all of Smyrna breathed a sigh of relief. With Hadjianestis in charge, a general of fine reputation delegated by the king himself, surely the army would at last celebrate a final victory, and all the uncertainty would finally be over.

On their way to the beach, the children, having seen the decorations, had begged Vasili to stay in town long enough to see the grand event that was about to take place. Even Dimitri wanted to watch, despite the fact that he'd been so eager for the beach and had been terrorized nearly out of his wits three years ago at the outbreak of gunfire when the Greek army first arrived.

They stood some distance off, barely able to see for all the crowds, as Archbishop Chrysostomos greeted the Greek general. But this time there was no gunfire and no panicked crowd. This time there was only the certainty that, with a general as famous as Hadjianestis on hand, the fighting was finally about to end. No one mentioned that he was perhaps a little crazy.

When the bands had played and the officials had made their speeches, Hadjianestis and his aides stepped into a touring car and drove off toward the Konak, and Chrysostomos led a triumphant procession of priests and followers back toward St. Photini's. By that time, Vasili decided, it was too late to go on to a farther-away beach, so he took the children on the ferry across to Kordelio, on the northern side of the bay, where he treated them to fish *kebabs* at an outdoor restaurant. Afterward, he hired a phaeton and they rode out along the seafront, past the last of the houses, to a place where the children could play in the sand, wade in the water, and climb on the rocks at the edge of the sea.

Watching them, the westering sun silhouetting their scampering shapes against the water, he thought of Hadjianestis and all the hopes that had been pinned on the general's arrival. He wondered what Emmanuel would have said about such hopes if he were still alive.

Some days he missed Emmanuel desperately, more than he could have imagined. Now he no longer had anyone with whom he could talk about serious politics. There was only Liana now, and in no way could he share with her the stories he had heard:

stories that circulated in Smyrna these days of Greeks and what few Armenians were left in the Turkish-occupied villages and countryside, once again driven from their homes, set on the road to walk impossible distances, dying of hunger and thirst and exposure and even worse things. One could barely imagine such things, though they had happened to Ara years ago. But perhaps none of it was true. Rumors always fed on uncertainty. Who knew what was true anymore?

CHAPTER 30

WHEN THE SUMMER HOLIDAYS FINALLY CAME, THE CHILDREN seemed suddenly to have sprouted wings. Dressed in summer cottons, they flew through the house and the garden, laughing, shouting, skipping, jumping. Manoush discovered the ladder-like branches of the tall old pine tree that hung over the barn roof, and he quickly figured out that he could climb half-way up the tree and then lower himself onto the roof and walk on all fours to the edge, where he would leap to the ground. Dimitri tried it a few times, before deciding he could make an improvement on the sport. He dug out an old rake from a corner of the barn and he piled enough straw and pine needles together to form a passable cushion. By then even Vaioush was climbing the tree and leaping down from the roof.

Giorgi stood on the ground under the tree, futilely raising chubby arms toward the lowest branches and crying out for help, until his brothers and sister took pity on him. Manoush pulled from above, and Dimitri and Vaioush pushed from below, and they finally managed to work him high enough to reach for the barn roof, whereupon he promptly lost his footing and fell screaming through the pine boughs, landing with an alarming thud.

Liana, hearing the panicked screams and the more alarming sudden silence that followed, looked out the window and saw her three oldest children crowded around the corner of the barn, as if examining something on the ground. She picked up her skirts and rushed out to investigate, fearing the worst, and found Giorgi writhing in pain, his right leg twisted at a bizarre angle beneath him.

"He wanted to," Manoush stated, as if absolving himself and the older two from blame.

Liana, ignoring him, laid her hand gently on Giorgi's forehead.

"Well, he did," Manoush repeated defensively.

"Dimitri, send Kafiye for the doctor," Liana said without looking up.

In terrified silence, Dimitri ran toward the house.

"Vaioush, have Hamdiye fix hot, wet towels."

Vaioush, transfixed, didn't move.

"Vaioush," her mother repeated sternly, and the girl hurried away.

Crouched beside his mother, Manoush reached a tentative hand and touched Giorgi's arm. "Will he die?" he asked, his voice a hoarse whisper.

"Maybe you'd better pray that he doesn't," Liana snapped, and she instantly regretted the meanness of her response. "No," she added in a calmer voice, "he won't die, but he's in a great deal of pain."

As if to prove her words, Giorgi, having overcome the shock of the fall, screwed up his face and began bawling, tears running down the sides of his dusty face.

Liana gathered him close in her arms, finding him heavier than she had imagined and wondering suddenly when she had last lifted him. She struggled to her feet and started carrying him to the house. She hadn't taken half a dozen steps before Hamdiye flew from the house, her slippers flapping against the soles of her feet.

"*Hanum! Hanum!*" she was shouting. "He's too heavy for you! Let me. Let me carry him." She tried to scoop the still screaming Giorgi from Liana's arms, seeming not even to notice the fuller pain her attempts were causing. But Liana clung to him, and together they managed to get the child into the house and onto a couch in the parlor.

Vaia, roused from her doze, looked in wonder as Hamdiye ran off and returned moments later with hot towels that she laid on Giorgi's legs, not only the injured one but the other one as well, for good measure. "What is it?" Vaia asked.

Liana, bent over the child, murmuring comforting words and rhythmically caressing his hair back from his forehead, said nothing. Dimitri and Vaioush stood together in guilty silence two paces back. Manoush hadn't been able to bring himself closer than the doorway.

"What is it?" Vaia asked again, her voice faltering on the final word, as if she had reached the last vestige of her strength.

"Giorgi fell," Liana responded this time, not even turning away from the child.

Vaia lay back in her bed, taking in, one by one, the faces of the other three childen, and she mumbled to herself a confirmation of all her worst imaginings.

The doctor arrived, preceded down the street by the coughing sounds of his reluctant automobile. Young Doctor Epimedes, only three years out of a French medical school, had taken over at the sudden death of Doctor Andreoglou, who had cared for the neighborhood for as long as Vasili could remember. Doctor Epimedes had a blond and very pregnant French wife and a black American Ford Model T automobile, and the people of the neighborhood whispered that it was difficult to tell which of the two made him proudest.

He pulled the towels off Giorgi's legs and tenderly probed them before announcing the expected word: "Broken." He had already taken in the expressions and the postures of the other three, and he turned to them now, his stern eyes peering over his pince-nez. "Your brother will need a crutch. Why don't you all go outside and find a stick or a branch that's stout enough and long enough."

Released from the house and therefore from imminent blame, the three children darted off.

"How did this happen?" the doctor asked Liana.

"They were playing—" she started. She hadn't even asked how it had happened.

"They were jumping from the barn roof," Kafiye said from the doorway, her face still flushed from the excitement of having ridden back in the doctor's automobile, her first ride in such an amazing contraption.

Liana's hands went to her face in astonishment. "Oh, my heavens," she whispered.

"What would you expect?" came the froggy voice from the bed.

"He is young. He will heal," the doctor replied. "In a few months you will never know it happened, but next time, use a cold compress."

DESPITE GIORGI'S ACCIDENT, LIANA WAS FEELING BETTER: The coming of summer and the presence of the children seemed to have revived her. She tended the rose garden again and played endless games of Chinese checkers with Giorgi, who made up his own rules and was milking his convalescence for all he could. When he napped, she flew kites with the older children and batted the badminton birdies back and forth and chased butterflies with a frothy net. And some days she left the baby and her mother-in-law in Hamdiye's care and took the older four to town to visit her mother, lifting Giorgi onto the horse trams while Dimitri obligingly carried the crutch Vasili had fashioned. No one had said a word about the jumping game, and it was forgotten in guilty regret.

Sometimes, if Theodora wasn't too busy helping Christina with preparations for Soula's wedding, Liana would leave Manoush and Giorgi with her for an hour or two and she would take the older two by horse tram to Vasili's shop. Since Emmanuel's death Vasili had promoted Hovhannes, one of the assistants, to the position of chief artisan, and he was letting him make the artistic decisions, allowing himself to settle back into keeping the accounts and acting as primary salesman.

It seemed to Liana that Dimitri loved coming to the store almost as much as before. He would climb onto a stool and watch spellbound as Hovhannes expertly twisted the silver threads. She did not know that her own son Dimitri had long ago decided that he would be a silversmith, like his grandfather had been, and now he had convinced himself that Hovhannes could teach him as he had once thought his grandfather would. When his mother was ready to leave, Dimitri usually begged to be allowed to stay, and sometimes, if his father wasn't too busy, his mother would let him. On those occasions he would watch Hovhannes until closing time, and then he would help Vasili close up and the two of them would walk to the horse tram station together.

Dimitri had grown nearly to Vasili's shoulder now, and Vasili was again discussing with Liana whether or not Dimitri should start at the English-speaking Evangeliki School in the fall. Liana was still resisting, wanting one more year of childhood for Dimitri. The boy himself was unclear what he would prefer. He liked the excitement of being in the city, imagining riding the horse trams by himself, how it would make him feel almost like a grown-up. But he also liked the freedom of running home from school in Bournabat, kissing his mother as she waited for him, throwing off his school clothes and tearing through the fields and exploring in the reeds of the creek that ran at the far end of the field, finding toads or birds' nests. If he went to school in the city, he would return home later, and there would be no time for play—only enough time to study— before dinner.

And he still enjoyed going to the beach. Nearly every Sunday Liana and Vasili took the children, and sometimes it was a big family outing, with aunts and uncles and cousins. The women would pack baskets of food to lay out on blankets, and the men would stand around drinking *raki* and talking politics, the younger children running along the edge of the shore, while the older ones would wade out far enough to dive under the water. Dimitri was not the best swimmer— Constantine was—but Dimitri was the most enthusiastic. He was always the first one in and the last one out, shivering from near exhaustion in the evening air when Liana finally called him back to shore and wrapped towels around him. "You are a fish!" she would exclaim, holding him close. On the rides home from the beach, he would lean drowsily against her, his body pleasantly emptied of energy, his arms and legs tucked close to his body, his eyes closed, hearing but not really paying attention to the sounds of the horse tram bells and the desultory voices of the grown-ups.

And as the summer slid by, Soula's wedding dress was finished and hung in all its lacy beauty in the wardrobe in her bedroom, and Marina, her cousin, was noticing more and more the young man who worked in the store across from her father's place of business, and Christina prayed that somehow Naso would be able to come back for the wedding. And Naso, far from home, burned in the Anatolian heat and wondered along with all his comrades how they could survive another winter.

EMMANUEL USED TO JOKE ABOUT BEING THE ONLY GREEK SILVER-smith on a street of Armenian goldsmiths. Now, with Hovhannes, Vasili joked about Demirgis & Son itself being invaded. Indeed, when Vasili sat with the taciturn Hovhannes over coffee, discussing orders and the degree of success Hovhannes was having in maintaining the store's reputation for fine filigree work, Vasili realized that the future of the business had already slipped out of the hands of the family and into the very capable hands of the artisan who had succeeded Emmanuel. At the same time, Vasili recognized his son's interest in the art. He had thought, when Dimitri used to hang over Emmanuel, that it had just been the attraction of the grandson to the grandfather, but now that Emmanuel was gone and Dimitri stayed nearly as close to Hovhannes, it had become apparent that the boy's interest was far deeper than Vasili had imagined.

Yet, for a man to become a true artisan, he needed to be apprenticed at a young age—younger, surely, than Dimitri already was. Emmanuel had been ten years old when he'd put himself into the hands of a master. Vasili was certain Liana had no idea of the strength of Dimitri's interest, and he himself had no idea what her reaction would be if he told her. What would she think of her son's leaving school before he even turned twelve to apprentice himself to a master filigree artist? Would she be proud he was following in her father's craft, or would she be disappointed that he hadn't gone further in school? Education had always been important to Liana, and she was proud of her children's accomplishments at school. On the other hand, perhaps Dimitri's interest was simply a remainder of his love for his grandfather. In a year or two he might develop new interests.

And anyway, where would they find a master craftsman to teach him? Emmanuel had been the best; Hovhannes was very good but not, surely, nearly as talented as Emmanuel. Fine filigree artisans were becoming scarcer and scarcer; perhaps in another generation there would be none at all. And perhaps in another generation there would be little call for any. These days machines could do work so fine that it was often difficult to distinguish it from handcrafted work. People bought more and more of their clothes and shoes ready-made now, instead of having them made to order. Furniture was built in factories; rugs were made by machines. In America, Henry Ford was teaching the world that you could even make products as complicated as automobiles on assembly lines, each worker responsible for only a tiny part of the whole; and the result could be products so modestly priced that huge numbers of people could afford to buy them. Would the day come when machines made jewelry as fine as any craftsman could make—and cheaper as well? What, then, would become of the seamstresses, the bootmakers, the cabinet makers, the fine craftsmen?

He gazed at Hovhannes over his cup of Turkish coffee. The man seemed so serious in detailing the work in progress that Vasili wondered once again if Hovhannes ever laughed, if at home he was warm and loving to his wife and new baby. "You have family in the east," Vasili said suddenly. "What do they say of conditions there? Are they worried?"

Hovhannes frowned. His family had been driven out of Marash in 1915, and the ones who had survived the long walk all the way to Aleppo had returned finally, after the Greek army landed in Smyrna. He seldom spoke of them or of any other family matter. "Excuse me if I say this, but your army made a very cynical move," Hovhannes said finally. "A foolish move."

Vasili raised his eyebrows, inviting more.

"The attack on Constantinople, I mean."

"Cynical? You mean they knew they would be defeated?"

"I think they believed they would be able to take the city, and then the Allies would almost certainly force them to withdraw, having gone so far beyond their original stated purpose of occupying only Smyrna and the surrounding area, and that would allow them to make a safe—and certainly a face-saving—retreat from all of Anatolia. But it didn't work out that way, did it? And now they're weaker by two divisions, and they're still strung out in Anatolia way beyond their capacity to support themselves. If the Turks ever decide to attack—"

"I didn't know you had such an interest in military affairs," Vasili said. And all that time, he wondered, all the time that Emmanuel was talking politics, was Hovhannes listening? Why had he never said anything before?

Hovhannes shrugged. "It's a matter of self-defense to keep oneself aware of the doings of one's enemies. So. Now, what is left for the Greek army?" It could have been Emmanuel sitting across the little table from him, dipping a spoon of cherry conserve into his water glass. "Your Greek army has no money," Hovhannes went on. "They've been at war constantly for more than ten years. A long time to be away from home, fighting wars against this one and that one. They're demoralized, poorly fed, poorly clothed, strung out beyond all reason. Meantime Kemal has been sitting in Angora, his men gaining strength, their morale high. It's only a matter of time."

"It is not *my* Greek army," Vasili said softly. It was the only argument he could make. The rest of it was only too true.

"You are Greeks; they are Greeks."

"I'm a native of Smyrna, as you are. *This* is our country."

Hovhannes shook his head. "It's not the same. You have another country you can go to. This is the only one I have."

Greece is not my country, Vasili wanted to say. *They're strangers to me, despite the shared religion and the shared language. I was born here, as were my father and my grandfather, and those before them, way into the distant past.* But how could he hope to explain this to Hovhannes, who had seen the Smyrniot Greeks cheer the arrival of the Greek army and, more recently, the arrival of General Hadjianestis? How could Hovhannes understand that Smyrniots felt themselves Smyrniots first, and Greeks second?

Vasili gazed at Hovhannes, with his angular face and his stiff demeanor, wearing the work apron that he never removed in the shop, and his long, slim, talented fingers, and his stern, judgmental manner, and he wondered how such a man could be of the same race as Ara—Ara, who had danced with wild abandon at Vasili's wedding, who had bombed the Konak so many years ago, who had gone east to fight for his people and who had married there and then lost all he held dear. Ara, whose latest letter had come today and resided now in his breast pocket, who had made a home for himself in California, halfway around the world. Who had found a new wife and who had written ebulliently of his new life and his fine new house and the two—*two!*—automobiles he owned and the marvelous business opportunities in California. It was as if Ara had shucked off all the old when he left; as if this were no longer his home; as if he had never had a family here—parents and a wife and a child whom he had loved and who had loved him: as if the only thin thread that tied him to his past was his friendship with Vasili.

When adults wage war, children perish.

—ELIE WIESEL

CHAPTER 31

THE WEDDING OF SOULA PAPAIOGLOU TO ADONIS MOUZAKIOTIS was held on August 25, 1922, at Aghios Giorgios Church in Smyrna, where her mother and all her aunts had been married years before. The day was warm but, thankfully, not hot, with Smyrna's clear, blue, crystalline sky hanging overhead. Soula walked boldly to the front of the church and stood before the priest, wearing a bright, wide smile of delight and pride, deep dimples pressing into her full cheeks. Soula's skin was fair and golden, like the flesh of a ripe peach, and her body was all soft curves, a woman meant to be touched, caressed. In her presence, women found excuses to stroke her arm, pat her back, lean close in whispered confidences. Men cleared their throats and looked away, fearing a lack of self-control, imagining full breasts and a rounded stomach, feeling the weight of Soula's full hips against their groins. In an age that dictated stylish women came in slim, boyish shapes, Soula was a throwback to a time of lush, fleshy delights.

Soula had been no more difficult to match than had her mother, Christina, before her, though the procedure was somewhat different. No longer did girls parade in the baths before the mothers of sons, though in fact girls still went to the baths—sometimes—and the mothers of sons went nearly always, in a manner much less ritualized but still fruitful. An aunt of Adonis's knew the Papaioglou family and had let slip that Soula might be to his liking. She'd been pointed out to him at Aghios Giorgios, and he'd felt an immediate short-ness of breath and a tingling in his hands and a strange, un-wonted sensation in his lower extremities, and he had asked to be introduced to the girl's parents. A week later he was invited to the Papaioglou home, and over brandy in the par-lor with Spiro he had declared his intentions and stated his prospects.

A modern father, Spiro invited Soula into the parlor—after having first waved as much cigar smoke as possible out the window—and Soula stared Adonis in the face and flashed her dimples, and Adonis could suddenly think of only one thing: how to hide his swelling member from the father of the girl he hoped to marry. He almost forgot to inquire about the dowry.

Both families thought them an admirably suited pair: the luscious Soula and the adoring and well-provided Adonis. Ev-eryone thought Soula was made for bearing children. Everyone thought Adonis would make a perfect husband. As the two of them stood before the priest, everyone felt a fullness of heart, as if God could not possibly have brought a better gift into these two young lives.

In the rear of the church, Soula's cousin Vaioush kept a close watch on the Jordan almonds she'd been charged with giving out to the guests at the close of the ceremony. She had been to weddings before and knew the ways of wedding guests. The men would palm a handful of almonds, rubbing them between their fingers as they did their worry beads, then pop them, one at a time, into their mouths. The children would grab up big handfuls and stuff them into their mouths and run back for more until their mothers shooed them away. The mothers would take a dainty one or two and hold them for a time, as if holding back the sensual pleasure of teeth biting through the thin white candy crust to the soft sweetmeat of the almond itself. And the young women, like her cousin, fifteen-year-old Doroush, would take two or three and surreptitiously slip them into a pocket or purse. Tonight, after the party, when they climbed into their beds, they would tuck their almonds under their pillows in hopes of dreaming of their future husbands. Vaioush imagined that even Marina, who was the same age as Soula and had already been spoken for, would sleep tonight over almonds in anticipation of dreaming of her fair-haired Christo. Vaioush herself had no such intention. She was going to become an actress. She would go to Hollywood, in America, where her father had a friend, and she would make moving pictures and become famous all over the world.

When the wedding ceremony was over, Soula and Adonis would climb into the town car rented for the occasion and ride off to Soula's parents' home for the party. All those who had been at the wedding would be there, and there would be music and dancing and tables filled with the food Soula's mother and grandmother and aunts had spent the last weeks preparing, and bottle after bottle of *raki* and *mastika* would be consumed, but at the end of the party there would be no sheet. That was another custom that the new generation was discarding in its headlong rush to modernity. The newly married couple would laughingly leave the party and the relatives would smile fondly, and the young men—Adonis's friends—would covertly nudge each other and try to imagine how Soula would be in bed, but no one would be indelicate enough to suggest proof of virginity from a bride of the 1920s.

And two hundred miles to the east—on the plateau of Dumlupinar, near the town of Afyon Karahissar—Soula's brother Naso slept on the bare ground one more night just like the hundreds that had preceded it, in a hard, mean, dreamless sleep, blessedly unaware that in the morning, at dawn, Mustafa Kemal's troops would finally strike, taking the Greek army by surprise, smashing through the lines and killing all but three of Naso's platoon.

THE GREEK ARMY, REELING FROM THE ATTACK, PLUNGED INTO retreat in some sectors and regrouped in others, trying a desperate counterattack, which almost immediately collapsed. Within twenty-four hours of the first attack, the Greek army was in a full and almost entirely disorganized retreat. The soldiers ran for the sea, for the boats that they trusted would be there to take them home: to Athens, to Lamia, to Patras and Piraeus, to Nauplion in the south and Ioannina in the north. And some of them ran no farther than Smyrna, where they had joined up in such high hopes—now all of them desperate to escape this God-forsaken, desolate land of Anatolia's interior, with its fierce winters and its scorching summers, its barren landscape and its villages filled with bitter and hostile Turks.

They burned the sparse fields behind them, telling themselves that they were protecting their rear, disallowing any aid or comfort to the Kemalists who pursued them. And for the same stated reasons they killed the inhabitants—human and otherwise—of the villages they passed, burning the houses and the stores of grain they held, throwing bodies—human and otherwise—into the wells to make the water unfit for those who came after, decapitating animals in the mosques and desecrating their walls with animal blood and human feces. Of all the towns and cities that had been held by the Greeks, only Afyon Karahissar survived intact, because at Afyon the rout had occurred so fast there had been no time to do anything but run. The rest of the towns were dynamited, burned, despoiled, and the countryside around them burned and salted into unproductivity.

The army acted in anger and hate, striking out blindly, redeeming their shattered manhood by killing all who fell into the path of their rampage, and though they never used the word "revenge," it was written in their hearts, and they barely noticed when some of the villages they devastated were Greek instead of Turkish. Their scant satisfaction lay in the knowledge that for more than one hundred miles they had left a trail of burned fields and smoldering towns and grisly death.

In Smyrna the populace knew little of this. The vast majority of the victims had been left behind, dead, unable to tell the tale, and the few survivors remained hidden in their villages, too terrified or too traumatized to speak.

What the people of Smyrna did know—what they saw— was the trickle of Greek refugees from the outlying areas, hurriedly come to Smyrna to escape the hordes that had descended upon them. They had brought their most precious possessions, gathered up in a frenzy of terror—rolled carpets and wooden trunks, sheets and blankets and wide tablecloths into which had been gathered family heirlooms and jewelry, precious family photographs and homely pots and pans thrown together hurriedly and haphazardly, an everyday tin coffee *jezveh* scraping against a cherished silver candlestick—the candlestick's mate having been lost in the rush—a kilo of rice wrapped in a silken scarf.

They poured into the city—hundreds, thousands every day—heading for the sea, for the hope it offered of escape, and there they stopped, camping at the seaside, lining its length from the Standard Oil depot in the north to Paradisia in the south, but mostly concentrated at the shipping quays in the center of town. Their detritus surrounded them: boxes, trunks, carpets, furniture even, an occasional wheelbarrow piled with crates. While some cooked their dwindling supplies of food over campfires on the quays, others begged for food and shelter, and their children wandered hollow-eyed and hungry from one encampment to the next, chewing on dirty fingers and casting covetous glances at crusts of bread and bowls of rice.

And the army came. A scant few at first, the advance guard of a legion that grew to overwhelming numbers in those last few days of August and the first week of September, hundreds of men—thousands—gaunt, ragged, empty-eyed, trudging through the final dispirited miles of their defeat. They were making for Cheshme, for the boats that were waiting there to take them away, leaving the great Greek dream in tatters on the unforgiving plains of Anatolia.

Christina, hearing of them, rushed out and searched their straggling ranks, looking for Naso, for his familiar, lighthearted gait, for his cocky grin, and was sickened at the sight of these walking dead. "Have you seen my son? Naso Papaioglou?" she asked over and over. "Did you know Naso Papaioglou? Robust, always making jokes?"

She was greeted only by the sounds of the other mothers: *Have you any news of my Eleftherios?. . . . Michalis—hair as blond as a German's? . . . Dino—tall and slim, like you? . . . Lambros? . . . Taki? . . . Niko?*

The soldiers dragged themselves past, unseeing, unhearing, and mothers like Christina watched them go, gazing longingly as these sons of other mothers moved on to other homecomings and other families, leaving the Greeks of Smyrna to mourn their lost and to gird themselves for what lay ahead.

CHAPTER 32

VASILI, HEARING OF THE ARMY'S ARRIVAL AND OF THEIR PITIFUL state, closed the shop and hurried down to see. On the Kordon, that most magnificent of Smyrna's many fine streets, refugees now crowded against one another and stared in melancholy silence as the never-ending line of ragged soldiers dragged itself along. He saw the vacancy of their eyes and their hopeless, shuffling gait, and those things told him more than the arrival of the refugees had, more than any of the news from the front had: that the Greek *Megali Idea* of a Greater Greece spread across the ancient Greek cities of Asia Minor had turned into disaster.

And that was when he knew he had made a horrendous mistake. All those years ago Ara had warned him, and Emmanuel had urged him, but he had allowed himself to be seduced by the rationalizations of a cautious and comfortable man: his mother, and Liana's ties to her family, and always a new baby. Always it had seemed that catastrophe was something that struck elsewhere but never in Smyrna—never in bustling, carefree, sun-spangled, rose-scented Smyrna.

He turned and ran up the street to the American consulate—and found its locked doors crowded with others who'd had the same thought. People were pounding and shouting at the barred doors, demanding visas, but from within the building came only silence. A sign posted on the door announced in large letters in four languages that the consulate had already ceased issuing visas for entry into the United States. Vasili rushed on, panic rising, and found similar crowds and similar signs at the French and British and Italian legations.

In the crowds that milled on the streets he heard the outrageous fares that were being asked for boat passage from Smyrna—two hundred pounds, five hundred, a thousand. Twice, five times, ten times what the fares had been only a few months ago. And all of it in cash, in stable foreign currency or gold. Or silver, perhaps? He thought of the silver in the store. Seven people, counting Vaia, he thought. Surely they wouldn't charge for Baby Dora—she was only an infant. And Liana wouldn't leave her own mother here. And Sophie, who had no one to look after her: nine people in all. Did he have that much silver? Surely it would cost hundreds—no, thousands of pounds—and the price would go up even more by the time he was able to gather it together, then convince the women they must leave. *Oh God*, he thought, *how many thousand pounds?* A fortune.

He took a taxi home; the horse trams were too slow. The taxi, in fact, was too slow. Anything would have been too slow. He would have flown if he could. He rushed through the gate, ran across the garden, and took the steps two at a time and burst through the door. And he found silence inside.

He peered in at his mother, who was drowsing in her bed, the curtains pulled against the afternoon sun. He stormed through the house and found someone at last: Hamdiye in the kitchen, briskly rolling out *yufka* with a thin dowel stick.

"*Effendim!*" she said, breathless with exertion and surprise.

"Where's my wife?" he demanded. "Where are the children?"

She stared at him, wide eyed, astonished at the almost accusatory tone of his voice. "The little ones are napping," she
responded finally. "Liana *Hanum* and the older ones have gone
shopping."

"*Shopping?*" He was dumbstruck that they could be shopping at such a time.

"School starts in less than two weeks," Hamdiye sniffed, as
if a man lucky enough to be able to send his children to school
rather than put them out to work by the time they reached the
age of eight should know such an important thing. "They've
all grown," she added, as if she thought he needed to be told.
"They need new shoes, new underclothes, new school uniforms."

School clothes? In Smyrna, then, almost certainly. Vasili
tried to remember. Why did he not know that? Had she told
him and he'd been too busy thinking of other things? Had she
not bothered to tell him?

"Did she say anything about stopping at her mother's?"

Hamdiye completed one circuit of rolling the thin dough
and leaned her hands against the table. "No." And then she
added, "But she quite often does, doesn't she?"

She could be in any of a dozen stores, he thought, or at her
mother's—or even at Christina's or Eleni's. Or on a horse tram
somewhere in between. By the time he returned to Smyrna,
she could be on her way home . . . His thoughts were interrupted by a banging coming from upstairs. Hamdiye sighed,
put down her dowel, and dusted her hands.

"Never mind," Vasili said. "I'll get him."

Since Giorgi's accident his leg had been in a plaster cast,
and he needed help getting in and out of bed and up and down
the stairs. Usually, he demanded help by banging his fists

against the wall. Liana worried constantly over Giorgi's leg, imagining it wasn't healing properly. Young Doctor Epimedes had taken to stopping by once or twice a week to reassure her. Vasili sighed. Liana would think no foreign doctor would be so caring and so competent. Certainly none would be as attentive.

It was nearly dinnertime when Liana and the children returned, finding Vasili seated in the parlor reading to Vaia while Giorgi cuddled in his lap and sucked his thumb. Liana raised her eyebrows, but Vasili shot her a glance that told her they'd discuss it later. Then he put on a smile of greeting at the inevitable onslaught of his other children.

"Papa, we got new shoes!" Vaioush shouted, pulling at his sleeve.

Her grandmother groaned from the bed.

Vasili put an arm around his daughter, briefly pulling her close and wishing only for normalcy. "Vaioush," he said softly, "I'm reading to your grandmother right now."

"We stopped at Pappagallo, and I had *baklava* and *rizogalo*!" Manoush said, his eyes still shining in delight.

"New shoes," Vaioush whispered to him. "And underclothes, and new uniforms!"

He brushed her hair back from her eyes. "Isn't that wonderful," he said to both of them. In the doorway, Dimitri stood next to his mother, too old to demand immediate attention but still young enough to want it. Vasili flashed him a smile and Dimitri shyly grinned back. Then Vasili resumed reading to his mother, as if nothing unusual at all was happening.

Dimitri turned to his mother. "Why is he home so early?"

"I don't know," she said, laying her hand on his back and ushering him from the room. But she had a feeling, an unpleasant feeling, in the pit of her stomach. As if for reassurance, she kissed him on the top of the head. Soon she would no longer be able to do this; he would be too tall. "Go wash your hands and face. It'll make you feel better after being in the city all day."

She found Hamdiye in the dining room, setting the table. "When did my husband come home?"

"Middle of the afternoon," Hamdiye said.

The two women looked at each other across the room. A subtle shift had taken place in the atmosphere, and neither one knew what to call it, nor how one addressed it or adjusted to it. "Why don't you go home to your own family," Liana said finally. "I can finish up here."

"It's no trouble."

Liana took the plates from her hand. "Please. Perhaps they need you."

Hamdiye stared at her for a long moment. "The bedding needs to be aired. I'll do it in the morning. And the rugs need beating. Kafiye can help me."

"Thank you," Liana said, recognizing the unspoken promise.

DINNER WAS FILLED WITH THE CHILDREN'S TALK.

"Papa, why does the city smell?" Vaioush asked.

"So many people, and so many animals—" Vasili began in response.

"I saw a man going poop on the street!" Manoush interrupted.

Vasili shot him a disapproving glance.

"Don't interrupt your papa," Liana said.

"Going poop," Giorgi repeated in his husky voice.

"Automobiles stink," Vaioush said vehemently. "I'm glad we don't have one."

"Not me," Manoush said. "I wish we did. I'd ride right up front with Papa. I'd have to direct him because he'd be going so fast he wouldn't even be able to see where he was going."

"Theodora *Yaya* says it's awful the way the people are living on the quays these days," Vaioush said. "She says they cook and do everything right out in the open, like peasants. She says it stinks down there now."

Vasili looked at Liana in surprise. "Did you . . . ?"

Liana shook her head.

"Mama wouldn't let us go see," Vaioush said.

"We wanted to, but she wouldn't let us," Manoush added.

"If I were a police man I wouldn't let them do that," Giorgi said.

"They haven't anywhere else to go," Dimitri said solemnly.

"They should go back home," Giorgi retorted.

"You're too little to understand," Dimitri said.

"Am not!"

"*Yaya* says she almost doesn't dare go out of her house anymore—she doesn't know what's going to happen next," Vaioush said.

"Vaioush," Liana said, "eat your dinner and stop talking so much. Give your papa a chance to rest after his hard day." She flashed a smile across the table at Vasili, and he felt his stomach turn over and the bile rise in his throat, and he had to swallow three times to force it back down.

"You didn't go down to the seafront, then?" Vasili asked later.

The children were all in bed, and the two of them were sitting on the veranda in the late summer dusk. Vaia had been asleep in her parlor bed for hours. Vasili could smell Liana's roses and the jasmine that climbed the trellis at one end of the veranda. Or perhaps it was the jasmine scent of Liana's hair.

"I didn't want the children to see."

"You didn't see the soldiers, then?"

"I heard about them. It sounded awful; I didn't want to see it. And I didn't want the children to see, either. Mama says Christina goes every day looking for Naso. Once, Mama went with her. It's terrible, Mama says."

"It's over, Liana. God knows what will happen now."

"That's why you came home so early?"

"We have to move to the city."

She felt a sudden panic. "*Why?*"

"You know why. It's not safe here. That's what all those refugees should be telling you. It may not even be safe in the city. We must find a way to leave."

"Vasili"—she leaned toward him earnestly—"this is not some little village; this is *Smyrna*."

"No one will protect us here, Liana. The Greek army is running away as fast as they can. Who do you think is coming after?"

"But Bournabat is safe. It's filled with foreigners—the Levantines and the English and French and even Americans—nothing's going to happen to us with them here. Do you really think their armies will sit by and let anything happen?"

"I think we should move to the city."

"Where would we go? We have no house there anymore."

"We could move in with your mother. Just for a while. Until I can get us completely away."

"All of us? In her little house?"

"It was big enough for your family."

"But our children are used to the country. You heard what Vaioush said. They would hate the city."

"Maybe only for a while."

"And your mother?"

"We'd have to take her along."

"You haven't asked Mama, have you? What would she say to all that?"

"You know what she'd say. She would want us to be safe."

Liana let out a long, impatient breath but said nothing.

"Maybe only for a while, Liana," he said in a softer voice. "What we really need to do is leave altogether."

"Leave?" A whisper.

"If Smyrna falls, we will be like those refugees. Homeless. Better to leave now—"

"*Leave?*"

"All of us. You, me, the children, my mother. *Your* mother, if she wants to go. Sophie."

"And go where?"

"America, perhaps. Ara says—"

"Ara! You haven't seen him in years."

"You know he's offered—"

"It's easy to write, Vasili. Easy to make offers. Besides, your mother would never go."

"She doesn't have a choice."

"You've decided it, then, haven't you?" A feeling of resentment had overcome her.

"Liana." He leaned toward her. "I want you to be safe. I want our children safe."

She looked around her, at the front of the house, and at her garden, barely seen now in the gathering dark. "I love this house," she said softly.

"I know you do."

"I can't leave it."

"We have to."

She was silent for a time, and he waited. She knew the logic of it; she could understand that. And yet . . . "Just to Smyrna, then, to my mother," she said at last, settling back into her chair. "No farther."

He took her hand and held it to his lips. "To Smyrna," he said into her skin. *One step at a time*, he thought. "Pack what you need in the morning. I'll arrange for a cart to come and get the things in the afternoon. We'll take only what's most important."

"Tomorrow? How can I decide what to take in only one day?"

"After we move the children, we can always come back and get more." *If it's safe.*

"But my mother doesn't even know. She'll need to get ready."

"You can send Hamdiye in the morning to help her."

She let out a sigh of exasperation. "But *I'm* not ready."

He knew what she meant. "Liana," he said softly.

"One more day here. Please."

One more day. *Well*, he thought, *it could wait one more day; the initial victory was won, at least.*

"Listen," she said.

He heard it then too: a nightingale, her favorite, singing its bright, sweet song, a song beautiful enough to break the heart. They sat together, listening to the bird and the sigh of the pines above them, enclosed by the darkness and the scent of roses and jasmine. Finally he rose and drew her with him. "The day after tomorrow," he said. "I'll stop by your mother's house in the morning and warn her."

"Do you really think it's necessary?"

"We wouldn't be doing it if I didn't think so."

She moved into the house beside him. "Perhaps the children

will think it's an adventure. Like camping out. I hope it isn't too long. Surely we'll be back by the time school starts."

"I hope so too."

The first victory, he thought: to Smyrna. And then, as soon as he managed to gather enough to pay for nine tickets . . .

CHAPTER 33

THEODORA'S HOUSE ONCE AGAIN BULGED WITH LIFE. OVER VAS-
ili's and Liana's fierce objections she vacated her own
room—the largest of the bedrooms—for the two of them and
the baby. She moved into Liana's old room, and a cot was set
up there for Vaioush, barely leaving enough space between
the beds to turn around. Theodora tried making a joke of
the cramped quarters. "Vaioush and I will have to help each
other dress," she exclaimed. Vaioush gazed at her in doubt, not
knowing—and not caring to learn—about the intricacies of a
grown woman's undergarments.

The three boys moved into the bedroom that Christina
and Sophie had once shared, and they took turns sleeping on
the floor, though it soon developed that both Manoush and
Dimitri preferred the floor to sharing the double bed with Giorgi, who flung his whole body—including the cast-enclosed
leg—with wild abandon in his sleep.

Vaia, of course, was given the parlor, its draperies drawn
against the summer heat.

When Liana had arrived with the children, she found that
Sophie had already moved into the tiny space in the attic that
had been meant as a maid's bedroom. "I won't have it," Liana
argued. "It's musty and cramped up here."

"Actually, it's quite pleasant," Sophie said cheerily. "In the old days I used to hope Mama would get rid of Despinise so I could have this room. It's so cozy and clever, nestled like this between the rafters."

"It's hot and it's close," Liana argued. "Sophie, it's impossible!"

"There're two windows up here, plenty of air. And it's not too hot. I rather like it. Maybe I'll stay up here even after you go back home."

"You'll do no such thing. You're only saying that to make me think you like it. But Sophie—"

"Relax, Liana," Sophie interrupted. "It's going to be like a party with all of you here."

Liana stamped her foot. "You always change the subject."

Sophie burst out laughing. "Liana, you are too funny! You used to do exactly that when you were little: Every time you couldn't win an argument you'd stamp your foot in exasperation and complain we were changing the subject."

"It's not funny. Here we are—"

Sophie was still chuckling, and suddenly Liana realized she couldn't remember when she had last seen Sophie laugh. With the children, yes, but with adults . . . surely not since before Themo left. She moved to a tiny window and looked out over the neighboring roofline. *I used to dream of my own house in this neighborhood, my children running back and forth between my home and my parents',* she thought. *I used to imagine impromptu parties and games between the cousins, and between us sisters and our husbands. I thought my adult life would be one long time of running back and forth to this house in which I grew up. I never dreamed that I would move to Bournabat and find a house and a life there that were so dear I can hardly bear to leave them, even for a few days. I never thought the parties and the picnics, the holidays and the name-*

day celebrations, would be at my house—not at Mama and Papa's, as they always had been. I never thought that Papa would die so young, or that Sophie would never have a child of her own.

She turned to Sophie then and hugged her close. "But I don't want to put you and Mama out like this."

"It's not putting us out," Sophie said. "We love it. And it'll only be for a short time, I'm sure. Let's enjoy it, Liana. It'll be just like old times, like when we were children."

Liana let out a long breath. *It's not at all like that,* she thought. *It will never again be like that.*

HAMDIYE HAD HELPED WITH THE MOVING, FROWNING HER DISAP-proval the whole time. "That house of your mother's is too small," she commented. "And where will the children play?"

"Vasili thinks it's best." It was all Liana could think to say.

"Humph," Hamdiye grumbled.

"It'll be all kinds of extra trouble for Mama, of course," Liana said. "If you're willing to come this far, I'm sure we could use your help."

Hamdiye gazed at her. "Every day?"

"Well, when you can manage it.

"And who will keep your house up? A house goes to rack and ruin if you don't take care of it."

"I thought we could just close it up. As if we'd gone somewhere for the summer."

"Dust still settles. And mice come. And worse things."

"Could you keep an eye on it then?" And then an idea came to her. "Hamdiye. Would you like to move in? Just for as long as we're gone? Your whole family?"

Hamdiye stared at her in astonishment. "*Madamjum . . .*"

"Think about it. The house would be lived in, kept up, and your children would have the whole garden—"

"I don't know . . ."

In the evening, Vasili would repeat those same words: "I don't know, Liana. What would the neighbors say?"

"Who cares what they say? These are strange times, aren't they? Why else would we move in with Mama? Hamdiye would keep the house up. And when we come back there won't be any of that bothersome airing out and cleaning up. It would be just like we'd taken a house at the beach for the week."

"But if we—"Then he didn't say more. He just stared at her and shrugged. "If you want to," he added at last.

Even Hamdiye finally agreed, though God knew what her husband and children would think, living in such a house. And until Vasili had mentioned it, it had never occurred to Liana to wonder what the neighbors would think.

That took care of the house, and Hamdiye would come twice a week to the city to help with the straightening up and to cook her wonderful dinners.

As far as the children's schooling was concerned, Liana had made up her mind not to be worried. School was not due to start until mid-September. Surely after a short time they'd be able to move back home—hadn't Vasili said from the start that they wouldn't be here more than a week?

And wasn't he at the shop long hours—longer than normal? Surely that meant things were settling down already, that business was better than ever, though God knew she had no other way of knowing it. Vasili had insisted she should not stray from her mother's home, not even as far as the neighborhood shop, and that she keep the children home as well. Poor Vasili, taking his responsibilities for this household of women so seriously.

ON THE FIRST DAY AFTER HIS DECISION, VASILI INVENTORIED THE shop. If he managed to sell everything on the premises—every piece of finished work, every work in progress, every gram of silver bullion and every length of silver wire—he might realize as much as twenty-five hundred pounds. If he sold the house in Bournabat and got a decent price—but who was buying houses in Smyrna these days? And Liana's jewelry at home, and his own mother's would bring something, and Theodora's and Sophie's would—but he had no idea how much they had, and if they would be willing to sell. If any of it could be sold. In fact, in these days, if any of it at all could be sold. Still, he told himself, there had to be a way, if only he could think of it. He thought of what he had at home and what was here. He counted again, hoping that his figures would come out differently. But no matter how he figured, it seemed that, even if he were fortunate, he might perhaps be able to gather four or five thousand pounds. It would probably take at least that, if not more, to get all of them just to America. In the worst case, he supposed, they could live with Ara until he found a job, but he would still need additional money to get to California, all the way across the United States.

Theoretically, it seemed he might realize enough if he was able to sell everything. But that was theoretically. Who would buy? Who wasn't trying to do the same thing—converting whatever was at hand into cash or gold in order to get out? And who—knowing the desperation of the situation—would pay full price? Who would not take advantage?

Stock worth two or three thousand pounds would realistically go for half that. A house in Bournabat, large as it was but vulnerable because of its distance from the city center, would go begging for buyers. Even if kept up meticulously by Hamdiye—who had moved her family into it two days after Vasili's family had moved out—the house would not seem an attractive prospect right now.

It was so easy to become discouraged, but he forced himself not to fall into such a trap. He put his calculations away. Nothing was certain. Everything was worth trying. He took the best of his pieces, the last of Emmanuel's work and the very best that Hovhannes had done, and he took a cab—*The rich are impressed with show*, Emmanuel used to say; *if you look prosperous they take you more seriously*—to the Karatass district and asked to speak to Socrates Economides. The Economides family—shipowners—was one of the wealthiest families in Smyrna.

But *Kyrios* Economides was not home that evening, nor could Vasili discover when he was expected to return. So he moved on. In two hours he had covered a dozen or more homes of Smyrna's wealthiest, and he found only three men who would even agree to see him. Two were loading up their own possessions even as they spoke—mounds of carpets and fine furniture, crates of china and crystal, silver serving pieces and gold jewelry—and they had no interest in trying to find space for more. The third examined Emmanuel's finest fruit bowl, tapped at it with his teeth—as if it were a piece of gold, as if he could thereby tell the quality of its workmanship—and then offered a tenth of its value.

Insulted, Vasili left.

Refusing to become disheartened, he promised himself he'd try elsewhere the next day. But the next day he had barely opened the shop when an elderly man came sidling in. He pulled from beneath his suit coat a platter of middling quality. "How much will you give me for this?" he asked.

Vasili stared at him. "I sell. I don't buy."

"You sell fine silverwork. This is fine silverwork. You can sell it. One hundred pounds." He thrust it into Vasili's unexpecting hands.

Vasili turned it over, as if looking for the artisan's mark, but in fact he knew it was not of a quality that any artisan would proudly claim.

"I bought it here, in this store," the man said, as if to establish the platter's value.

"I don't believe you did," Vasili said as gently as he could manage.

The man stiffened in umbrage. "What? *What?* This is the work of Emmanuel Demirgis, the best silversmith in the city his whole lifetime, God rest his soul. What do you know of such work? Could you possibly have done better?"

Vasili lifted his head in disagreement. "Emmanuel Demirgis was my father-in-law; I know his work very well. This is not his. His mark is not on it." He offered the platter back to the man.

"Fifty pounds," the man said.

"I'm sorry," Vasili said. "There is no market for it."

"There's always a market for fine silver. Thirty pounds, my last offer."

"There is no market," Vasili repeated.

The man waved his arm wildly around the store. "There is no market? What? You have a shop here! Why do you have a shop if there is no market?"

"Not today," Vasili said. "Everyone is selling; no one is buying. *I* am selling, and no one is buying."

"They will buy this!" The man shook the platter at him. "They will buy this if you offer it!"

"I'm sorry."

"Twenty pounds!" the man shouted at him.

"I'm sorry."

The man threw the platter down onto the floor. "Are you telling me it's worthless?"

Vasili bent down, picked up the platter, and held it out to the man, but the man backed away as if it were a snake.

"Keep it! Keep it!" he shouted. "If it's so worthless, you might as well keep it with all your other worthless things!" And he stormed out the door.

Still holding the platter, Vasili looked around, at the finely engraved cups and the intricately woven silver baskets, at a jeweled filigree chalice fit for a king, at matching bracelet and earring sets, at an engraved tray whose diameter matched the length of Vasili's arm, at a biscuit bowl with dainty handles and a set of twenty napkin rings each with a different design, at a silver mesh handbag and three small filigreed jewelry boxes. Surely it couldn't be true that they were all as worthless as this poorly made tray. Surely there were still people in this terrifyingly uncertain time who would pay for beauty, for fine workmanship.

That afternoon he tried Paradisia, the American enclave near the American school, and the French one clustered around the French cathedral, and the British in Bouja. Long after it had grown dark, he returned home, having sold two pieces, with twenty British pounds in his pocket—not enough to pay the boat passage for even one of his children.

The next day he took a horse tram—because a taxi would have cost too much—out to Bournabat, ostensibly to check on the house. He walked down the familiar street and smelled the familiar smells, but when he stood in front of the gate and saw the big stone house gleaming in the summer sunshine—the house where he had been born and where all his children had been born—still sheltered by its pines as if nothing had happened, and Liana's garden in front, the roses exploding in extravagant blooms, he couldn't bear to step inside.

Instead, he went from door to door, to all his neighbors' homes, the Levantines and the British and the French who had remained, and showed napkin rings and necklaces and earrings to wives of wealthy men, and they looked askance at him, as if he were an itinerant peddler, as if they hadn't known him as their neighbor, living on the same street as they, longer than they had lived there, as if his family hadn't been one of the first to settle under the cool pines of Bournabat.

And then he went back to the city and played with the children and ate dinner, just as if it had been an ordinary day in an ordinary week. And in the night, in her parents' bed, he made quiet and fierce love to Liana.

CHAPTER 34

THE LAST OF THE GREEK SOLDIERS TRAILED THROUGH SMYRNA on the evening of September 8, on their way to the boats that waited for them at Cheshme. By then rumors held that Kemal and his army were on the outskirts of the city, and that he had warned the League of Nations that after the terrible depredations in the countryside he could hardly be held accountable for any actions of his troops when they took the city.

The Greek officials had left earlier that day, slipping away without the fanfare that had accompanied their arrival. Even the impeccably dressed General Hadjianestis, with the manners of an aristocrat and an eye for beautiful women, he who had run the war from the comfort of the residence he'd requisitioned along Smyrna's seafront, had fled. Panic spread across the city as their terrifying state of vulnerability dawned on the people, and they turned against each other, hoarding precious food supplies, fighting over loaves of bread pulled from neighborhood bakeries. Peddlers strolled the streets, doing brisk business selling fezzes to the desperate populace, as if the mere wearing of a fez would disguise a Greek or an Armenian, as if a Turk couldn't tell the difference. Turkish flags flew in desperate hope from Greek homes and businesses.

Frantic crowds had formed permanent clots around the American and British and French consulates begging for visas, but the doors remained locked, the officials refusing to process any more visas. They were, after all, too busy making arrangements for the evacuation of their own citizens.

By daylight on Saturday, September 9, nearly fifty foreign ships were floating in Smyrna Bay—battleships and transports and freighters of nearly every maritime nation in the world. Only Greece was not represented, its last ships having skulked away under cover of night. And every foreign ship bristled with guns, its sailors under strict orders to maintain the integrity of the ship and of the taking of Smyrna by the Turks, as if suddenly every foreign nation had, overnight, become partisan to Turkish interests. In some cases, foreign soldiers appeared on the streets, guarding foreign enterprises: the American theater and the Standard Oil repository, the Belgian power plant, the British and French railways. But otherwise, they all seemed to be playing up to the Turks, as it had become clear that the Greeks had already lost Smyrna.

The city that morning was breath-holdingly still, doors closed and bolted, shutters locked tight, streets nearly deserted, everyone inside, waiting to see what would happen. No *bahchevans* made their rounds, no nut sellers or *gevrek* vendors walked past, no camels plodded through the streets; nor did ships' horns sound, nor did any dogs bark. The tens of thousands of refugees who had made camp along the quayside and whose detritus lined it were almost the only ones in sight as noon approached and the Turkish cavalry rode silently along the quays under the hot midday sun to its new barracks in the Konak area at the center of the city. They rode ramrod stiff at a dignified pace, as if on parade, and they looked well fed and fresh, their mounts in precise military order with hooves clattering on the cobblestones, the soldiers' curved scimitars drawn and raised, glistening in the sun. The captain commanding the cavalry division had been the target of three bomb attacks on the outskirts of Smyrna. The first two had killed his mounts and wounded three of his men, and each time he had changed mounts and continued on. The third bomb had exploded close enough to have left cuts on his face and head, but he had not even paused, riding on through the city, leading his men, looking neither to the right nor to the left, the blood on his face drying in the sun, a magnificent and terrifying display of severe determination.

Other than those few bombs and some scattered and mostly unthreatening gunshots in the distance, the city was taken with barely a token of resistance. By nightfall, the full Turkish contingent was settled into the Konak and the foreign soldiers guarding their nations' commercial interests breathed a sigh of relief. Control had passed uncontested into Turkish hands.

Vasili stayed at home that morning, leaving his shop closed. He had brought home in the previous days nearly all of the smaller items—bracelets and earrings and brooches. *If all else fails,* he told himself, *we could barter our way onto a ship.* He had collected nearly three thousand pounds, mostly in British pounds sterling, but lesser quantities in French francs and gold sovereigns. These he had secreted in the pockets of his clothes, not yet telling even Liana of his plans, for fear she would refuse to go. But certainly, he thought, she now understood the gravity of the situation.

But as Saturday passed, encouraged by the control that Turkish officers seemed to exercise over their troops and gaining renewed hope of weathering the events of the moment, he took Liana aside. She'd been sitting on the floor of the parlor, reading stories to Manoush and Giorgi. Liana's back leaned against the bed in which Vaia slept—or lay with her eyes closed—her most common practice these days. He had more than once joked to Liana that perhaps his mother had hit upon the cleverest solution: sleeping away the most unpleasant parts of one's life.

"I'm going to the shop," he said to her now.

Liana looked up at him and frowned.

"I'm going to the shop," he repeated, thinking she hadn't heard.

"Why?" she demanded.

He turned and left the room, and she rose and followed, suddenly flooded with panic. "*Why?*"

"Things seem under control here," he said quietly. "Keep everything closed up; nothing will happen. But there's a great deal of value at the shop—"

"Vasili, you can't be serious." How could he leave now? Who knew what would happen in the next hours?

"Perhaps in a day or two we'll even be able to open again."

"You can't know—"

"Liana, please. It's asking for trouble leaving the place empty like that. Unguarded."

"Hire someone to guard it, then."

"Who could I hire these days?"

"You don't even have a gun!"

"Yes, I do."

"You do?" She gaped at him. "Where did you get a gun?"

But he ignored her question. "It looks as if it's not going to be as bad as we thought." He hoped that was true.

"Vasili, you can't go. You don't know what they're going to do." She reached out to hold his arm.

"They? It looks as if *they* have kept things pretty much under control."

"For now." She pulled at him, trying to make him understand the fear she felt. "Vasili, don't go. *Please.*"

He held her shoulders and gave her a quick, dismissive kiss. "What can I take along to eat?"

"Eat?"

"I may be there overnight. A day or so. Until everything seems settled down for sure."

"It's crazy!" *Don't leave us here!*

"What is there?"

"I won't let you go!" *Please, please. Stay with us.*

"What is there?" He started toward the kitchen

She hurried after him. "Vasili, just wait a few days—*please!*"

He rummaged in the pantry, spooning *rizogalo* into a small yogurt pail, breaking off part of a loaf of bread, taking a bunch of grapes the children had picked from Theodora's grape arbor.

She took hold of his arm again. "Please, listen—"

He pried her fingers away. "It's all right. Everything's going to be all right. Just make sure everyone stays inside until I get back."

"*Please,*" she whispered, the urgency clear, "don't go."

He bent and kissed her—a longer kiss this time, his free hand wiping the tears from the corners of her eyes. "Don't be afraid. Nothing's going to happen."

Then he was gone, out the back door, through the garden and out the back gate, slipping between the houses, making his way furtively by way of side streets and alleys. *She's glad now,* he thought, *that I made her move into town, where she can keep company with her mother and sister, where she doesn't have to be in the house all alone with the children.*

A house full of women and children to care for, he thought. And then, more hopefully: *In the best of all possible worlds, surely this transition of power will continue as smoothly as it has started.*

Then there would have been no need for the panic and the fears. Then he could rest easy because it wouldn't matter that he hadn't raised enough money for all of them to leave. Then life could go on as it had always been.

Back in the kitchen, Liana was left all alone, staring into the darkness. *Vasili*, she pleaded in her mind, *don't leave me*.

LIANA STOOD AT THE BEDROOM WINDOW, AND DESPITE THE warmth of the night, she shivered in her nightgown and robe. Through the shutters' louvers she could see only strips of the pale buildings across the street, lit by a moon still nearly full. From a distance she could hear gunshots and the breaking of glass, more now than earlier. And she heard footsteps running down the street, then silence again. The clock in the sitting room struck midnight.

She hugged herself to drive away the sudden chill that ran down her arms, then she turned and stepped to the basket, where eight-month-old Baby Dora slept, her hair a dark halo around a pale, round face, one hand curled close to her chin. Liana smoothed back the hair from her forehead, then turned and crept out of the room and across the hall to the room where her boys slept, Giorgi on the floor this night and Dimitri and Manoush in the double bed. Giorgi slept on his back, one leg— newly removed from the cast but still stiff—stuck out straight, the other one bent at the knee. His arms lay limp at his sides, as if in exhaustion. In the bed, Dimitri tossed restlessly while Manoush curled close to the far edge.

Then she tiptoed downstairs and checked the door and its bolt one more time, peeking in at Vaia in the parlor.

"Who is it?" Vaia's voice croaked from the darkness.

"It's me." And then she thought to add, "Liana." She had long wondered if Vaia lay awake nights, unable to sleep after dozing most of the day.

"Who are they shooting at?" Vaia asked.

Liana came into the room. "I don't know."

Vaia let out an impatient breath. "Here you are in perfectly good health and you don't even know."

Liana pulled the sheet up, tucking it under Vaia's chin.

"Well, *I* know," Vaia went on. "They're shooting at the Turks, that's what. The fool Greeks have finally decided to fight back."

Liana wondered vaguely what Vaia could possibly understand. It would do little good to point out that the fool Greeks had run away, had gone back to where they'd come from.

"And it's about time too," Vaia grumbled. "Misled you all, didn't they?"

"Try to get some sleep," Liana said, turning away.

"That's all I get, sleep," Vaia said at Liana's retreating back. "Sleep, and more sleep, in this God-awful house."

Liana climbed back up the stairs, deciding not to look in on her daughter for fear of waking Theodora. It would still be hours before daylight, before she had any sense of what was happening. She slipped back into her room and sat down on the bed, knowing she still would be unable to sleep.

Even more hours before she would see or hear from Vasili.

IN THE MORNING, THE CITY WAS EERILY SILENT: FOR THE FIRST time in centuries, no church bells rang. There could not have been a worse omen for the situation in which the city found itself. Liana ached to go to Aghios Giorgios, to light a candle in prayer for Vasili's safety, but she could not even do that. And since she had no idea of the conditions beyond the small view she could get between the louvers of the shutters, she stayed home.

Still, the streets of her neighborhood seemed almost normal, except for the silence. Late in the morning she noticed a man going house to house, slipping handbills under doors, and when he came to her mother's house, she scooped up the paper almost as soon as it slid under the solid oak door. The lettering was in Greek and Turkish and Armenian: Mustafa Kemal had ordered that no civilian was to be harmed. Any of his soldiers caught disobeying this strict order would receive the death penalty.

She folded the handbill slowly. Surely that would mean that ordinary shops could operate safely. Surely by this evening, Vasili would be able to come home. Feeling more lighthearted than she had in days, she organized Sophie and the children to pack a picnic lunch to eat in the garden. "We'll pretend we're at the beach!" she suggested.

"But there's no water," Manoush pointed out.

"You can wear your swimming suits anyway. We'll pretend about the water. It'll be a pretend beach picnic."

"It's too hot," Vaioush complained.

"Well then, anyone who doesn't want to can stay inside." She was already peering into the cupboard to see what she could find for such an outing. "I think we'll have pickled eggs," she said, choosing a jar of rose-colored eggs from the shelf. "And, of course, stuffed grape leaves."

"And pickles?" Giorgi asked.

She scooped him close and planted a kiss on the top of his head. "Oh yes, of course, *Yaya*'s pickles." Beyond him, in the doorway, Dimitri stood silently. She winked at him, and he grinned. "Dimitri, could you find a nice place to lay out the picnic blanket?"

"I could help!" Giorgi announced.

"Ask Dimitri. He's in charge of finding a good spot." She turned away. *Tomorrow*, she thought. *Maybe tomorrow we can go back to our own house and our own garden and our own beds.* The clock in the hall struck twelve noon.

At precisely that moment a convoy of five automobiles decorated with olive branches drove through the streets of Smyrna. In one of them, an open touring car, sat Mustafa Kemal, the conquering general, surrounded by an escort of cavalry.

And at precisely that moment as well, Vasili sat, tired and alone, and heard the first crash of breaking glass and the shouts of the irregulars who had come to Smyrna on Saturday and who were now claiming the victor's spoils at the far end of this street of shops belonging to Armenian goldsmiths and one Greek silversmith.

BY SUNDAY NIGHT THE SILENCE HAD ENDED, AND DESPITE ALL OF Kemal's assurances, the chaos began. Irregulars and uniformed soldiers alike rampaged through the Armenian neighborhoods, breaking into houses and shops, looting and burning. They ran through the streets, their pockets stuffed with watches and jewelry, robbing at gunpoint or knifepoint anyone they could find. They shot into the lighted windows of private homes, killing and wounding randomly. They dragged women and girls from their beds and raped and gutted them. They decapitated the men, or rounded up whole neighborhoods and drove the men off, bound together, into the countryside, to be shot carelessly there, the living still tied to the dead. But inside the house, Liana and the rest knew nothing of all that. Certainly, they heard gunshots and shouting, but there was no way of knowing whether it was only street noise or if their world was ending.

Liana tossed in her bed a second night and roamed the dark hallways of the house. She met Sophie on one of her forays, and the two of them clung together. "I can't stand it!" Liana whispered, pressing her hands against her ears to shut out the sounds of running footsteps and gunshots in the street outside.

"He'll be all right," Sophie murmured, rubbing her sister's back.

"Why doesn't he come home? What's happening to him?"

"He'll be all right. He'll be all right."

Liana pulled away from her. "I can't stand it. *I have to know!*"

"In the morning—in the daylight—things will settle down," Sophie said. "Didn't they say Kemal would execute anyone who disobeyed his orders? They won't have the nerve when it gets light."

Liana slumped against her sister. "Oh God," she whispered. "Oh dear God, don't let anything happen to him."

Sophie wrapped her arms around her sister and led her back into her bedroom, and the two of them sat on the edge of the bed and clung to each other, listening to the shots and the shouts and the screams. "It's far away. Listen to how far away it is," Sophie said.

"*His shop* is far away."

"You're safe. Your children are safe. Mama and Vaia *Hanum*. We're all safe. Vasili will be safe too; you'll see."

"Oh God. Oh God." Liana buried her head in her hands, and Sophie rocked back and forth with her, crooning as to a baby.

"Remember how Mama used to do this when we were scared?" Sophie whispered. "Remember having bad dreams in the night, and Mama would come and hold you and sing to you?"

Liana squeezed her eyes tight, trying not to hear the sounds and thinking: *But this isn't just a bad dream.*

"Remember when we were girls, and we older ones used to tease you because you always got so scared when you woke up in the night?"

"I did not."

"Yes, you did."

"I liked waking up in the night."

Sophie laughed softly. "You hated it."

I hate it now, Liana thought. *How much longer before daylight? And will it be any better when it is?*

CHAPTER 35

HAMDIYE CAME LATE IN THE MORNING. SHE STEPPED INSIDE, breathless, already pulling off her dark scarf and taking from her pocket a light-colored one for covering her head indoors. "I had to walk the whole way," she announced, her mouth tight in anger. "No horse trams running today. No trains, either. The foreigners are all deserting us."

Running home to be with their families, Liana thought.

"What's it like out there?" Sophie asked.

Hamdiye stared at her for a moment and then spit out the word: "Terrible." She took Liana's arm and pulled her aside, into the kitchen. "Something you should know, *Madamjum*. They were in your garden last night—*chettes*. The soldiers wouldn't dare, I suppose, but those irregulars have no idea of right and wrong. I stepped outside and yelled at them to go away, and when they saw I was a Turk they came right up on the veranda and asked why I worked for an infidel, and I told them it was my house. They backed off at that, but it was clear they didn't believe me. I don't know if I should let my children sleep there another night."

"Do what you think best," Liana said. *Oh God*, she thought. *Oh God, my house too.*

"And . . ." Hamdiye went on. She caught Liana again by the arm and pulled her closer. "And that isn't all." She bent near, so that her breath felt hot against Liana's face. "They killed the English."

Liana stared at her.

"The English. The English man and woman. The old ones in the little square house at the end of the street."

"Mr. and Mrs. Ferguson?" Liana asked.

Hamdiye nodded. "Dead in the garden, they were, their throats cut. Blood all over." She made a face. "They're animals to do such things."

"Hamdiye, you shouldn't have come."

Hamdiye straightened, and she brushed her arms as if sloughing lint away from them. "It's my job."

"They might have killed you. You should have stayed home. What about your children?"

"I took them to my sister."

"You should have stayed with them."

"They won't hurt me. They wouldn't dare. But it's not safe for you people out there."

"Hamdiye, Vasili went to his shop."

Hamdiye bent close in alarm. "When?"

"Night before last."

Hamdiye straightened again, her mouth a tight line.

"And he hasn't come back," Liana whispered.

Hamdiye pulled the pale scarf from her head. "I'll go see."

"I'm going too."

Hamdiye turned back. "You wouldn't be safe."

"I'd be as safe as you."

"You're not a Turk."

Liana stood her ground. "It's my husband."

"Your children need you."

"I'm going."

Hamdiye gave her a long look. "Do you have anything black?"

It was a question meant to defeat. Turkish women of Smyrna wore black outdoors as a matter of course; Greek women never did. Theirs were the light, bright colors; even in the dead of winter they wore bright colors. But Liana was not about to be defeated. "I can wear the things Mama wore when Papa died."

Hamdiye stared at her for a moment in silence and finally said, "Then hurry." Her voice was terse and cold.

PANDEMONIUM RULED THE STREETS IN WAYS THAT LIANA HAD never guessed, shut up in the house as she had been. The two women walked hurriedly down dusty passages between houses, looking neither to the right nor to the left. Where once there would have been women out washing marble steps, and little old men sitting at tables writing letters for those with a few piastres but no skill with words, and blankets hanging from open windows, airing in the sun, now there were only closed shutters and palpable fear. Hamdiye's dark scarf was pulled down over her forehead; Liana's face was fully encased in black. They clung to each other's hands, fearing separation in the unruly streets. Men ran this way and that, shouting, shooting pistols, brandishing dark-stained knives. Once or twice Liana flattened herself against a wall, wide eyed in fear, but Hamdiye jerked her hand until she looked away as a good Turkish woman would, not daring to challenge a man with her eyes.

They ran from one corner to the next, peering around it, hoping not to be stopped, not to be looked at too closely. Once a man stopped them, but Hamdiye muttered something and he let them pass. As they moved, they began to see more and more bodies littering the streets: men slit from ear to ear, women cut from throat to crotch, blood pooling in the street, puddles of blood muddying the summer dust. At one corner they ran nearly head-on into a long troop of men under guard: Greeks of all ages. Unable to look away, Liana scanned their ranks, desperately hoping not to see Vasili, and was relieved that she saw no one she recognized.

As they approached Eski Buyuk Pazar, they saw shop windows broken, the cobbled streets littered with glass, the stores themselves emptied of merchandise. Hamdiye said nothing, pulling Liana along with her, and Liana, too frightened for Vasili, dared not say anything either.

When at last they turned onto his street, Liana stopped dead still in despair. Every shop window was broken, and all the stores had been looted. "They wanted the gold," Hamdiye said tersely. "You can hope they don't appreciate silver so much."

But as they approached the store, Liana knew. Though she could hardly bear to think it, still she knew. And when she finally stood before it, she felt as if she had always known, as if there had never been a time when she hadn't known how it would end. Hamdiye tried pulling her away, but she wrenched her arm from the woman's grip and stepped into the store.

Like in all the other shops, glass shards littered the floor. All the display cases had been broken or forced open. Nothing remained, except, unexplainably, the frail handle of what had once been a fruit bowl. Liana picked it up and turned it over in her hand. Perhaps two looters had fought over the bowl, breaking it in the process. She recognized the handle. It was a bowl her father had made, one he'd priced too high to sell because it was a particular favorite of his. She held the handle in her hand, pressing it tightly, the broken edge of it cutting into her palm, and she walked forward into the dimness of the shop.

She found him in the back, where perhaps he had dragged himself after they had shot him, leaving a trail of blood that had dried to a dark stain on the wood floor, a stain amid all the others: coal oil and kerosene and, perhaps, paint and coffee and food accidentally dropped and, now, blood. His hair was matted with blood and the perspiration of his effort. His lips were turned down in concentration and pale from loss of blood. His hands—so broad, with the wide, flat wrists she loved—seemed in death larger than life, large all out of proportion to his body.

She knelt and held him close, feeling an emptying within her, a loss of all bone and tissue and flesh, a sudden dryness so great there were not even tears for his loss. Nothing. There was nothing at all inside her except a thin wail that escaped from her lips, unbidden, unknowing. She was enveloped in the nothingness, pulled by it into a cloud of incomprehension, drowning in it, lost in its depths. Nothingness rose around her, blocking out all seeing and hearing, all sense of touch except his body in her arms, the feel of his clothing and his hair and his skin on her hands, all sense of smell except the scent of his skin against her own, all sound except the beat of her own heart against his silent one.

When Hamdiye finally pulled her away, there was nothing left within her, only death, only the smell of it and the feel of it and the silence of it.

"There's nothing here for you now, *Madamjum*," Hamdiye said gently.

"We have to bury him." The voice came from within her, as if she had spoken, though she was sure she hadn't.

"No."

"Yes."

"If they find you here they will kill you as well," Hamdiye said. "Or worse," she added.

"We have to."

"They rape infidel women. Cut them open. You saw on the street."

"We have to." A determination. Nothing for it but to do it.

Hamdiye sighed. "You haven't even a shovel."

"Find someone."

Hamdiye sighed again. "They will want money."

"I will pay." A voice from far off, someone else's voice, not even her own. "We have to."

Hamdiye turned and picked her way through the broken glass and the splintered display cases, and Liana went back to Vasili. She gathered him once again in her arms, whispering to him, whispering promises she couldn't understand, and couldn't have kept even if she could have understood them.

When Hamdiye at last returned she had two boys with her, barely older than Dimitri. They hardly glanced at Vasili, their eyes resting instead on Liana.

"Ten pounds," the taller one said.

"All right," Liana said.

"Money first," he demanded.

"It's at my house."

"First."

"I haven't money here."

The boy looked at Vasili now for the first time. "Maybe he has some."

He knelt and reached a grubby hand into Vasili's pocket, but Liana shoved him away. Tenderly she felt in Vasili's pockets, but there was nothing there: His clothing had already been rifled by whoever had killed him. Or by whoever had come afterward, a scavenger of the dead.

"Without money first, we don't do it," the boy said, his face close to Liana's as they knelt together.

Then his eyes fell on a glint of silver at her neck, and before she understood and had a chance to move back, his hand snapped out. He grabbed the necklace and yanked it from her neck, the fragile connectors between the links breaking, three linked hearts falling away from the others, landing in Liana's lap. Quickly she scooped them up, holding them tight in her hand.

"Give me the rest," the boy said. His face was inches from hers.

"No," she said.

"Give me." His hand, dirty and scarred, was thrust in her face.

"You have enough. More than you asked for."

He looked down at the partial necklace in his other hand. "Worth nothing if it isn't whole."

"You know nothing," she spat at him. "It is the work of Emmanuel Demirgis. It's worth more than you asked, even broken like that."

He stared at the links in his hand. "How do I know that?"

"Ask anyone on this street."

He laughed. "They're all dead."

She narrowed her eyes at him. "And that makes it even more valuable, doesn't it?"

He rose slowly, jamming the necklace into a pocket, and took his shovel, and Hamdiye showed him out the back of the shop where he could dig a grave. Liana took Vasili's hand in her own and held it tight.

By the time they left the shop they could smell the smoke. The fires had already started in the Armenian quarter.

CHAPTER 36

LIANA LAY IN BED, THE HOUSE QUIET AROUND HER, ONLY MUF-
fled sounds coming from the street, and she was unable to
remember how she had gotten there, how she had managed to
come back home. It was almost as if someone else had insisted
on Hamdiye taking her to Vasili, someone else had found him
lying in his shop, someone else had cradled him, had insisted
he be buried, someone else had faced those ruffians, and she
herself had only been a silent witness.

How many times? How many times had he said it: *Liana,
we should leave this place.* But always there were reasons—her
family, his mother, the children, a baby on the way. Always reasons. And finally he had stopped saying it. Only a few months
ago she'd come upon the men discussing it—Vasili and Spiro
and Aleko—and she'd been frightened Vasili would bring it up
again. Indeed, he had, just last week, but she'd put him off,
fearful that he would force her to go, and when he hadn't insisted, she'd felt relief. She had been a fool. She'd never been
willing to leave, never imagined anyplace else could be home
for her, never imagined she could have a life without her family
close around her. And now he was gone, he who had been her
life, her morning and her evening, the one with whom she'd

shared laughter so many times and tears more than once. He who had measured out her days, the structure of her life built around his comings and his goings, the mirror of her hopes, the river of all her dreams.

She squeezed her eyelids tight, but he was still there, the agony of his death still written across his face, dead in his own shop, alone, untended, just as her father had been, but so much worse. So much, much worse.

And it was her fault. If she had gone. If she had smiled and said, *Yes, Vasili, of course, Vasili,* he would be alive now, sitting under a palm tree in California with Ara, drinking *raki,* the children laughing in the California sun, playing at the California beaches. Did they have *raki* in America?

She longed for one last chance. One more time: *Liana, we should leave this place.* And this time she would say yes. *Yes, Vasili, anywhere. Anywhere you want.* She ached for him, for the touch of him, his lips against hers, his hands on her, the secret language of their love making, for his calm, gentle voice, for the way he seemed to make everything right, for his voice and his touch and his smell.

She rose from the bed and opened the wardrobe, breathing in, imagining his scent. She touched his shirts, clean and smooth, and buried her face in them and smelled sunshine and warm breezes and the faint scent of laurel. She lifted the sleeve of his suit coat and held it to her face. She pulled it from the hanger and draped it over her shoulders, hugging herself close in it, smelling him, imagining him.

She stepped to the dresser and opened the top drawer. His collar box, his handkerchiefs. She smoothed them with the palm of her hand. His father's watch fob and a medal Vasili had won when he was a child. She fingered it in her hand. Vasili. A photograph of herself, and another of her with the children before Baby Dora was born. Taken last summer in the garden, she only just beginning to show. All of Ara's letters, written first from eastern Turkey and then from Syria, and finally from America. From California. The second drawer: his undergarments, pale and smooth. "Vasili," she whispered, "yes, I'll go. Wherever you want. Yes, please. Yes."

She felt the tears coming again and she lifted the undergarments to her face, burying herself in them, crying great, heaving, hysterical sobs. She leaned against the dresser and wept for him, for herself, for the children, for all those dead in the streets and in their shops and along the country roads and in their own homes. And finally, when she was sobbed out, when the tears had turned to gulps of pain and anguish, she wiped her eyes and face with the pile of undershirts still in her hands and she laid them back in the drawer, and that was when she saw the packet.

It was made of a sheet of newspaper, folded and folded and folded yet again. Curious, she opened it, and a profusion of coins spilled out. Gold coins. She gathered them into her hands, heavy, as if announcing their own value. Gold? Vasili had never told her about gold.

She lifted the other things in the drawer but found nothing more. Then she opened the top drawer again and lifted the handkerchiefs. Looking for what? More gold? A note? Something of explanation? And found nothing. She pushed aside the photographs and the collar box and Vasili's father's watch fob and Vasili's medal. Nothing more. She opened the collar box, a note there perhaps? *Liana, if I die, there is money for you all.*

Inside the collar box there was another packet, this one bulkier. She opened it now, her fingers trembling. *Vasili? What secrets did you have?* Three pairs of earrings, each with a matching bracelet or brooch. Her father's work. Beautiful. The most beautiful jewelry in all of Smyrna. She laid them out on the top of the dresser, each set together. Vasili . . . ?

She scooped them up suddenly and jammed them into the pocket of his suit coat, still draped around her shoulders, and she felt the stiff rustle of paper there beside them. Paper? A note, then? She pulled it from the pocket: not a note, and not one piece but many, and from the other pocket as well. Money. Paper money. She sat down on the bed and laid it out before her: British pound notes, French francs. And more from the inside pocket, dozens of them. She started to count them and then stopped in wonder. Hundreds of pounds, thousands, perhaps. She stared at the money in front of her and began to cry again, and without thinking she wiped her eyes on the sleeve of the coat.

She gathered up the money slowly, methodically, the British pounds together, the French francs together, even some American dollars hidden among them. When she had finished, she thrust them into the left pocket of the coat, then she walked to the window and stared out between the louvers. Smoke from the fires drifted into the sky. Unbidden, her hands slid into the coat pockets, the left one with the money and the right one with the jewelry. "Yes, Vasili," she whispered. "Yes."

She went down the back stairs, hoping to avoid the others for now, and found Hamdiye just getting ready to leave. Was it so late then?

"I'm taking the children away," she said, a new determination in her voice. "Vasili left money, and I'm sure it's enough to pay for all of us."

Hamdiye nodded, as if this were the first sane thing she'd heard all day.

"I may need you to help me get to the quays. Could you come again in the morning?"

"You should leave now."

"I can't. There's Mama and—Hamdiye, would you take Vasili's mother with you? If I give you gold?"

"You will need the gold."

"She needs someone to look after her."

"Your mother—"

"Mama and Sophie will be going with me."

"I'll take her, then."

"Thank you. I wish I could give you more—"

"What will happen to your house?"

"What do you think?" Liana asked. "Is it something you want?"

"It's your house."

"It won't do us much good if we're somewhere else."

"It's Madame Vaia's house as well."

"Do you want it in exchange for keeping her?"

Hamdiye shrugged.

"You decide," Liana said finally. "If you want it, take it."

Theodora, having heard voices, walked into the kitchen. "Liana, for heaven's sake, you shouldn't be up. You should be—"

"Mama, we have to leave."

"Leave?"

"We have to get on one of the boats and leave Smyrna."

Theodora was shaking her head in confusion. "Where would we go?"

"Wherever we can. We could go to America. Ara was always writing to Vasili, telling him to come."

"*America?*" Theodora's eyes were wide with horror.

"Why not? There's nothing for us here anymore," Liana said bluntly. "You know that—there's hardly even any food in the stores."

Theodora shook her head. "No. I'm not going. My family is here."

Liana took a step forward. "You have to. I've seen it out there; you haven't."

Theodora raised her chin: *No.*

"You have to. The children and I are going, and you have to leave too."

Theodora narrowed her eyes. "I can't help what you and your children do, but I can't leave *my* children—my other children. Don't ask me to."

"Mama, listen: Vasili begged me to leave. If we had left then, he'd be alive now."

Theodora stiffened. "Do what you must do, Liana, but this is my home."

"For God's sake, Mama, people are being killed here! In their own homes!"

Theodora came close and put her arms around Liana. "You're upset, dear. In the morning things will seem different. You'll see."

Liana pulled away from her. "Please, Mama, you haven't been out there! Men and boys are being taken away. Women are being raped and killed."

Theodora stared at her, blinking her eyes, unable to register Liana's words. Finally she said, "I'm too old to leave. Maybe Sophie will go with you."

"I can't leave without *you*, Mama. Please."

Theodora's arms closed around Liana again. "It would be good for you to leave, make a new life, but not me. I'm too old."

"You could die here, right in your own home."

Theodora held Liana at arm's length. "Have you thought about Vaia? What will happen to her?"

"Hamdiye already said—"

"Hamdiye! Can you imagine what Vaia would think of that? I will stay with Vaia. You go if you like. I can understand that you'd want to, though to tell you the truth I should think you could wait a month or so, until things settle down."

"They won't settle down! They'll only get worse! You'll die— you'll all die! Hamdiye"—she turned to the silent woman— "tell her."

Hamdiye looked up from her work, her lips a tight line. "Everyone must do what she thinks is best," she said at last.

"Dear," Theodora said, looking at Liana again, "surely you don't think all those foreign ships in the harbor will sit there and do nothing if things really get bad."

Liana shook her mother off and stalked out of the kitchen. Things *were* really bad, and the foreign ships *were* sitting there in the harbor doing nothing to stop it. It was absolutely clear to her now: A person had to save herself, a person had that responsibility to her children.

CHAPTER 37

HAMDIYE CAME FOR HER IN THE MORNING, AND LIANA IMME-
diately sent her to Christina's house with a note saying that
Liana and the children were leaving and strongly encourag-
ing Christina and Spiro's family to join them. But Hamdiye
returned strangely shaken. No one was home, she reported.
She didn't mention that the door had been broken in and that
she had seen blood splattered on the foyer floor. Liana could
only hope for Eleni, who had recently moved closer to the sea,
to a wealthy neighborhood, but also close—uncomfortably
close—to the Armenian quarter of Smyrna that was now
burning. And the *imbat*—the southeasterly wind—had come
up, blowing the flames north and west, toward the center of
the city.

Liana had spent half the night urging her mother and Sophie to leave with her, but both remained adamant. Theodora
steadfastly refused to leave the home that had been hers for
forty years, and Sophie insisted on staying with her because—
well, because she couldn't bear to leave her mother alone. And
they would keep Vaia with them.

Liana no longer had the energy to argue. Instead, she
woke the children early. "We're going on an adventure!" she

announced as she dressed Giorgi, but her gay voice did not match the expression on her face.

Vaioush grinned, but Dimitri looked askance, surely wondering what madness had suddenly overtaken his mother. Liana noticed and chucked him under the chin. "On a boat!" she said, forcing a smile.

"With Papa?" Manoush asked, a question that hit like a blow to the gut.

She recovered enough to say simply, "No, not with Papa." She looked then at Dimitri's anguished face. "Come with me a moment," she said to him, leading him out into the hall. Her mind tumbling, unsure what to say or do, she placed her hands on his shoulders—such small shoulders, she thought—and then she pushed herself through. "You are the only one I can depend on," she said to him. "I am sorry, but there's nothing for it. You must help me now. You must be the man of the family." She could hardly bear to see the shadow of worry on his face. "You and I must be strong. Can you do that, do you think?"

He nodded solemnly, but she felt his body shake beneath her hands. "It is a terrible time, Dimitri, and you are far too young for this, but it can't be helped. We must get through this, all of us. I must get us onto a boat. You will not like what you see when we leave Theodora *Yaya*'s house, but you and I must be strong, just until I get us onto a boat. Until we are safe. Can you do that?"

"Yes, Mama." His voice was ragged, but he was no longer shaking.

"I will give you something," she said. "A letter, from your papa's friend in America. It is important that we keep it safe, do you understand?"

He nodded.

And then she had an inspiration. Taking the three linked

hearts from her pocket, she said to Dimitri, "This is a good luck charm, from your Emmanuel *Papou*. Remember when he gave me the necklace? And now, since you are to be the man for a time, you must take it, to shelter us all. Keep it in a safe place, and whenever you feel afraid, touch it to remember who made it and how much he cared about you."

His eyes were on her face as she spoke, and she closed his hand around the hearts. He looked at her for a moment longer before he thrust his hand into his pants pocket.

"Fine, then," she said, nodding. "And you will help me with the children, I know. Help me keep them safe." She gave him a kiss on each cheek, and his arms wrapped around her as if he would never let go. They stayed together for a long moment, then she gently removed his arms from around her neck and gave him one more kiss before returning to the others.

They ate a quick breakfast of tea and toast with Theodora's rose-hip jelly, the children silent and Sophie holding Baby Dora on her lap, and a tearful Theodora hovering around them, barely able to imagine what horrors the young ones would see on their way to the port. All the time, Hamdiye stood stolidly in the background, saying nothing, until Liana finally lifted her bag, embraced her mother and sister one last time, and walked to the door. She paused there and looked at each of her children, their eyes on her, their lives dependent on her. Then she handed Giorgi over to Hamdiye and she took Baby Dora from Sophie, and she ordered Dimitri and Vaioush and Manoush to hold each other's hands, and they left Theodora's home in a silent and fearful parade, Theodora and Sophie watching through their tears. Liana dared not think what a pitiful group they made, for fear that all her courage would dissolve in tears and regret.

All the way to the quay, she tried to shield the children's eyes from the bodies lying in the streets, bloating in the late summer heat, but there were too many bodies, and all she could do was to hurry the children along, looking neither to the right nor to the left, refusing to acknowledge the stench that hung in the air.

The quay was absolute chaos, crowded now with more than two hundred thousand angry and terrified people spread out along the two miles of the quay. Overnight, more fires had started, and now it seemed half the city was in flames, and the smoke burned their eyes and drove their lungs into fits of coughing, and the heat of the flames drove them closer and closer to the edge of the quay. Liana took one look at the wind blowing behind them, fanning the flames forward, and once she even started to turn back for her mother, but Hamdiye forced her to turn once more toward the sea. "They have made their decision," she said sternly, "and you have made yours." And indeed, Liana knew she had.

Giorgi, in Hamdiye's arms, his eyes wide at the sight of all the fire and smoke and the screaming crowds at the quay, asked, "Mama, are we going to meet Papa here?"

"I hope so," she answered.

Hamdiye looked away, as if unwilling to see the face of deception, but Dimitri stared full at her. *Is Papa dead?* he had asked last night. He had seen Hamdiye bring his mother home, had watched as she was put to bed, had helped keep the younger ones quiet while she lay in her bed and mourned for Vasili.

I don't know, she had answered him then, unable to put such a finality to Vasili's life for his son.

"He is, isn't he." Not a question.

"Terrible things are happening," she had answered. "He wants us to do what's best."

"What are we going to do?" he had asked.

You will have to be the man for a while, she had said. He was only eleven, too young to be the man, but she had hoped it would give him strength.

She had no idea where her own strength—her own determination—had come from. Unless it had come from Vasili himself, unless he had willed it to her, passed it to her as she held him in her arms or, later, when she had clasped his clothing to herself. Now she wore, under her summer dress, one of his undershirts—a foolish notion, perhaps, but she had thought it would give her strength. She also carried the jewelry he had secreted—she had found two more packets of it—and the money he had collected, as well as more gold and jewelry from her own mother and from Sophie.

Is Papa dead? Even now, even in the crush of this crowd, with the flames of the city behind them, having left her mother behind, and her sisters and her mother-in-law and all her nephews and nieces, and having set her face to the sea—to the only hope of escape—she couldn't bring herself to say the words.

SHE HAD EXPECTED TO SEE BARGE-LIKE LIGHTERS MOVING BACK and forth to the ships in the harbor, carrying passengers as quickly as they could to safety. Instead, the big ships—dozens of them—remained still in Smyrna Bay, as if they were only mirages in the sea, and even though caïques and lighters and rowboats and all manner of other small craft circled the ships, no one was boarding. No gangplanks had been let down, no rope ladders hung over the sides, no refugees crowded the decks. One could almost believe that the vessels in the harbor were ghost ships, except that from across the water came the sound of music—a marine band aboard one British dreadnought was playing patriotic marches.

It was then, finally, that reality struck her. The ships had not come to save the people of Smyrna, as she and all the others had thought, neither to take them away nor to rescue them from fire or gun or knife or to prevent rape or pillaging. They had come simply to observe.

She turned then to Hamdiye, who stood beside her, as awestruck as she herself was. "You must find a way," Hamdiye said to her.

How? Liana wondered. "How?" she asked.

"You must." Then Hamdiye set Giorgi down on the ground between them. "You must," she repeated, staring Liana full in the face.

Liana felt Giorgi's arms wrapping around her legs. "How?" she asked again.

Hamdiye's eyes still bored into hers. "You are strong," she said. "And you have money."

And I must save them, Liana thought. *Yes, Vasili.* "And you must go," she said to Hamdiye. "You have your own family to care for."

"Yes, *Madamjum*, I do," Hamdiye said. She turned from them then and disappeared into the mass of people around them.

ON THE QUAY, IMPOSSIBLE CROWDS JAMMED THE SEAWALL AND THE docks, screaming to be taken aboard. All along the length of Smyrna Bay scores of thousands stood, begging the ships to take them away, and the harbor was strewn with the bodies of those who had jumped in, trying to swim to safety, while the small boats that plied their way from British dreadnought to French cruiser to American destroyer shoved aside bodies of the dead in the water as those boats made their fruitless rounds. In that throng, Liana and her children were six more refugees, a woman and five children, with little baggage, with no man to push them forward, with no visas for entry into another country, with nothing more than hope and the absolute terror of complete despair. And that was how they spent the rest of the day and the night, as the fires, whipped by the wind, drew close enough that the smoke filled their lungs, and they could feel the heat on their backs as they pressed themselves closer and closer to the sea, willing themselves onto one of the ships. The crowd around them surged forward and broke into screams of agony and despair, their cries rising to the smoke-filled sky and drifting out to the ships, where the sailors had been ordered to take no passengers, no matter how desperate, unless they were under the official protection of their own government.

CHAPTER 38

BY THE NEXT MORNING, NEARLY ALL OF SMYRNA WAS IN flames—an unbroken wall of fire two miles long: the city that had been called the City of Roses, the city on whose proud, broad streets the finest wares of the world could be purchased, the city that had prided itself on its gentle climate and its cosmopolitan ways. In the city itself, unspeakable terrors had taken place. Archbishop Chrysostomos had been taken by an angry crowd and torn, literally, limb from limb. Countless men and boys—including Christina's husband, Spiro, and their fifteen-year-old son, Constantine—had been taken away, marched into the countryside, where they fell to sword and gun and were left to the vultures. Women and children had been raped and killed, knifed sometimes from neck to crotch. Families, taking shelter in churches, found themselves engulfed in flames as the churches were set afire. Unknown numbers died in unknown ways, their bodies never recovered, never identified, their relatives, lucky to have escaped with their own lives, never knowing what had happened to them. Terrifying sounds filled the air: the sharp reports of gunfire, the roar of the wind-driven flames, the crash of collapsing buildings, and above everything the desperate screams of more than two hundred thousand souls trapped between the fire and the sea. That sea had turned copper colored, though no one could tell if it was from the reflection of the flames or from the blood of those whose bodies floated in it, and the sky was so blackened by smoke that it was completely dark by seven o'clock in the evening of a summer night, and the people coughed and gasped for breath in the smoke that surrounded them.

And, somehow, as the sun rose bleakly on that third day of the fire, Liana found herself and her children at the front of the crowd, nearly shoved into the sea by those pushing from behind, trying desperately to escape the smoke and the scorching heat of the flames that were now just across the street. In Smyrna, nearly all the buildings had been constructed with timber frames, because wood timbers could more easily take the repeated shaking of Smyrna's occasional earthquakes. Now those buildings were heated so high from the surrounding flames that their interior timber frames caught fire, hiding behind their walls until those fires finally burst out in unquenchable flames, destroying the buildings from the inside. Firefighters could only stand and watch, their rubber hoses melting in their gloved hands from the heat.

Then, suddenly and without warning, like a miracle sent from heaven, a lighter appeared beside the quay, and Liana pulled out a handful of gold coins, showing them to the boatman, and he grinned an almost toothless smile and held out his hand for her. But instead she pushed her children forward, then she handed over Baby Dora and she herself scrambled aboard, filling the already overcrowded vessel far beyond its capacity.

The boatman stood his ground until she poured out her coins into his hands, and then, because he still stood there, she pulled British pounds from her pockets and gave him those as well. The American dollars and the French francs she kept to herself. They would be needed for passage on whichever ships were willing to take her and her children to America. Those and the jewelry would pay their way across the ocean and across America to California. As would the gold coins she had sewn last night into the hem of her dress and into the seams of Dimitri's jacket.

The boatman signaled to the oarsman at the stern, who started immediately to pole away from the quay, but then, suddenly, from somewhere on the quay, someone threw a bucket of liquid onto the barge, splashing all those aboard, including Liana and the children, and that was followed almost immediately by a burning torch. In an instant, all those on the boat knew—the sudden smell rising to their nostrils—and the quicker witted dove into the sea. Liana, seeing them, understood just as the first flames licked up the hem of her frail summer skirt—*benzine*—and her eyes widened and she saw the small, round faces of her children. Dimitri stared at her, uncomprehending, seeing the flames now eating their way up her dress and smelling the smoke, the acrid smell of benzine smoke, his face full of fear, and she turned quickly to the others, the force of her turn seeming to disorient her. In her arms, Baby Dora was screaming from the heat of the fire that was eating its way into her blanket, and she heard the children's coughs and screams and she felt Baby Dora in her arms trying to kick off the flames. With one arm, she batted at those flames and at the ones eating at Dimitri and the others, but she could not put them out, and it was as if she was in another world, one in which there was no fire and no smoke and she was not fainting, and the last thing she said, the last thing she did, was to push Dimitri off that flat-bottomed vessel, screaming, *"Jump! Swim!"*

And then there was nothing, save a vision of Dimitri, in a garden, surrounded by roses.

CHAPTER 39

"JUMP!" SHE HAD SCREAMED. "SWIM!"
And he did.

He swam. Weighted down by his clothing and the coins sewn into it, gulping seawater, he swam desperately in water turned too warm by the fires, water that smelled of blood and death, littered with the bloating bodies of those who had tried to swim to the boats and failed. After a few moments he paused long enough to look back, to see if his sister or any of his brothers had survived, but all he saw was the lighter in flames, and beyond it the greater flames and the black smoke of the city. Then he felt a nudge at the back of his neck, and he turned in hopes of seeing Vaioush or Manoush, but what he saw was the head of a horse, dead, floating in the water, its belly distended by bloat, and he struggled away in terror, sinking, feeling the water pull him into its warm embrace, and he almost gave in to it, letting it wrap around him like a mother, letting it hold him now and forever.

And then something turned over in his mind, and he struggled away, pulling himself toward the surface, and though the water's warm, liquid fingers kept trying to pull him back, he thrust himself away, driving himself to the surface, to the light and the air, gasping for breath. And he swam away from the grasp of the sea, away from Smyrna, away from his mother and all those he loved.

He didn't know one boat from another—could not, from the water, make out a flag, could not read the foreign writing on the sides of the ships—but he headed for the nearest, a tall gray one with numbers and letters in Western script on its sides and an anchor rope as thick as his leg. He saw ahead of him a man trying to climb that rope, reaching halfway to the deck, but then someone on deck poured steaming water down on him and he lost the grip of one hand and then the other, and he fell back into the sea. Dimitri saw that, and he saw now other ships' crewmen throwing refuse and even human waste onto those who tried to climb anchor chains, using poles and bayoneted guns and boiling water to keep from being boarded. Exhausted, he swam from one ship to another, looking for the one that would take him aboard, losing hope, losing strength, losing all sense of time or place. Finally all he could do was cling to a rope at the side of one ship and stare back at the city, where the dense smoke made twilight of midafternoon, where the moans of the dying and the terrorized rose to the sky, and where he had lost everyone he knew.

And that was when he heard someone calling to him. At first he thought it was his father, or his Emmanuel *Papou*, looking down from heaven, urging him not to give up. He looked up, hoping to see them, hoping, in his near exhaustion, even to see God. What he saw instead was a sailor leaning over the side, motioning to him, and though he couldn't understand the words, he understood the meaning, and he wrapped his arms and legs around the rope and allowed himself to be pulled up, his arms aching with all the unaccustomed effort, sodden, dripping, weary, smelling of the sea and of human and animal waste and blood. And when he was finally on deck, the sailor stripped off his own shirt and wrapped it around Dimitri, then he led him to a corner where he hid the boy amid a coil of rope. "I'll be damned," the sailor said in words Dimitri could only have understood if he'd had a chance to attend the Evangeliki School and learn English. "I'll be damned if I'm going to watch a little kid die, orders or no orders."

And Dimitri, exhausted and uncertain whether he was alive or taken up to heaven, closed his eyes.

THE NEXT THING HE KNEW, A MAN IN A SUIT WAS STANDING CLOSE, staring down at him. Behind the man was the ship's captain, frowning, and beyond the captain was the sailor, looking worried, and for a moment Dimitri thought they were going to throw him back into the sea.

"*Pos se lene?*" the man in the suit asked.

"Dimitri," he whispered.

The man crouched down closer. "Eh?"

"Dimitri Melopoulos," he said, his voice rasping, as if it had been choked by sand, as if he had lost it at the bottom of the sea. Then in a sudden inspiration, he thought of the letter, and he pulled it from the pocket of his jacket and handed it to the man.

The man opened the oiled paper packet and pulled a damp letter from an envelope that had lost its glue and was itself now merely damp, folded paper. But the ink was still legible.

"Who is this from?" the man asked in Greek.

"My father's friend."

"Where does he live?"

"In California."

"What is his name?"

"Ara Fayroyian."

"He's Armenian, then?"

Dimitri nodded, staring up at the man, trying to decide if

the man would think it good or bad that his father's friend was an Armenian.

"But you're Greek," the man said, still speaking in Greek. "Dimitri Melopoulos. Dimitri—Aghios Dimitrios. Saint Dimitri. One of our Lord's good friends."

Dimitri nodded, suddenly daring a bit of hope. Surely such a man would never throw him off the boat, would never have poured boiling water on him, despite the ship's captain, who stood behind him.

The man waved the letter at the ship's captain. "In these conditions, I call it as good as a visa." Then the man turned back to Dimitri and spoke again in Greek. "Do you want to go to America?"

Dimitri nodded.

"How old are you?"

"Almost twelve."

"Eleven." The man nodded. "But in America, you know," he said, his voice confidential, his hand brushing back the hair that had plastered itself over Dimitri's forehead, "you will have to take an American name, a boy like you. Aghios Dimitrios in English is Saint James." The man smiled at him. "In America, I suspect, they will call you Jimmy."

EPILOGUE

Detroit, 1982

THESE DAYS, SOMETIMES, HE LAYS HIMSELF OUT ON THE COUCH in the living room, blue-green cabbage roses on the wallpaper. He wears a clean white shirt, his shoes polished, and his black suit—the only color he has ever owned: black, because survival is serious business. In his hands he holds three linked silver filigreed hearts, graduated in size, the smallest no bigger than a child's fingernail. He remembers his *papou*, who made them, and he grips them tighter and imagines someone will find him like this one day, the tips of his shoes pointing heavenward: telltale markers left behind by a fleeing soul. It almost makes him smile.

He never made it to California, to his father's friend Ara. Some street urchins in New York City had beaten him up and stolen his coat from him, and with it, the coins sewn into its lining, as if they had known that immigrants to America had such things sewn into the lining of their clothes, which indeed they probably did, because immigrants almost always came with money sewn into their clothes. But, even more important than the coins, in the pocket of that stolen jacket was the letter from California; without it, he did not have the name of the city where his father's friend lived.

Instead, from New York he had been lucky enough to make his way—by accident and good fortune—as far as Detroit, to the home of Costas Stamatis and his wife, Soula, who had the same name as Dimitri's cousin, who was married less than two weeks before what the Greeks in America now called "the Catastrophe." And their son, Alex, who was his best friend all his life.

He lies there now, in his own living room, in his own house, still as stone, just as he had back then on the boat. Not the first one, though, the boat that departed slowly from Smyrna Bay, leaving everything behind. Everything, and everyone. Still, on that first boat they treated him like a little prince. He thinks they did, anyway, but he hardly remembers. What he does rememer is that he couldn't sleep. He tried to, but he couldn't: the first time in his life without his mother's kiss, without the scent of jasmine on which to dream.

It was on the second boat, the one all the way across the Atlantic, that he had first experienced what they call these days shock. Post-traumatic stress syndrome—that's the new way of saying it. He and Alex talked about that once, when there'd been something in the papers, Alex spitting the words out like something he'd hawked up from the back of his throat. Alex, God bless his soul, as close to a brother as he had in America. Alex, who had never in his life seen dead bodies lying in the streets in the summer sun. Never even heard a gunshot fired, except for the day when that Greenburg—Greenbaum?—guy got it right outside on the street, a dozen people walking by at the time. Coming out of Atlas Meat Packing next door, where everybody including the cops knew there was a speakeasy behind the freezer room. You just walked in the front door and said something like *"My buddy Tony tells me you got good meat here."* Then somebody looked you up and down, and they'd take you into the freezer, where there'd be another door at the back; and when you went through, there was a whole room back there, gin flowing like water from a faucet and tables for gambling.

What would Alex have known about post-traumatic stress syndrome? He wasn't even there in '67 for the riots, having left earlier in the month for a trip to New York City, taking Carol there for a final fling before sending her off to college—just the two of them then, Maroula dead by then, and they'd stayed in Astoria with relatives. No, it was he—Jimmy—who'd had to go down and hold a gun in his hand, terrified he might have to shoot someone, and watch the city burn, or at least watch what people said was the city burning, though almost none of them had any idea what a burning city was really like.

But Alex, dead now, and all the rest. Oh God, so many.

Still, he tells himself, it's in the bones. Some things you don't have to tell in words; it's in the bones. All a person has to do is look. Think. Why might a grown man be afraid to walk deeper into the lake than his knees? Why might a person fear fire—even something as seemingly simple as a bonfire of autumn leaves? Why might a person have to go on living, even when it seems there is no one else left.

Because there needs to be someone to come after, someone to know, even if that someone is not yet aware of it. Because when your mother shouts, *Jump! Swim!* what she means is: *Survive.*

ACKNOWLEDGMENTS

THERE ARE SO MANY PEOPLE AND INSTITUTIONS WHOM I COULD thank for making it possible for me to write this book and for making it what it is that I could not begin to thank them all. But I would like particularly to thank my agent, Jennifer Weltz, of the Jean V. Naggar Literary Agency, whose wisdom and advice and enthusiasm seem never to wane and who has been a steady advocate for this book and the others on which she and I have worked. And, as well, thanks to Jennifer's assistant, Cole Hildebrand, who stepped in to help me when I direly needed it.

Again, thank you to my editor, Sara Nelson, of Harper-Collins, who fell in love with this book and who paved the way to publication so smoothly. Her suggestions, unusual as they sometimes were, opened my eyes to new possibilities. And kudos to her team at Harper: Sara's amazing assistant Edie Astley, designer Milan Bozic, marketing director Lisa Erickson, and associate publisher Amy Baker, all of whom have made me a real partner in this publishing experience.

I could not have researched and written *Children of the Catastrophe* without the help of some great libraries, especially the University of Michigan Library and the fabulous Michigan Electronic Library, and the small but mighty Leelanau Township Library—and, of course, the diligence and effort of some outstanding librarians, including Deb Stannard, Nellie Danke, and Julie Preneta.

I want to thank my writers' group cohort, whose comments helped to improve what I originally wrote: Alison Arthur, Karen Casebeer, and Karen Mulvahill. And thanks to the several friends and relatives who read early versions of my books over the years and whose suggestions and support have encouraged me toward publication: Sue Landes, Betsy Wilson, Coralyn Riley, Susan Ager, Pamela Grath, Sarah Olson, Laurel Riley, Dan Shoemaker, and, of course, Kent.

And, finally, thanks to all the wonderful and interesting people I knew or crossed paths with while living in Turkey and Greece, for without your being aware of it, my experiences with you and your countries helped make this book richer.

About the author

About the book

Read on

Insights,
Interviews
& More . . .

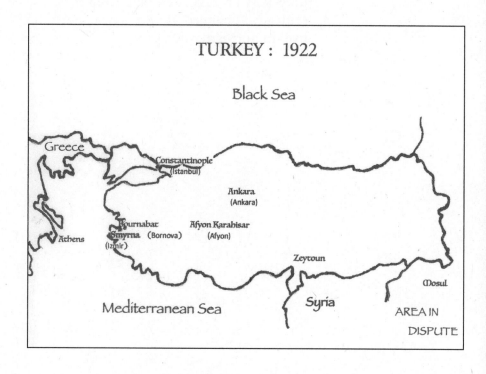

TURKEY : 1922

Black Sea

Greece

Constantinople
(Istanbul)

Ankara
(Ankara)

Kournabat
Smyrna   (Bornova)
(Izmir)

Afyon Karahisar
(Afyon)

Athens

Zeytoun

Mosul

Mediterranean Sea

Syria

AREA IN
DISPUTE

About the Author

Sarah Shoemaker is a former university librarian and the author of critically acclaimed *Mr. Rochester*. She lives in northern Michigan.

Author's Note

SMYRNA WAS A Hellenistic city of ancient times—its establishment dates back at least to the third millennium BCE. Over time, it was under the control of various world powers, including the empires of Alexander the Great and the Romans. In 1084 of the Common Era, the Turks captured it for the first time, but it was subsequently recovered by the Byzantines, then retaken and taken and retaken again over the centuries, until it was at last overwhelmed by the Ottoman Turks in the fifteenth century.

During those years, and due to its location at the conjuncture of the rich Anatolian plain and the eastern Mediterranean Sea, Smyrna grew to be the major commercial city—and the richest—of the Mediterranean region. Over that time, there remained in Smyrna a predominant Hellenistic (what we would today call Greek) population of traders centered around Smyrna's fine harbor. After the victory of the Ottoman Turks, more and more Turks arrived in the city, and the Turkish community developed farther back toward the mountains and away from the harbor, allowing the Greeks to maintain control of most of the commerce into and out of Smyrna. In those days, the Turks thought of themselves as military men and conquerors, and they were mostly content for the Greeks to remain in the ▶

Author's Note *(continued)*

commercial district while the Turks themselves kept what seemed more important at the time: dominance in military and political affairs. This was not an uncommon arrangement throughout the Ottoman Empire, which, at its height, stretched from the gates of Vienna southeastward to the edge of India and around the Mediterranean Sea as far as the Atlantic Ocean, and including nearly all the Balkans, the Middle East, and North Africa.

Smyrna, today's Izmir, had historically been multicultural, and by the late nineteenth and early twentieth centuries it held large populations of Armenians, British, French, Italians, Jews, even Americans, but virtually half the city's population was still Greek. Each of these groups generally kept to themselves in their own parts of the city, the political ramifications of which the Turks dealt with as the issues arose. And, by that time, Smyrna had long been the largest and wealthiest city on the Mediterranean Sea.

However, as time passed, the vast Ottoman Empire weakened until, by the end of the nineteenth century, it was mostly a shell of its former self, having lost portions around the Black Sea to Russia in 1829, Greece having won its independence in 1830, and France having taken Algiers in the same year. In the next ninety years, what had once been one of the world's largest empires lost territory over and over. By the end of the First World War, with the Ottoman Empire on the losing side, the winning European powers—and to a lesser extent, the Americans—pounced on what was left of that domain, especially the oil-bearing areas. In the various peace agreements after the war, Britain gained sovereignty over the island of Cyprus plus mandates over Mesopotamia (Iraq) and Palestine, and the French got mandates over Syria and Lebanon. The United States was given no land, per se, but its commercial and oil entrepreneurs were quick to stake out areas of strategic interest. And Greece was given permission to occupy Smyrna.

Despite their losses after the war, the Turks were used to thinking of themselves as the denizens of a huge nation, particularly the proud residents of Smyrna, which was still the wealthiest and the most cosmopolitan and important city in the Mediterranean world. But when the Greek army came to occupy Smyrna, and then proceeded to take, as well, the coastal areas to the north and south of the city, the Turks were rattled. And when the Greek army marched deep into the heart of Anatolia, the Turks began to fight back.

Although the Greek residents of Smyrna assumed that the European and American naval vessels in Smyrna's harbor in the summer of 1922 were there to protect them from the Turks, the reality was, as they were to discover, that those ships were there, in an exercise of ▶

Author's Note *(continued)*

realpolitik, simply to assure that their nations' own political and economic interests in the former Ottoman Empire were protected.

And then came the Catastrophe. ᕫ

Questions for Discussion

1. Liana and Vasili grew up in two quite different families. How do you think this affected them as adults and parents?

2. How much did you know about the burning of Smyrna before you read this book?

3. Liana's father, Emmanuel Demirgis, warned that the Greeks were making a mistake in killing Turkish residents of the outlying areas and destroying their crops. Do you think that the outcome might have been different if they had acted differently?

4. What role did the Allied Nations (Great Britain, France, Italy, and the United States) play in the Catastrophe? Why do you think that was?

5. What parallels do you see between Liana's world in 1922 and our world today?

6. What do you know about any reasons or difficulties that your own family/ancestors had when coming to America? ∾

Glossary*

Aghia—female saint, as in Aghia Elisabet (*Greek*)

Aghios—male saint, as in Aghios Giorgios (*Greek*)

bahchevan—a greengrocer who rides around a neighborhood on a horse-pulled wagon, selling fresh produce (*Turkish*)

baklava—a dessert made of filo pastry, butter, chopped walnuts, sugar, and syrup

charsha—marketplace (*Turkish*)

dolmathes, dolma—stuffed vegetables, i.e., *lahano dolmathes* (stuffed cabbage) (*Greek, Turkish*)

effendi -m—sir, Mr. (*Turkish*)

elinize saalik—"Long life to your hand," a high compliment to the cook (*Turkish*)

Eski Buyuk Pazar—literally "Old Grand Market" (*Turkish*)

galactoboureko—a Greek custard pie (*Greek*)

gevrek—a six-inch-wide crunchy ring of baked dough sprinkled with sesame seeds (*Turkish*) ▶

Glossary (*continued*)

hamal—a porter, one whose job is to carry heavy loads (*Turkish*)

Hanum—Mrs., madam (*Turkish*)

imam bayildi—a stew of eggplants stuffed with chopped onions, tomatoes, parsley, and plenty of garlic, cooked in a lot of olive oil. The name of the dish translates to "the imam fainted" and there are several explanations for the name. My favorite one is that an imam was courting a young woman, and the first meal she fixed for him was this one, and he loved it so much that he asked for it again, but she warned him that it used a lot of olive oil. Yet he still wanted it. So, for her dowry, she brought to the marriage five large jugs of olive oil. For the first dinner of their marriage, he asked for his favorite dish and she made it; the next day he asked for it again, and again the third day, but on the fourth, when he asked for it, she told him she couldn't make it because she had run out of olive oil. And the imam fainted. (*Turkish*)

imbat—a very strong wind in the eastern Mediterranean (*Turkish*)

itch pilav—a savory pilaf made with rice, lamb, liver, onions, tomato, pine nuts, and currants (*Turkish*)

jezveh—pot for making Turkish coffee (*Turkish*)

-jim, -jum—added to the end of a first name to express a close relationship to the speaker that might be expressed as "my dear," as in Madamjum (*Turkish*)

kayit kebab—chopped lamb, onions, tomato, green pepper, and dill wrapped tightly in greaseproof paper and cooked in the oven (*Turkish*)

Konak—government buildings (*Turkish*)

Kordon—the main street (*Turkish*)

Kyria—madam, Mrs. (*Greek*)

Kyrios—sir, Mr. (*Greek*)

Levantine—an inhabitant of the eastern Mediterranean area, called the Levant, whose family roots go so far back in that area that they do not think of themselves as having another nationality

lokum—Turkish delight, a type of sweet (*Turkish*)

Mashalla—Praise God (Allah) (*Turkish*)

mezes, mezthakia—appetizers (*Turkish, Greek*)

mitera—mother (*Greek*)

narghile—waterpipe ▶

Glossary *(continued)*

-oush—affectionate ending for a child's or close friend's name, like Jimmy or Susie (*Turkish*)

papou—grandfather (*Greek*)

pekmez—a molasses-like syrup used as a sweetener (*Turkish*)

piastre—a monetary unit of several Middle Eastern countries, whose value is 1/100 of a pound

politakia—traditional Greek music played on traditional Greek instruments (*Greek*)

Pos se leni?—What is your name? (*Greek*)

proika—a bride's trousseau (*Greek*)

raki—an alcoholic drink, flavored with anise (*Turkish*)

rizogalo—rice pudding (*Greek*), called *suitlach* in Turkish

sim—silver or gold metallic thread used in embroidery work (*Turkish*)

tavli—backgammon (*Greek or Turkish*)

theia—aunt (*Greek*)

tulumba tatlisi—a fried cookie-like sweet, made with flour, shortening, and lots of sugar and eggs (*Turkish*) *tzadziki*—a dip or spread made of yogurt, grated cucumber, garlic, and lemon juice (*Greek*)

yaya—grandmother (*Greek)*

*Spellings may vary, due at least in part to the fact that pronunciations of specific letters vary from language to language and alphabet to alphabet, as well as the fact that English, Greek, and Turkish all have different numbers of letters, including vowels, in their alphabets, so that often one can only approximate the sounds from one language to another.

Further Reading

FICTION

Birds Without Wings by Louis de Bernières

Middlesex by Jeffrey Eugenides

The Ashes of Smyrna by Richard Reinhardt

NONFICTION

Paradise Lost: Smyrna 1922 by Giles Milton

The Smyrna Affair by Marjorie Housepian

Levant: Splendor and Catastrophe on the Mediterranean by Philip Mansel

Discover great authors, exclusive offers, and more at hc.com.